LEMON BIRD

BIRD

Can Help!

Lemon Bird was penciled, inked, colored, and lettered in Photoshop.

Text, cover art, and interior illustrations copyright © 2022 by Paulina Ganucheau

All rights reserved. Published in the United States by RH Graphic, an imprint of Random House Children's Books, a division of Penguin Random House LLC, New York.

RH Graphic with the book design is a trademark of Penguin Random House LLC.

Visit us on the web! RHKidsGraphic.com • @RHKidsGraphic

Educators and librarians, for a variety of teaching tools, visit us at RHTeachersLibrarians.com

Library of Congress Cataloging-in-Publication Data is available upon request.
ISBN 978-0-593-12267-9 (hardcover) — ISBN 978-0-593-12533-5 (lib. bdg.)
ISBN 978-0-593-12268-6 (ebook)

Designed by Patrick Crotty

MANUFACTURED IN CHINA
10 9 8 7 6 5 4 3 2 1
First Edition

A comic on every bookshelf.

LEMON BIRD

BIRD

Can Help!

Paulina
Ganucheau

To Mamaw and Papaw

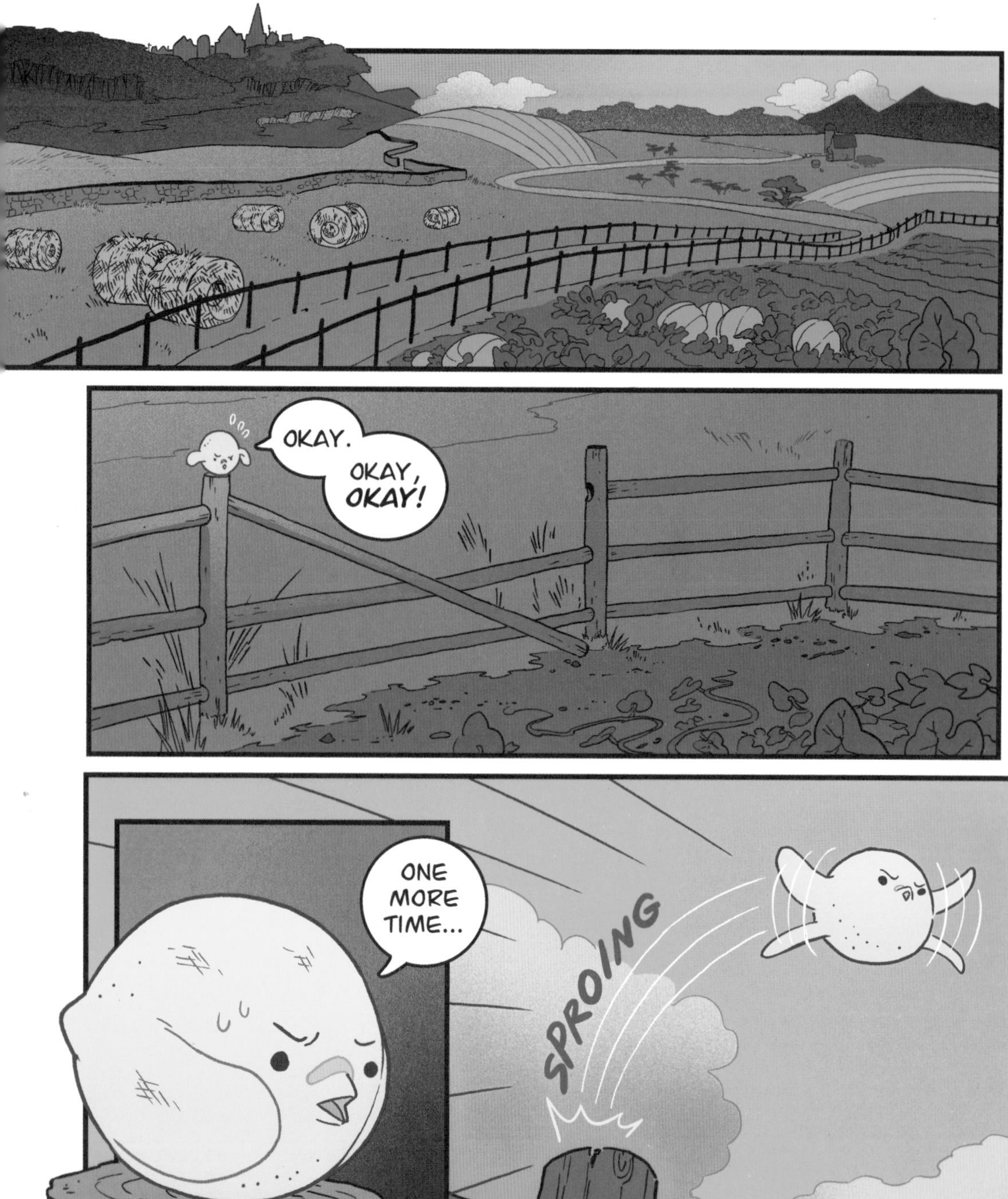

OKAY.
OKAY, OKAY!
ONE MORE TIME...
SPROING

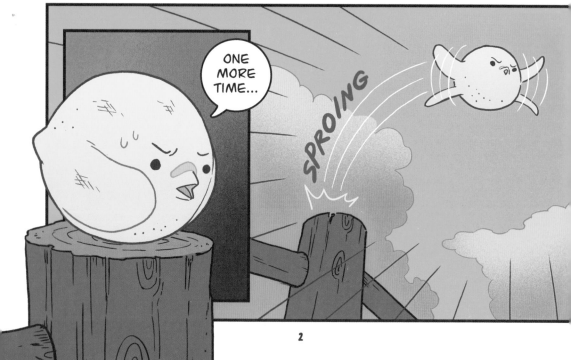

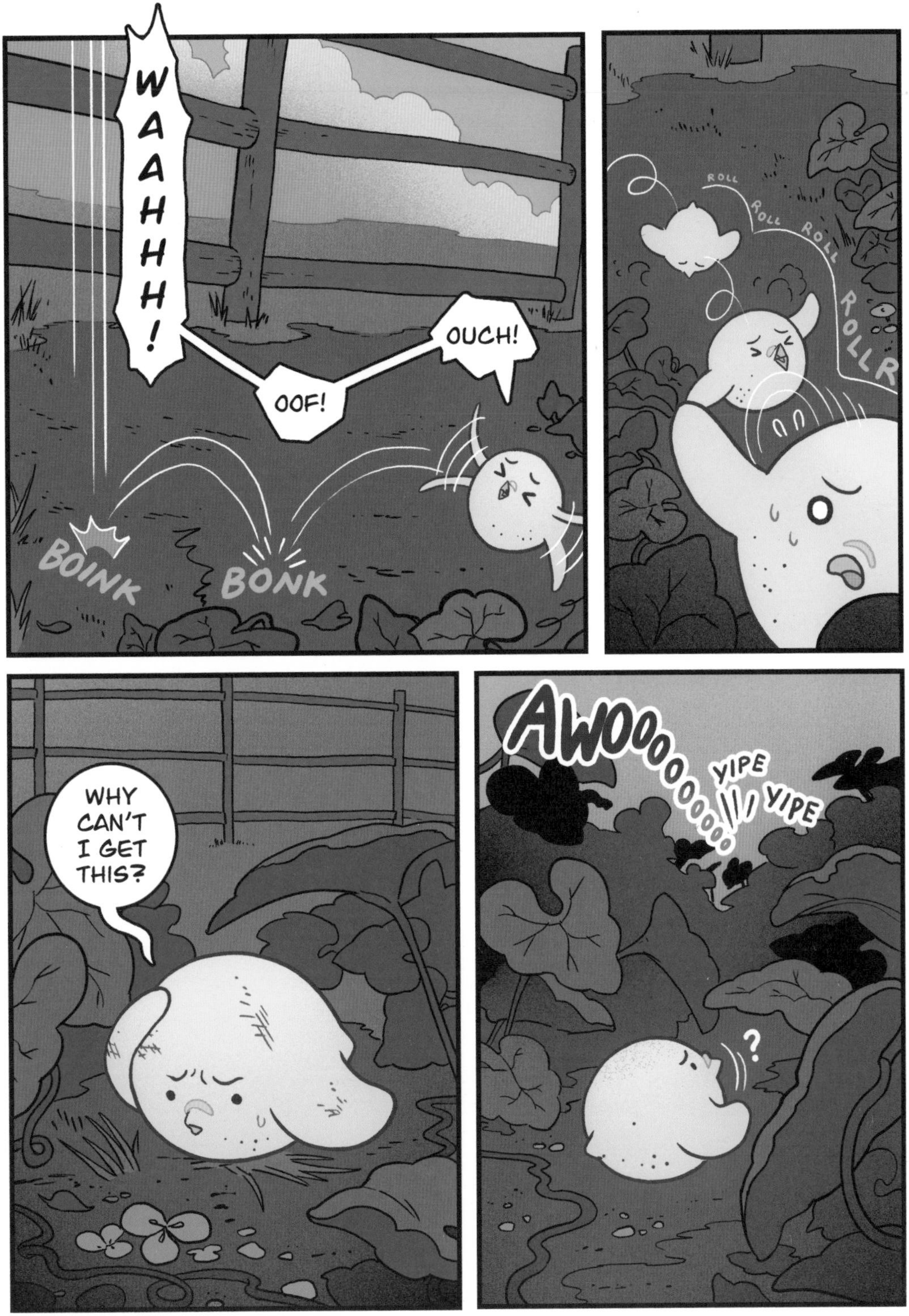
WAAHHH!
OOF!
OUCH!
BOINK
BONK
ROLL
ROLL
ROLL
ROLLR
WHY CAN'T I GET THIS?
AWOOOOOOOOO
YIPE
YIPE
?

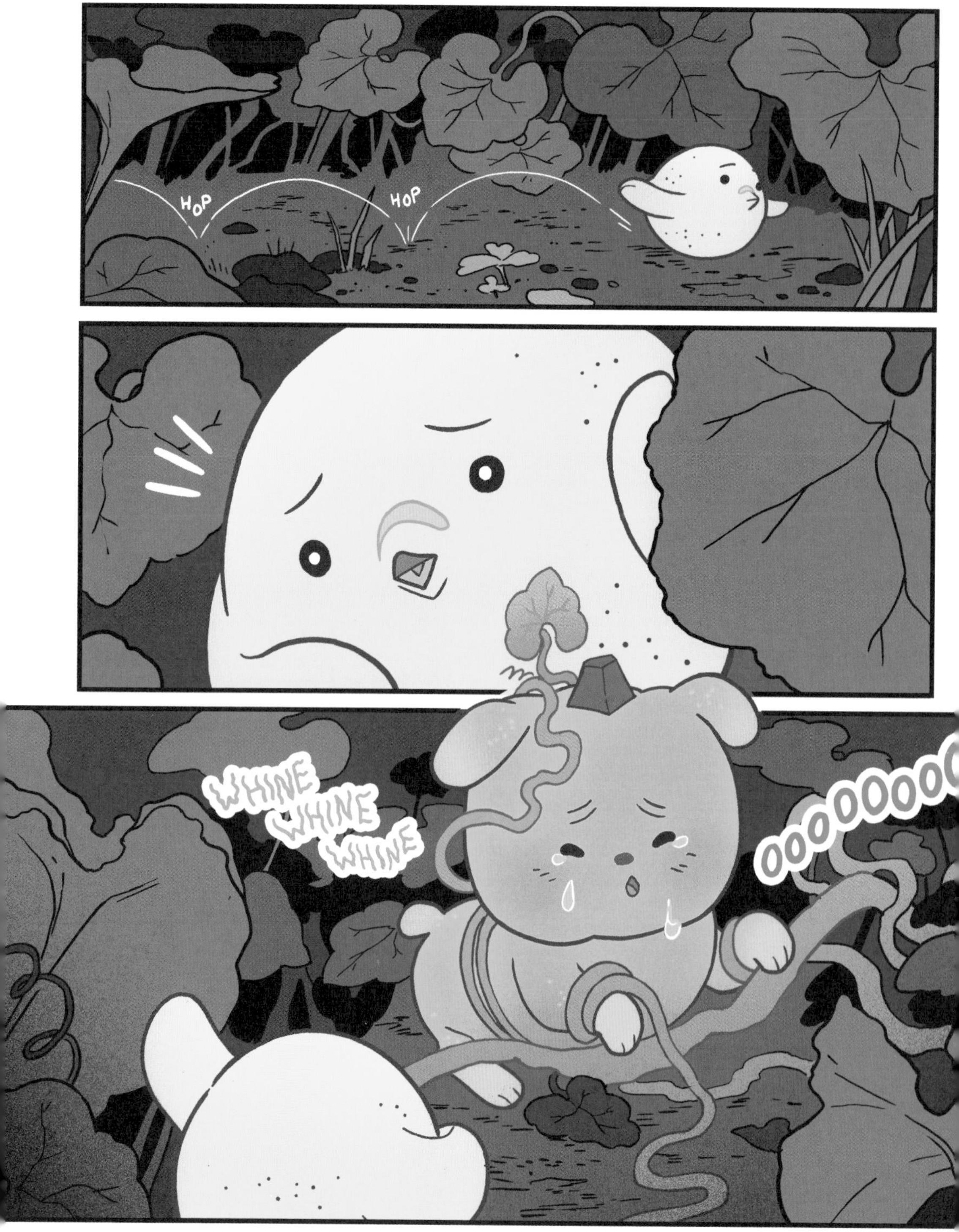
HOP
HOP
WHINE
WHINE
WHINE
OOOOOOOO

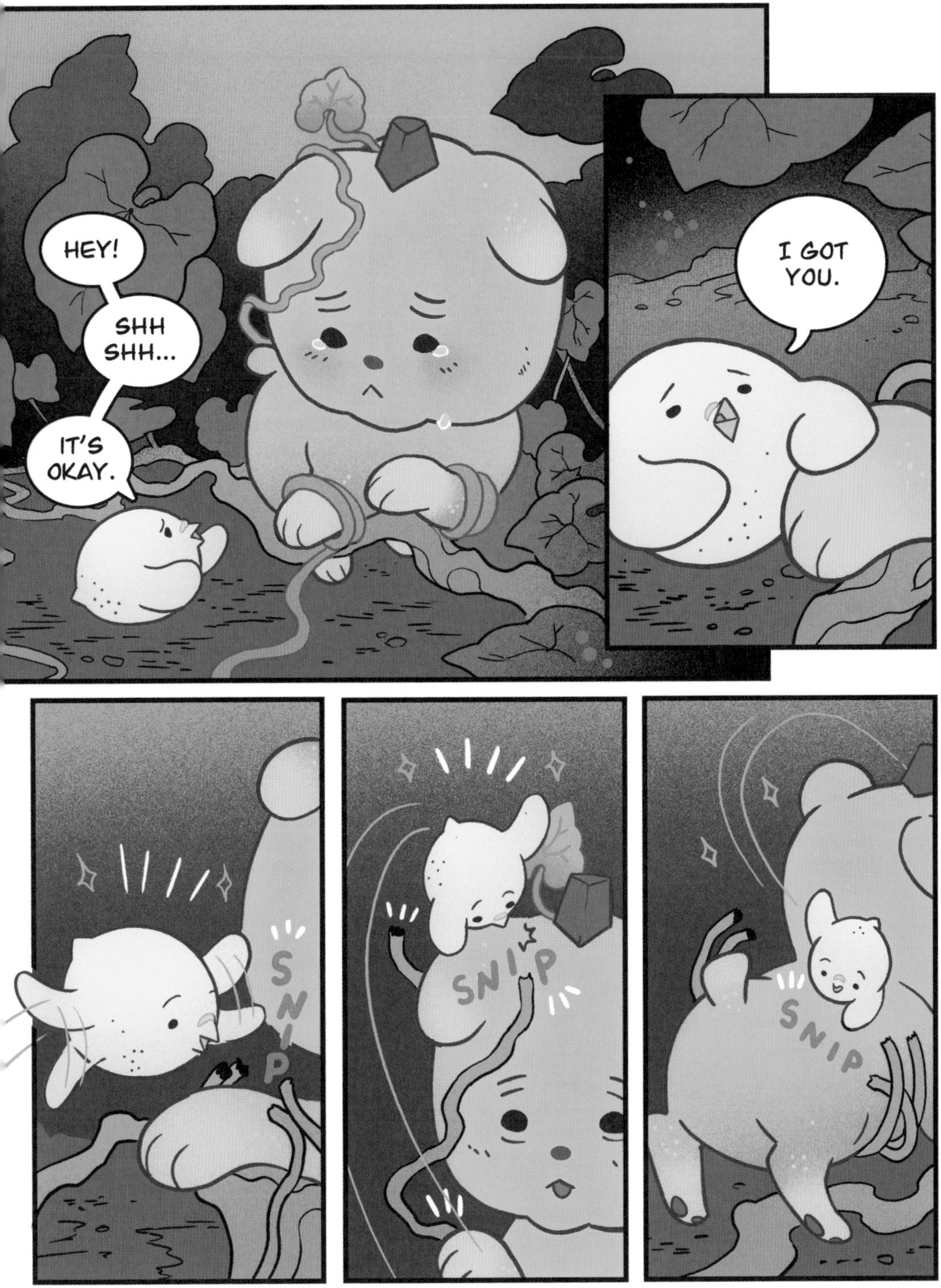
HEY!
SHH SHH...
IT'S OKAY.
I GOT YOU.
SNIP
SNIP
SNIP

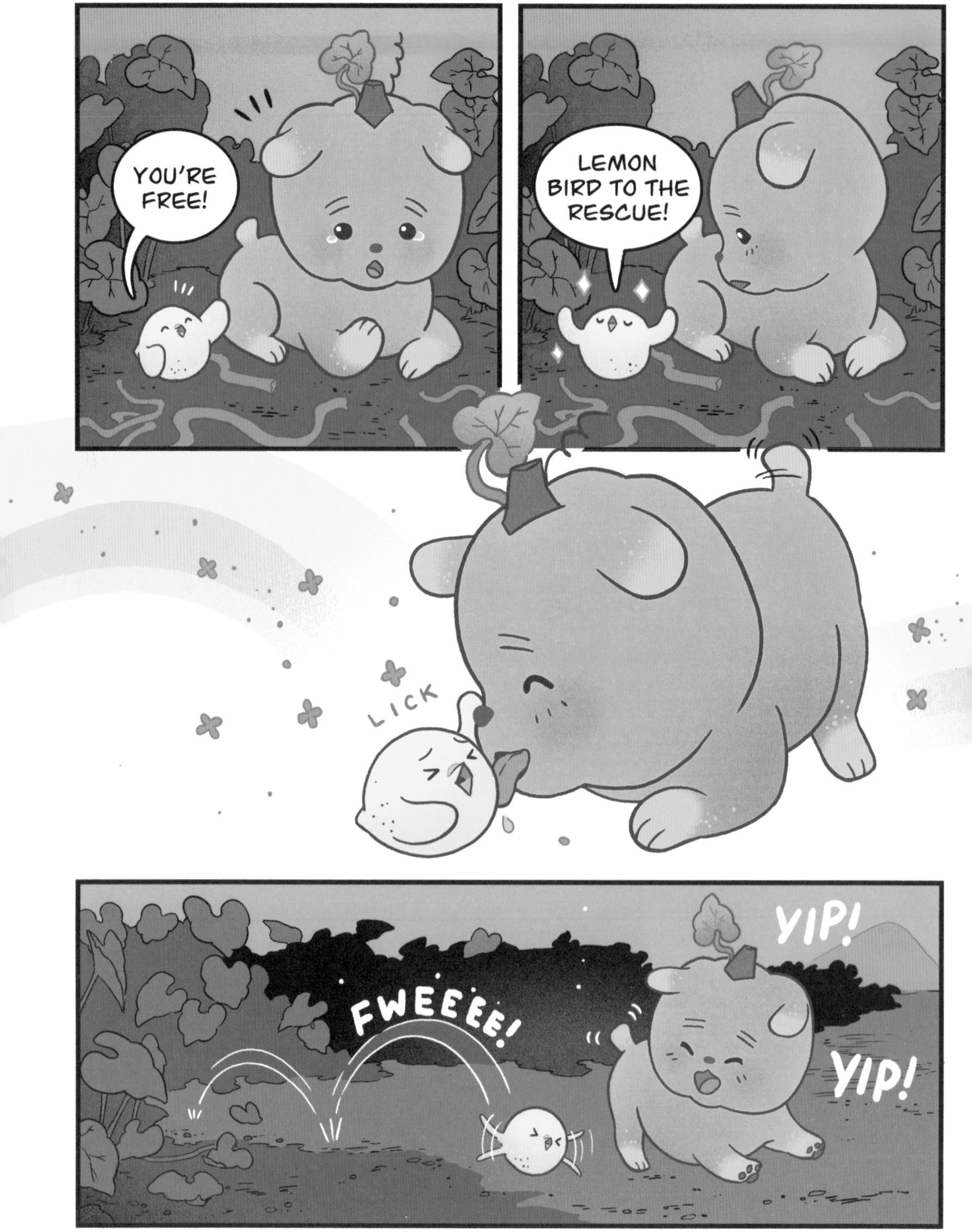
YOU'RE FREE!
LEMON BIRD TO THE RESCUE!
LICK
FWEEEE!
YIP!
YIP!

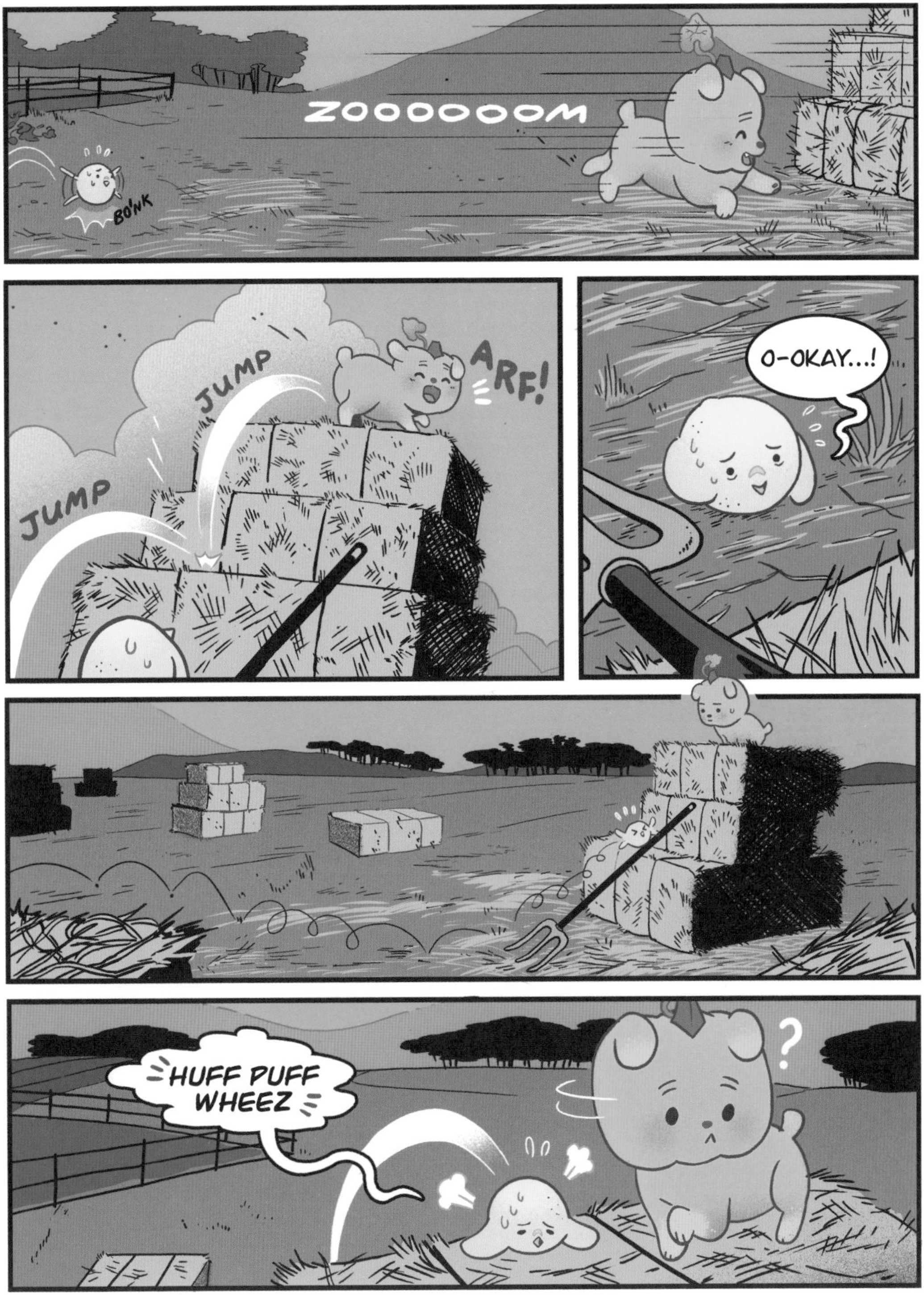
ZOOOOOOM
BO'NK
JUMP
JUMP
ARF!
O-OKAY...!
HUFF PUFF WHEEZ
?

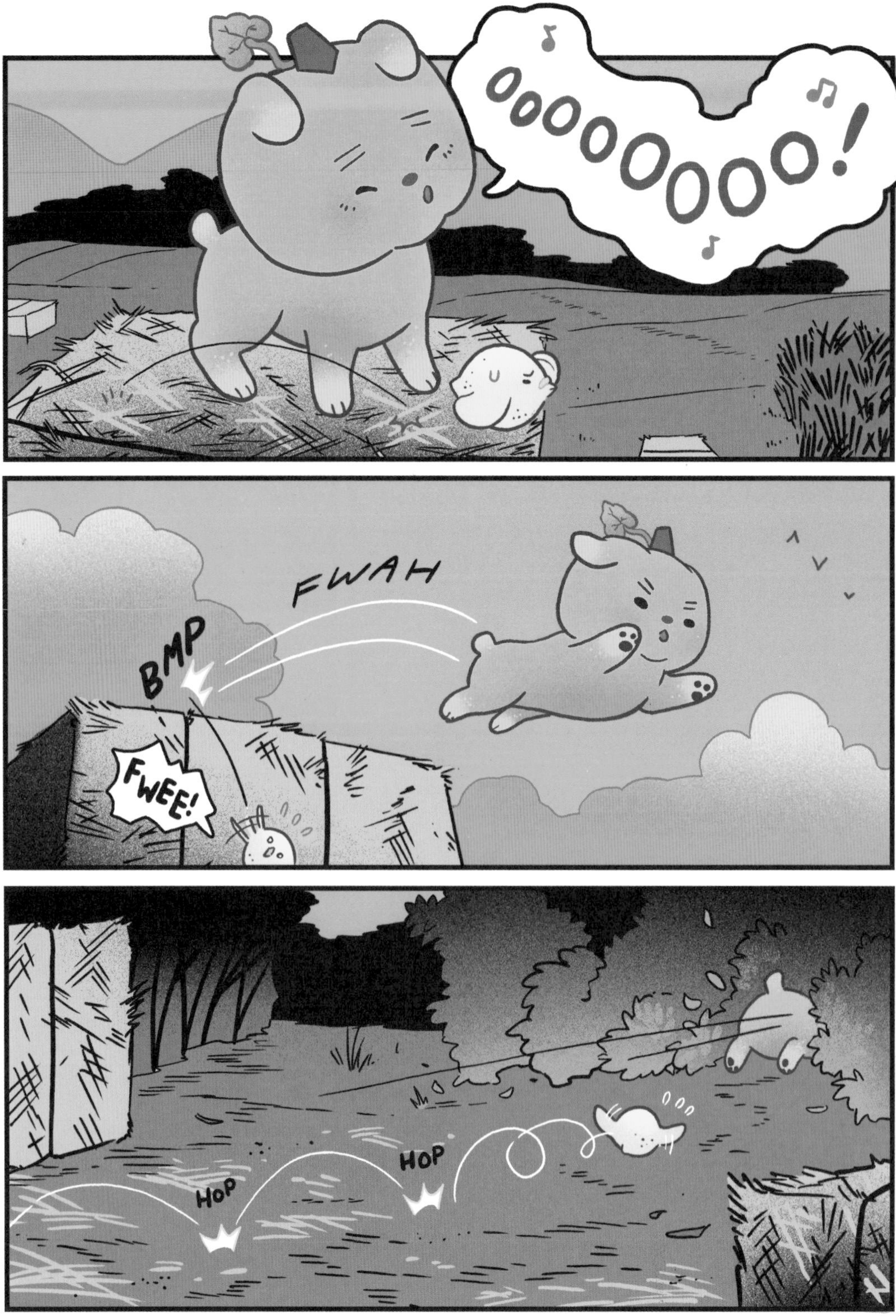
OOOOOOOOO!
FWAH
BMP
FWEE!
HOP
HOP

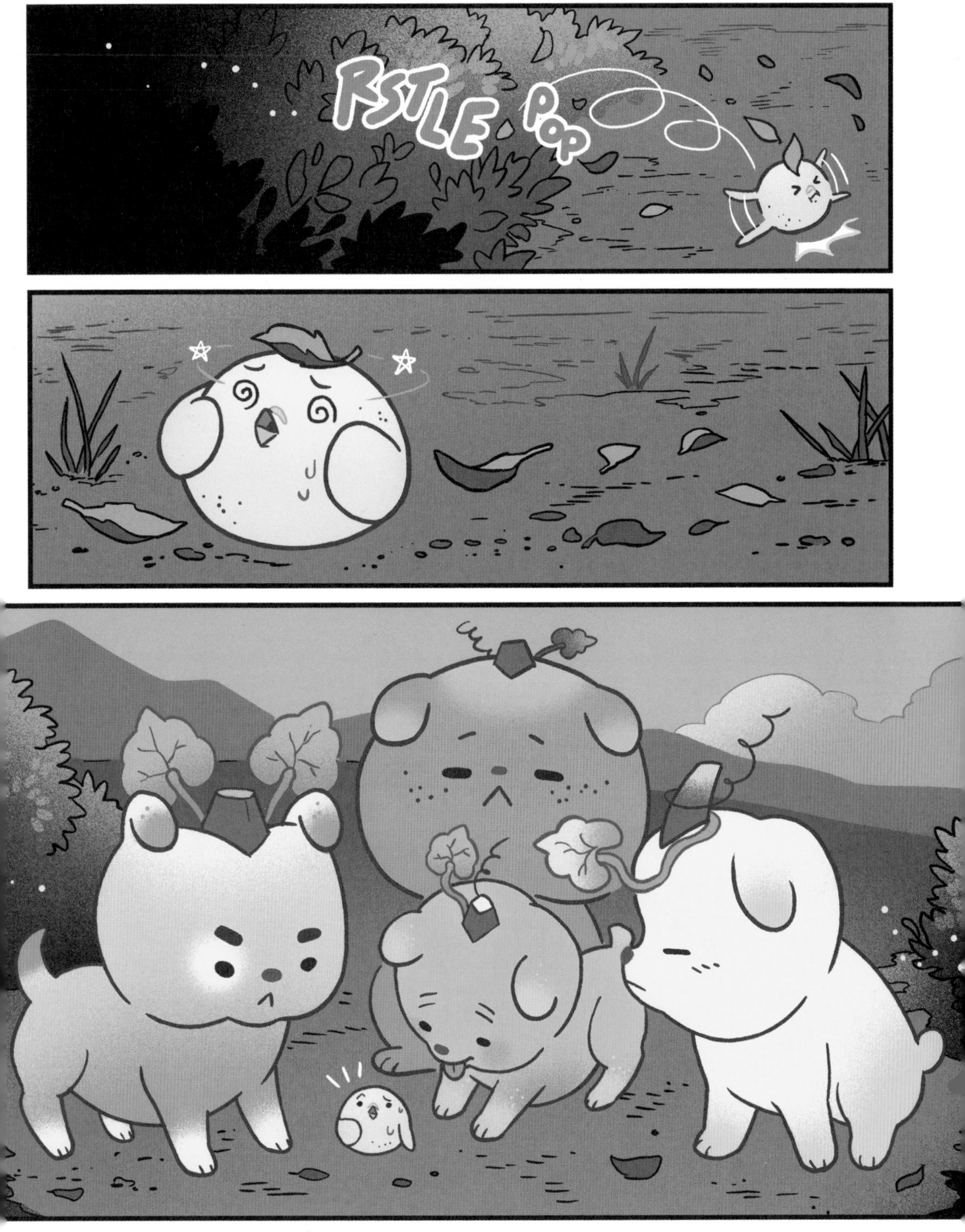
RSTLE
POP

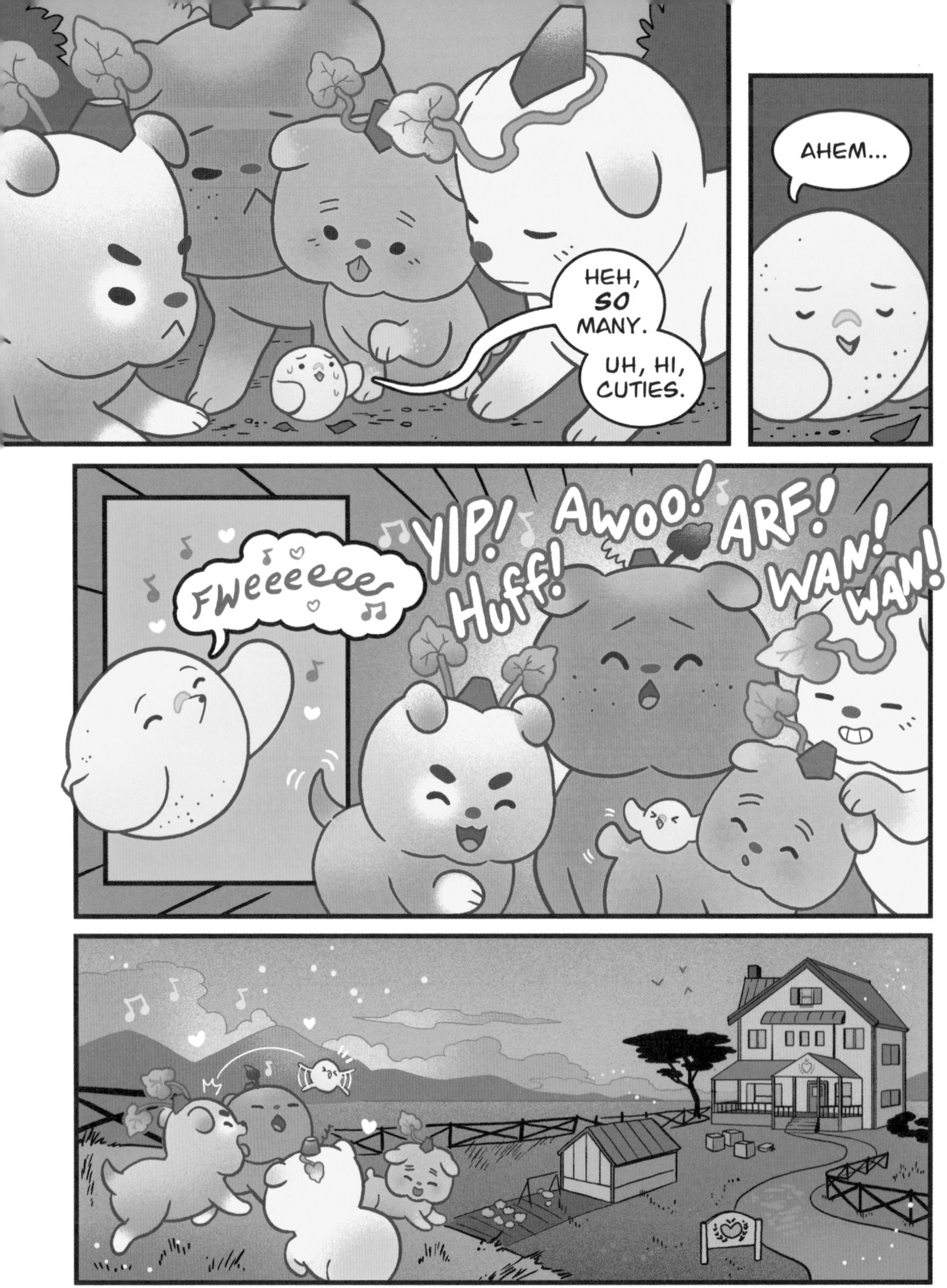
HEH, SO MANY.
UH, HI, CUTIES.
AHEM...
FWeeeeee
YIP!
Awoo!
Huff!
ARF!
WAN!
WAN!

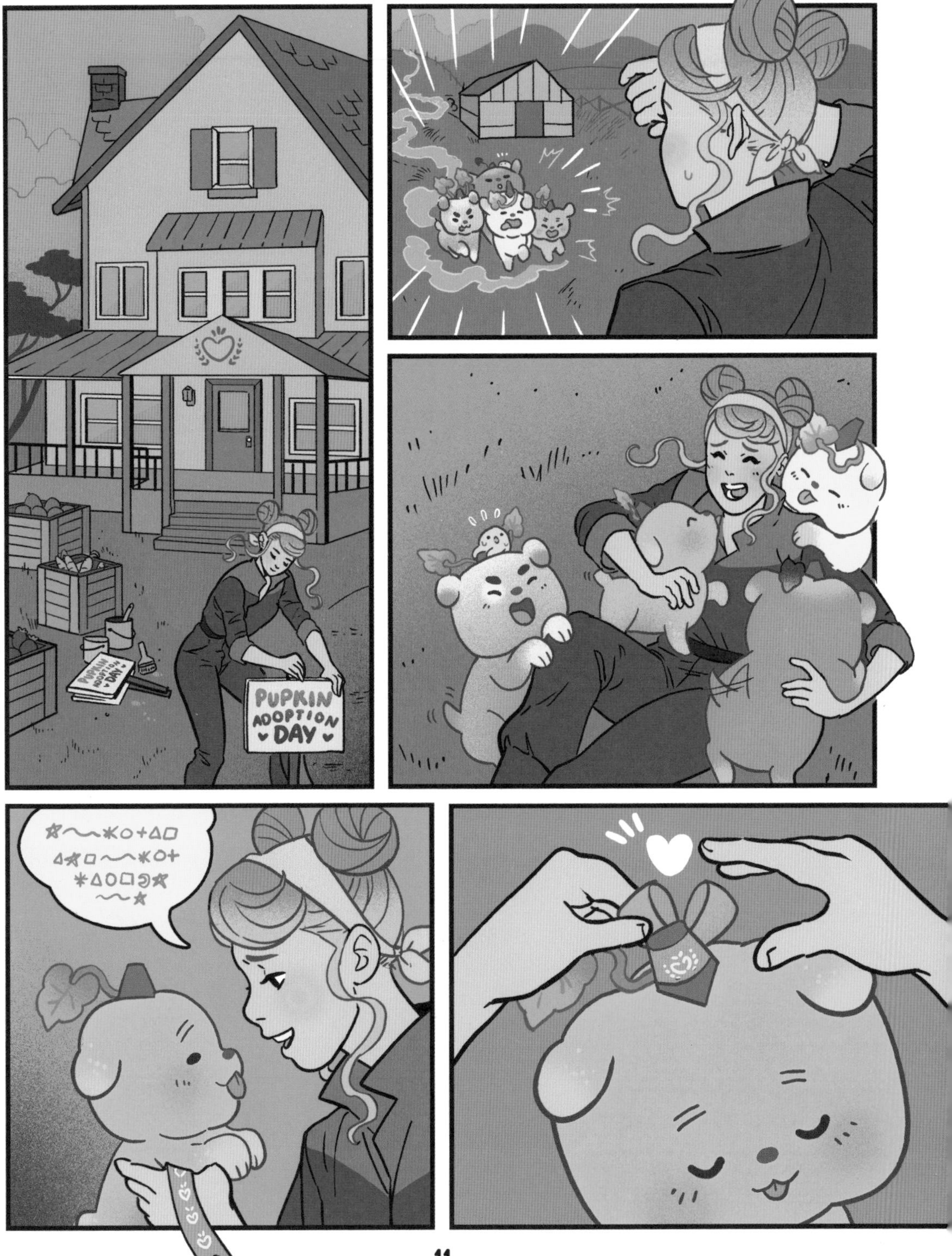
PUPKIN ADOPTION DAY
PUPKIN ADOPTION DAY

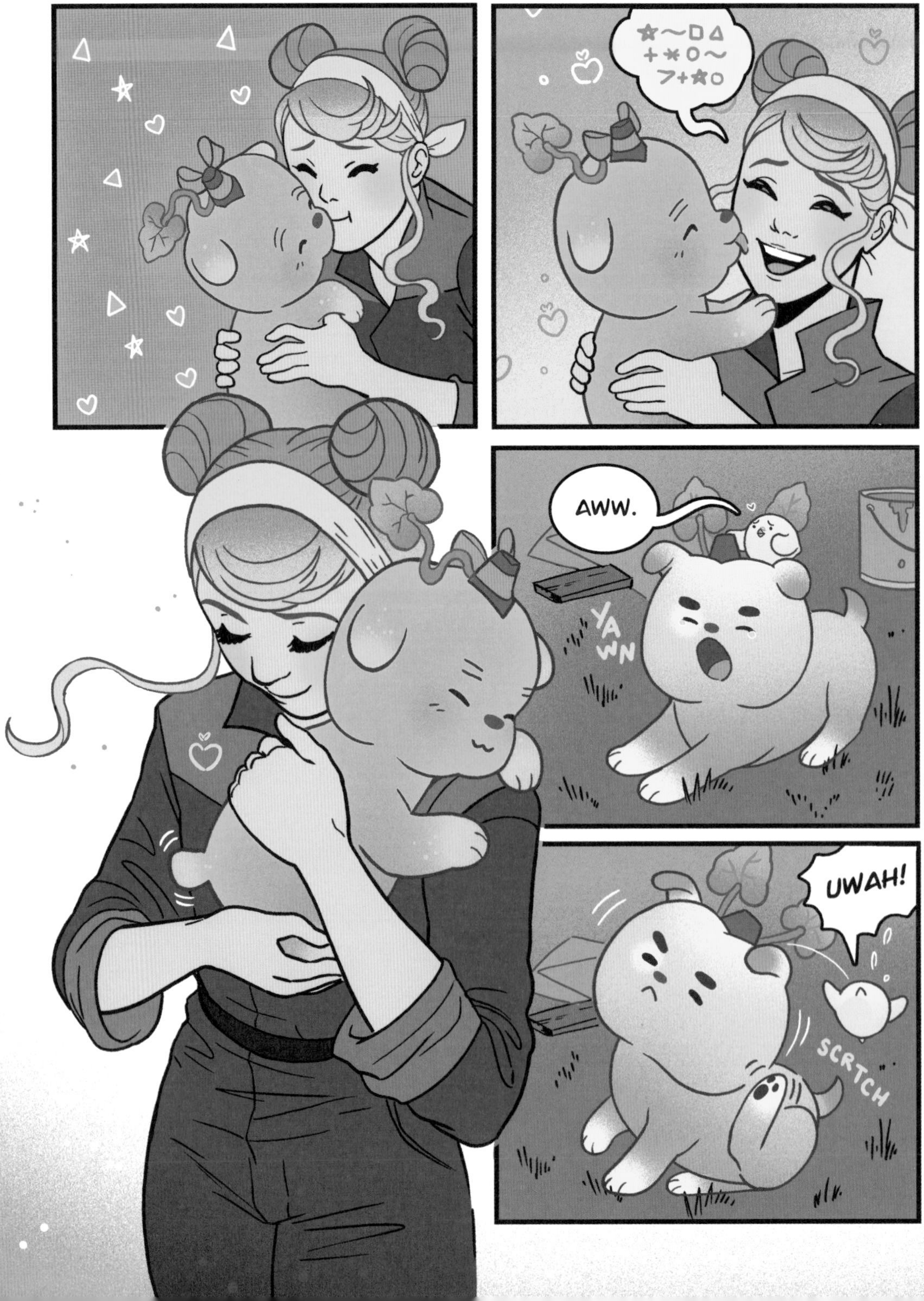
★～□△
+✱○～
⁊+★○
AWW.
YAWN
UWAH!
SCRTCH

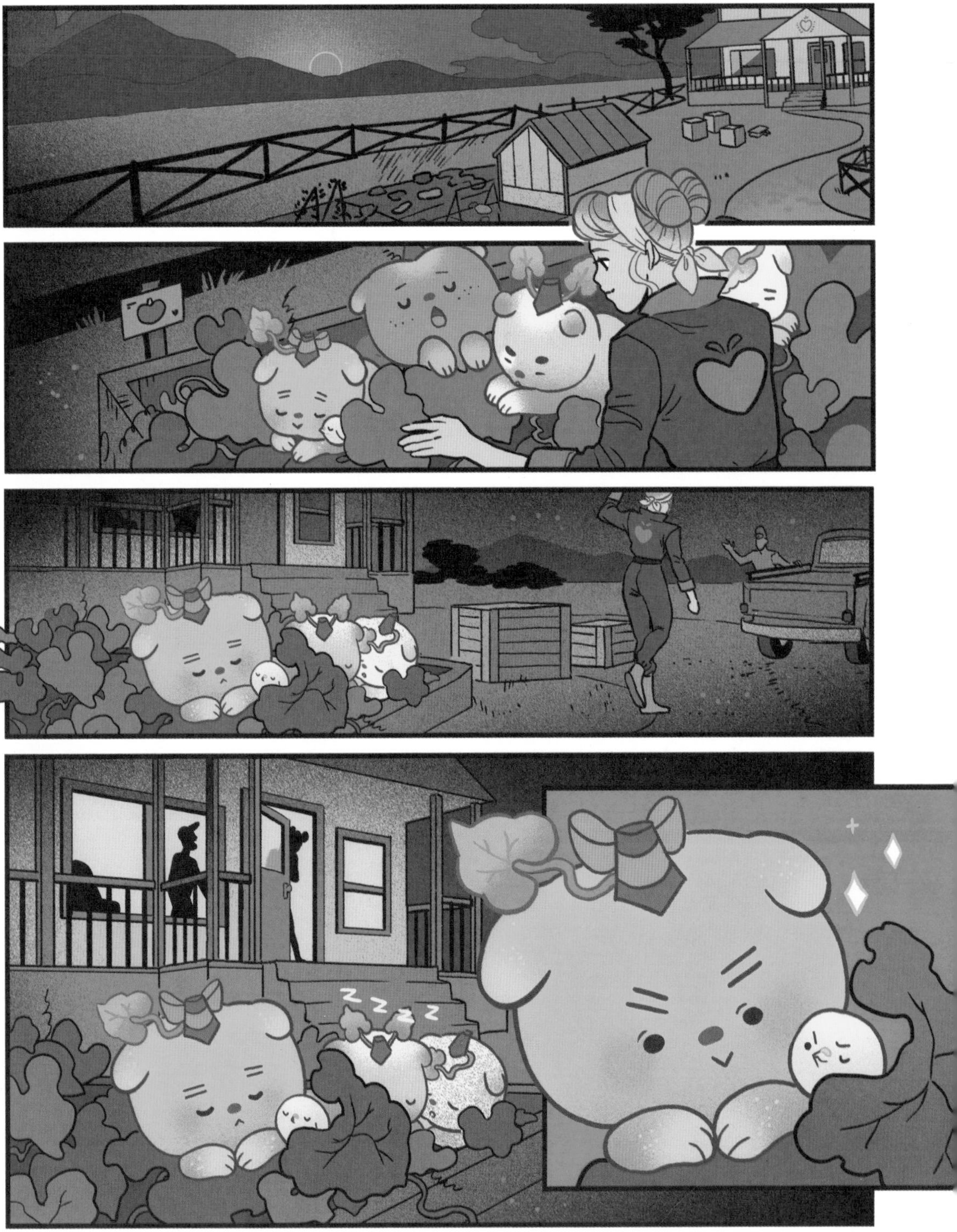
ZZZZ

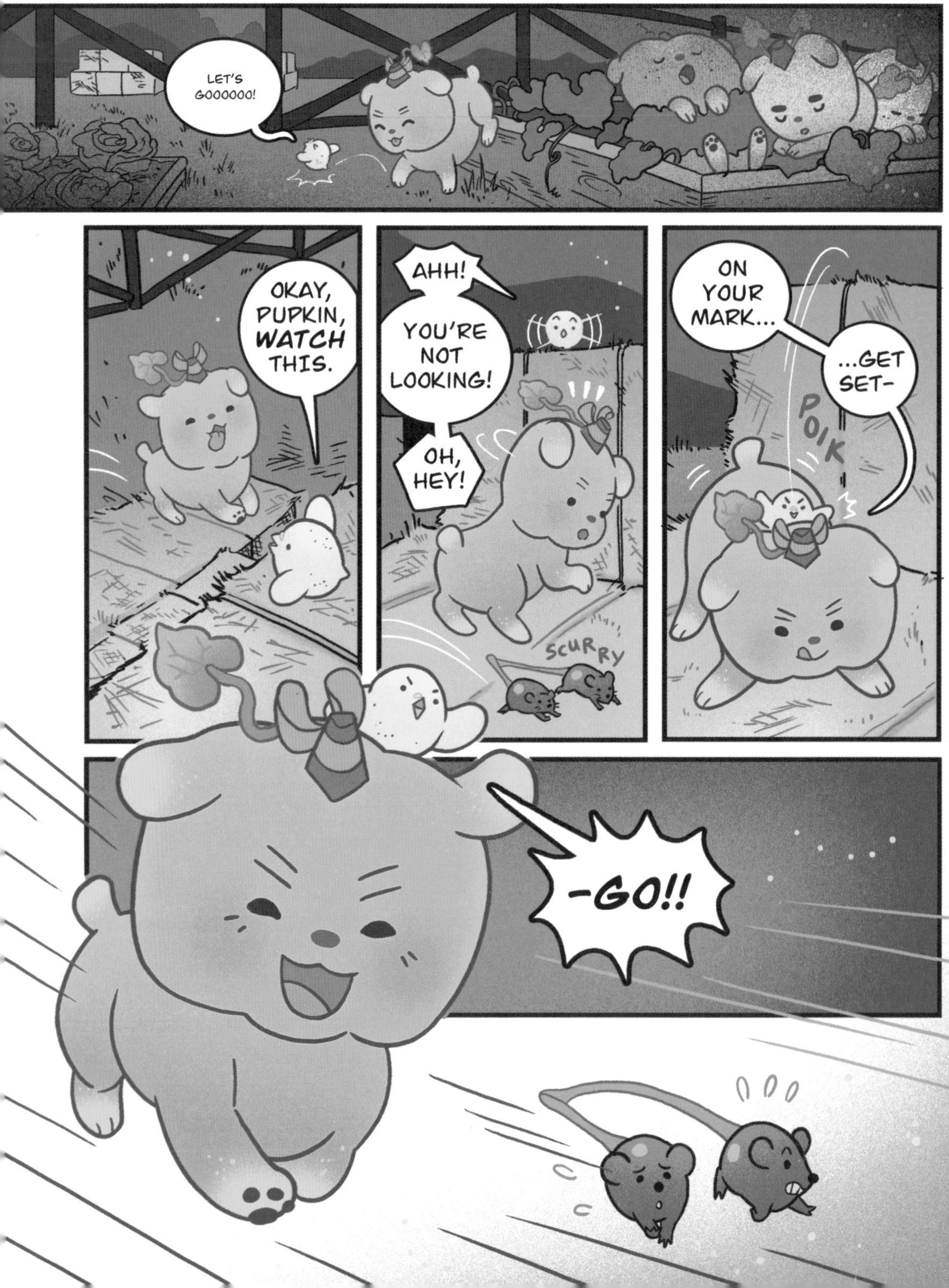
LET'S GOOOOOO!
OKAY, PUPKIN, WATCH THIS.
AHH!
YOU'RE NOT LOOKING!
OH, HEY!
SCURRY
ON YOUR MARK...
...GET SET-
POIK
-GO!!

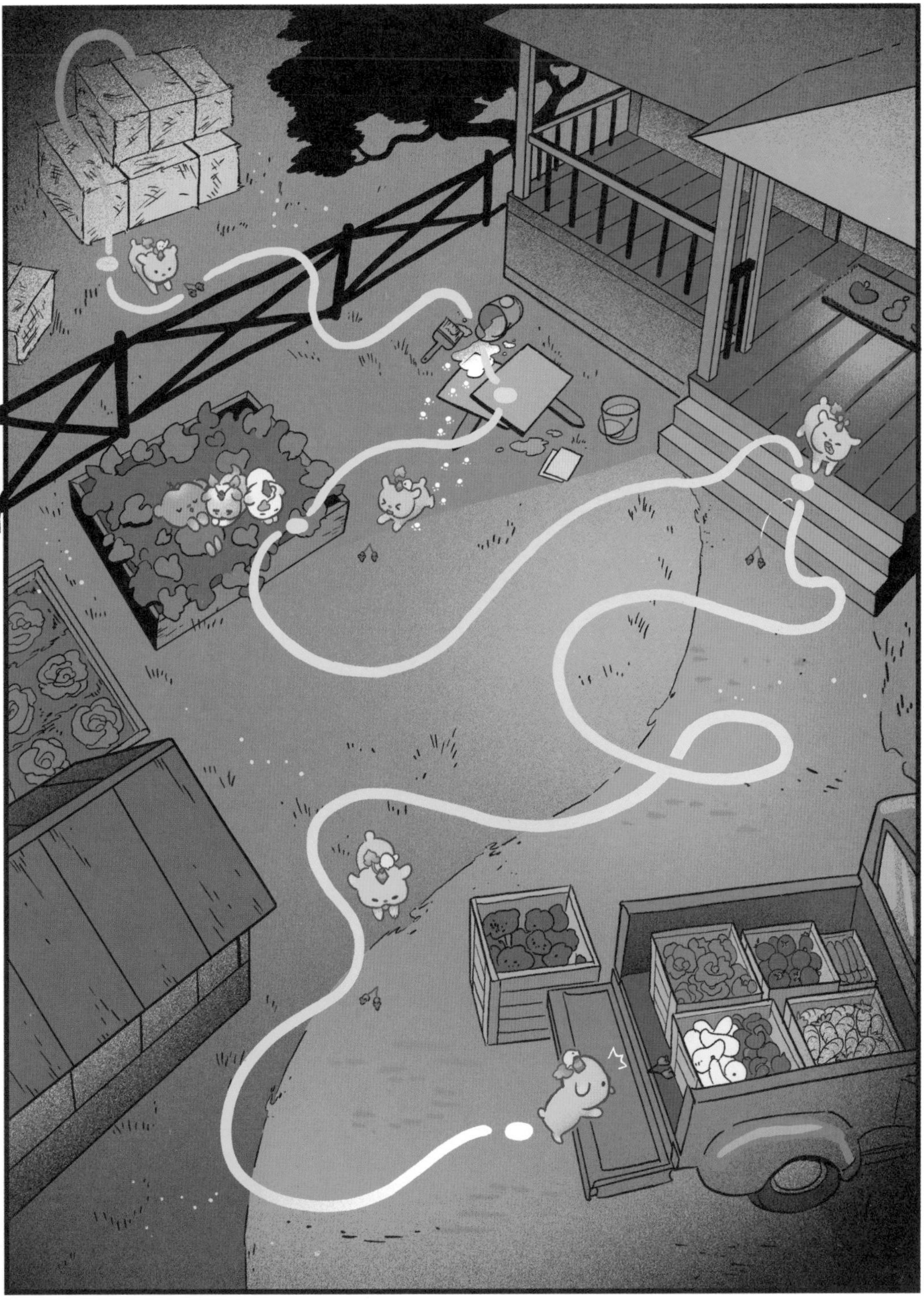

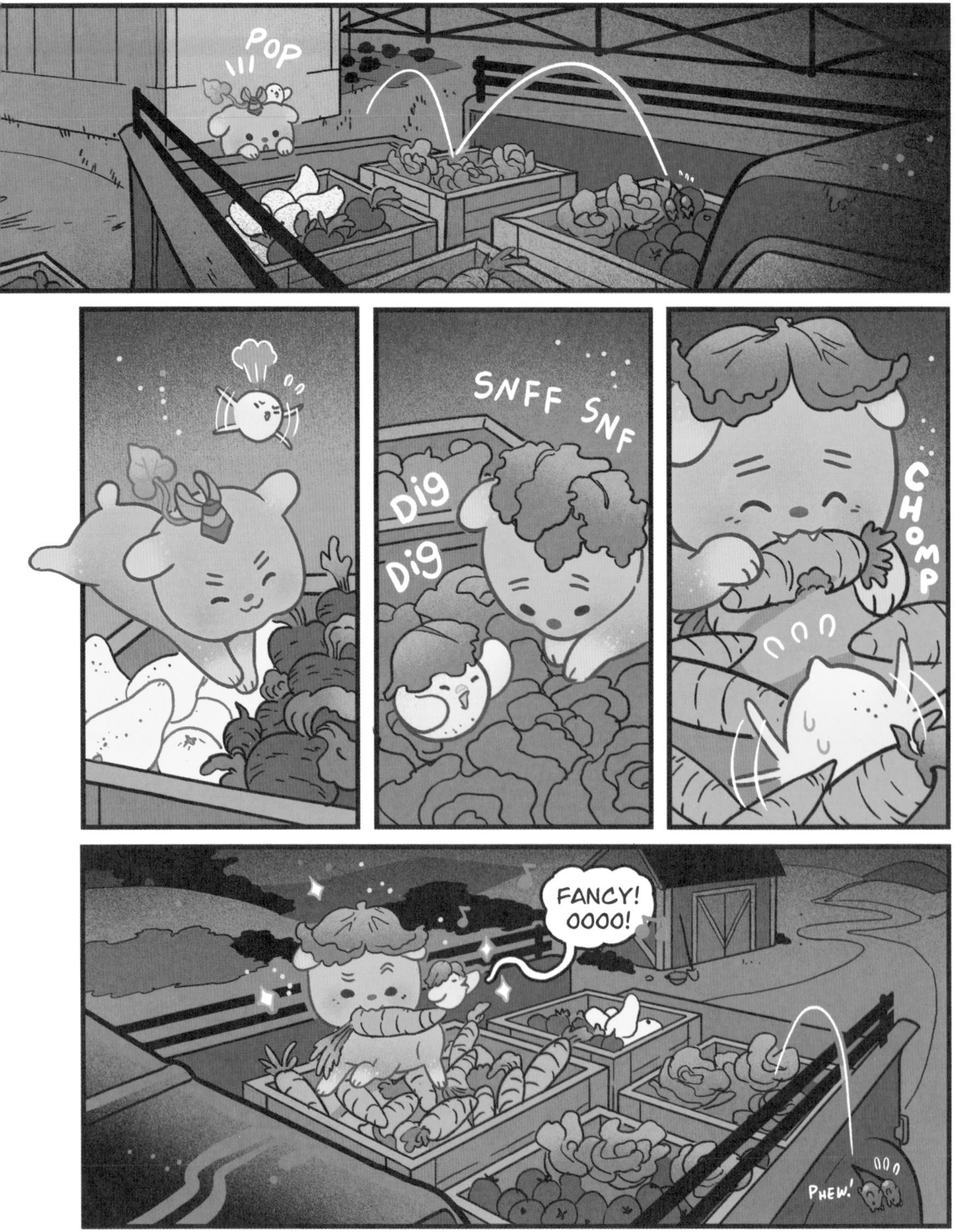
POP
SNFF SNFF
DIG
DIG
CHOMP
FANCY! OOOO!
PHEW!

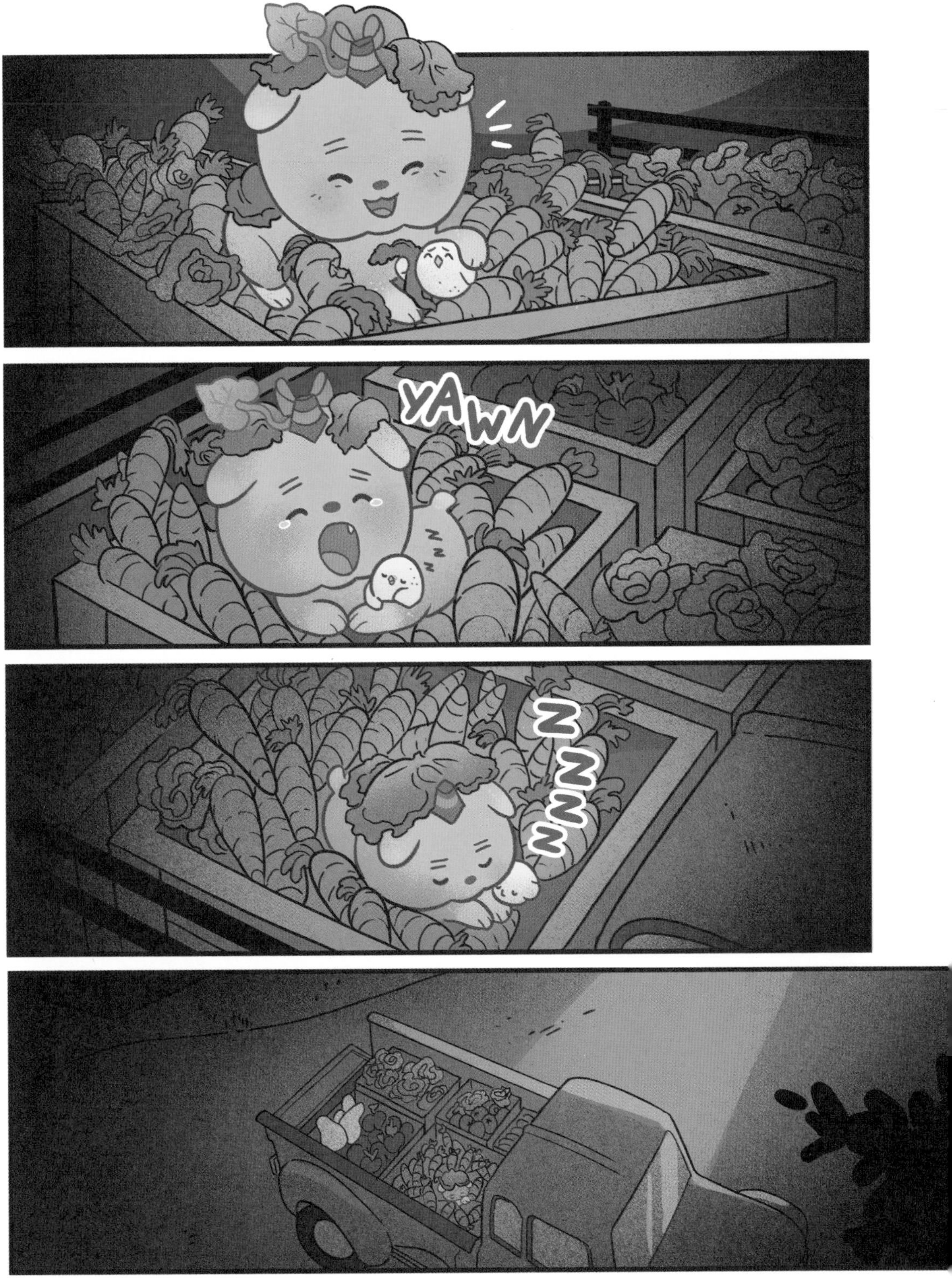
YAWN
Z
Z
Z
Z
Z

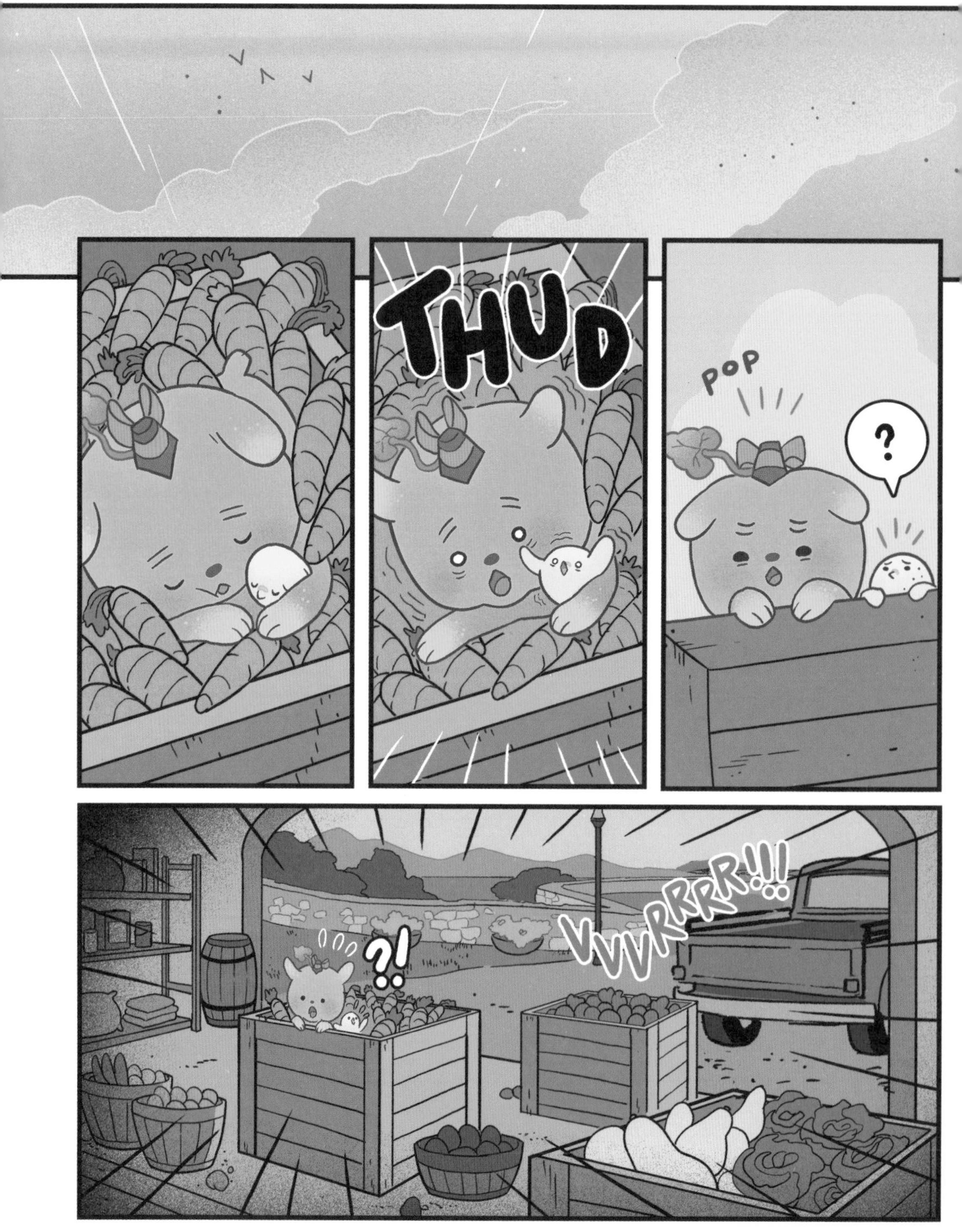
THUD
POP
?
?!
VVVRRRR!!!

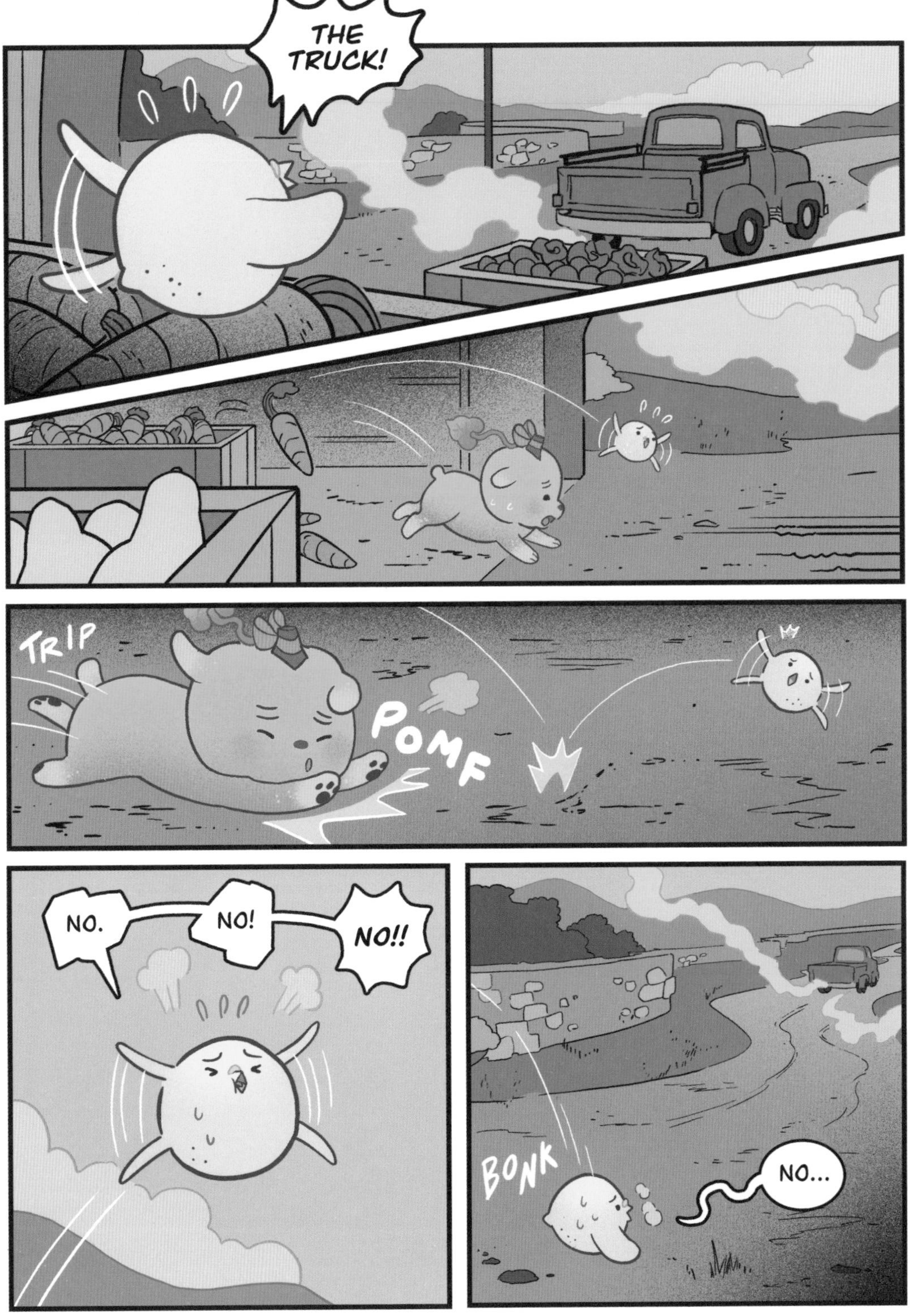
THE TRUCK!
TRIP
POMF
NO.
NO!
NO!!
BONK
NO...

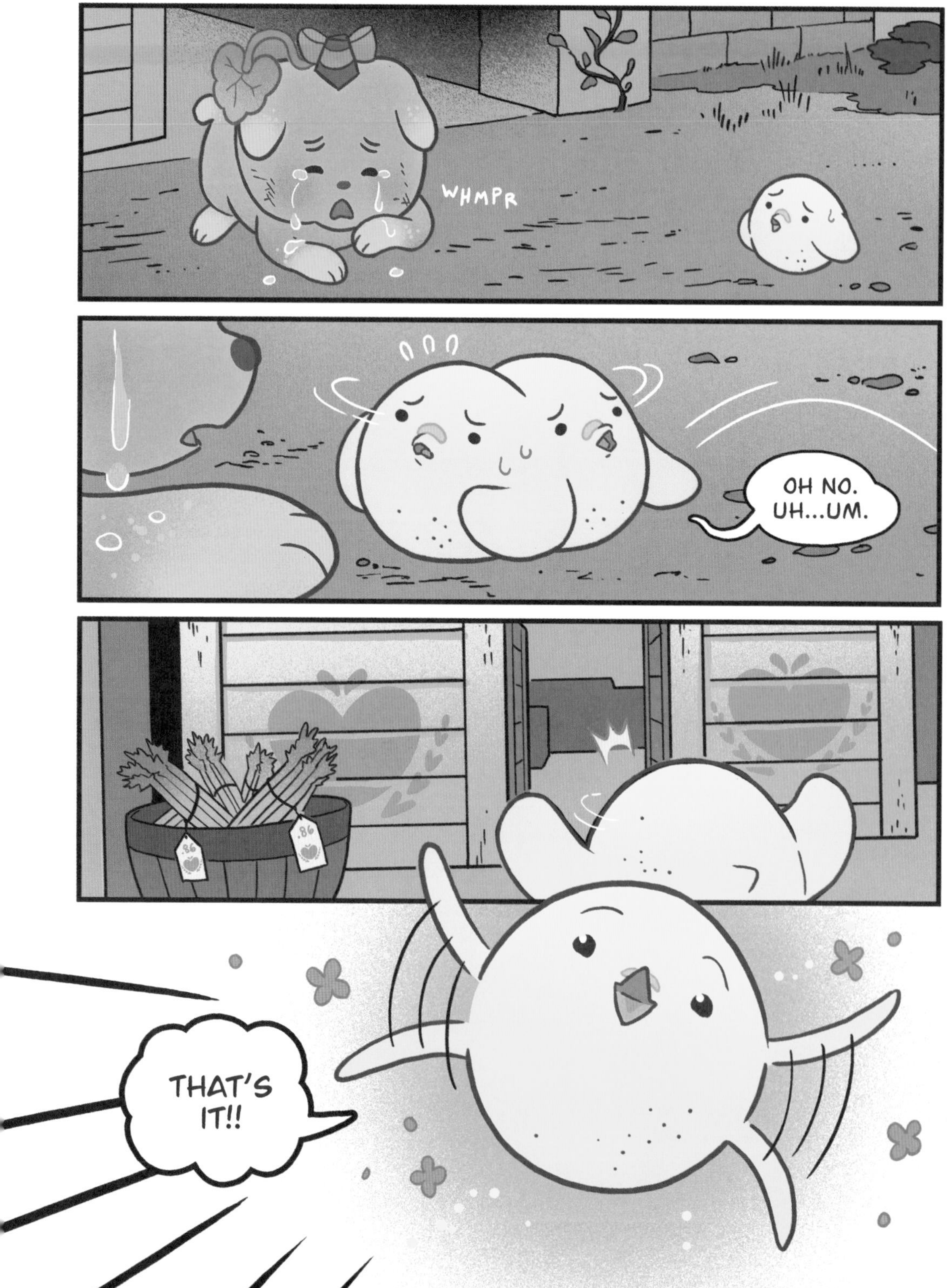
WHMPR
OH NO. UH...UM.
THAT'S IT!!

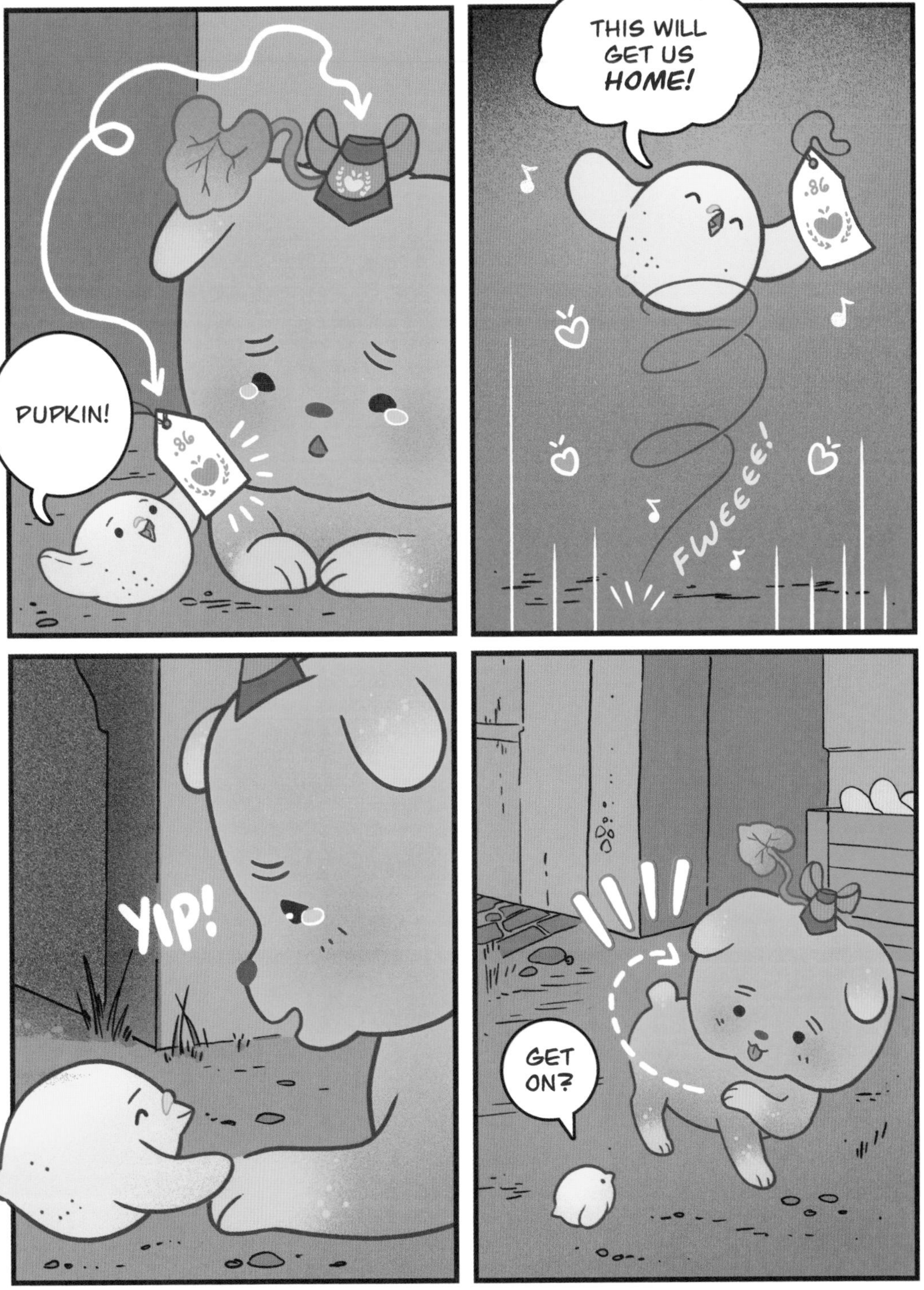
PUPKIN!
.86
THIS WILL GET US HOME!
.86
FWEEEE!
YIP!
GET ON?

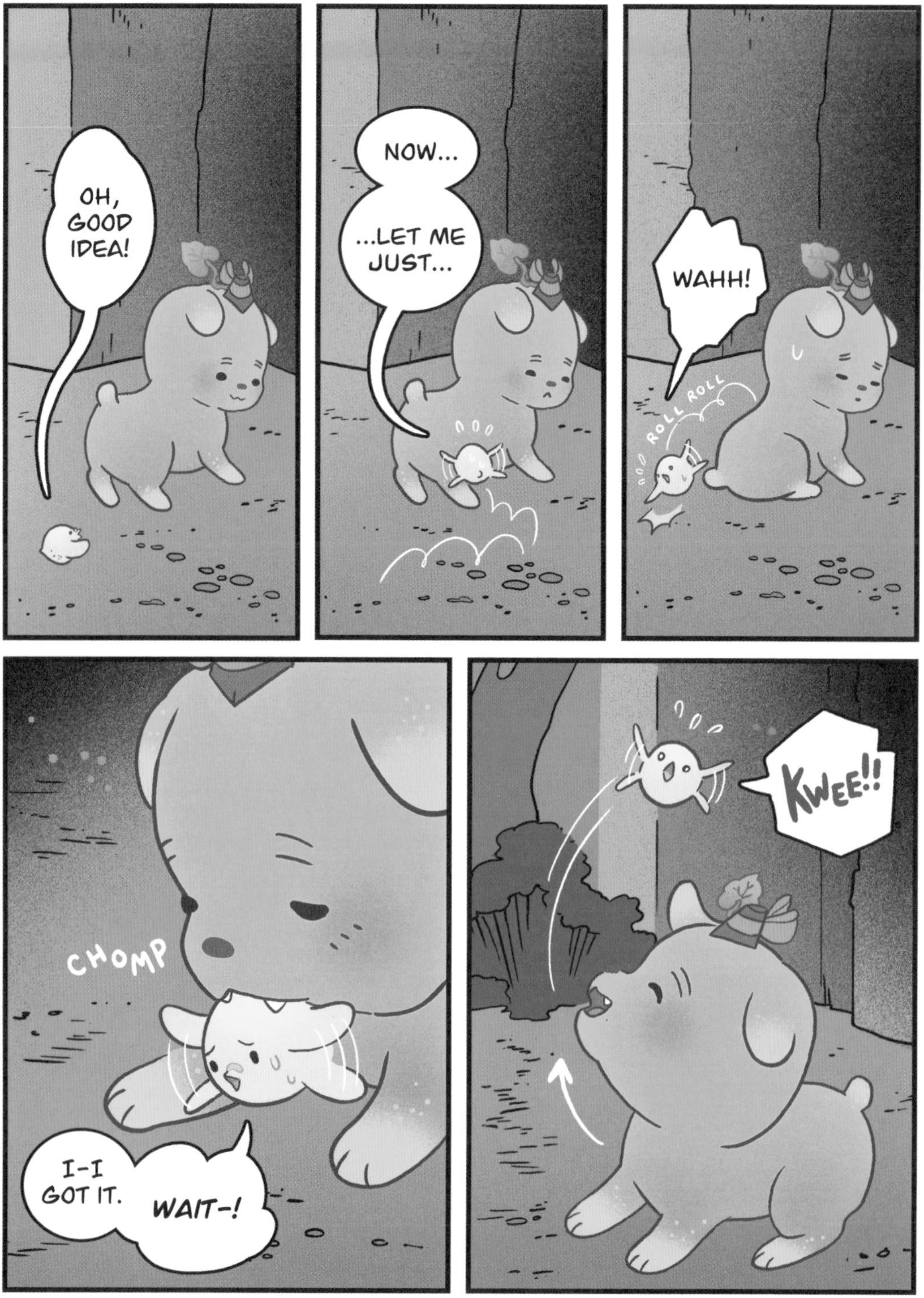
OH, GOOD IDEA!
NOW...
...LET ME JUST...
WAHH!
ROLL ROLL
CHOMP
I-I GOT IT.
WAIT-!
KWEE!!

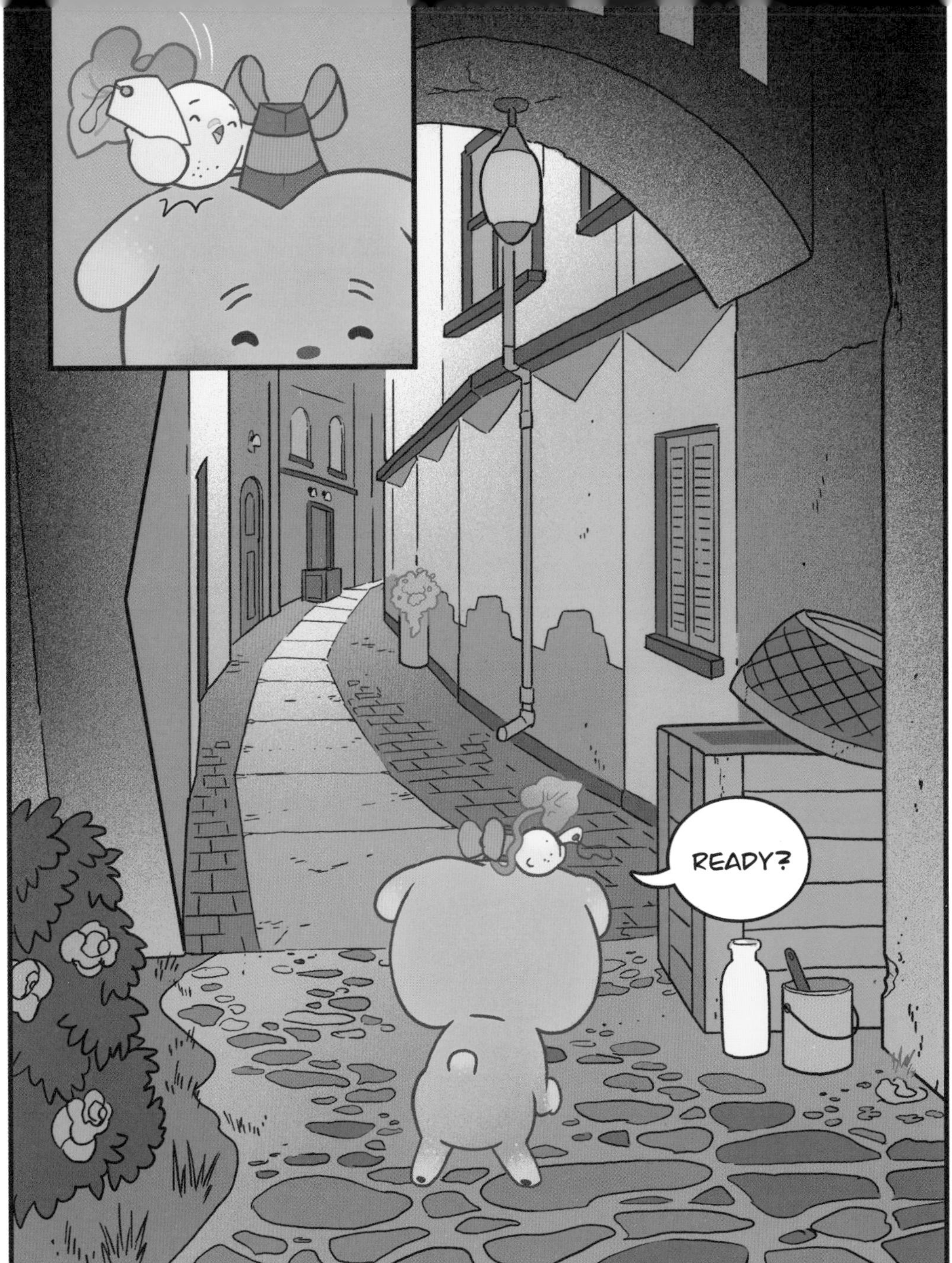
READY?

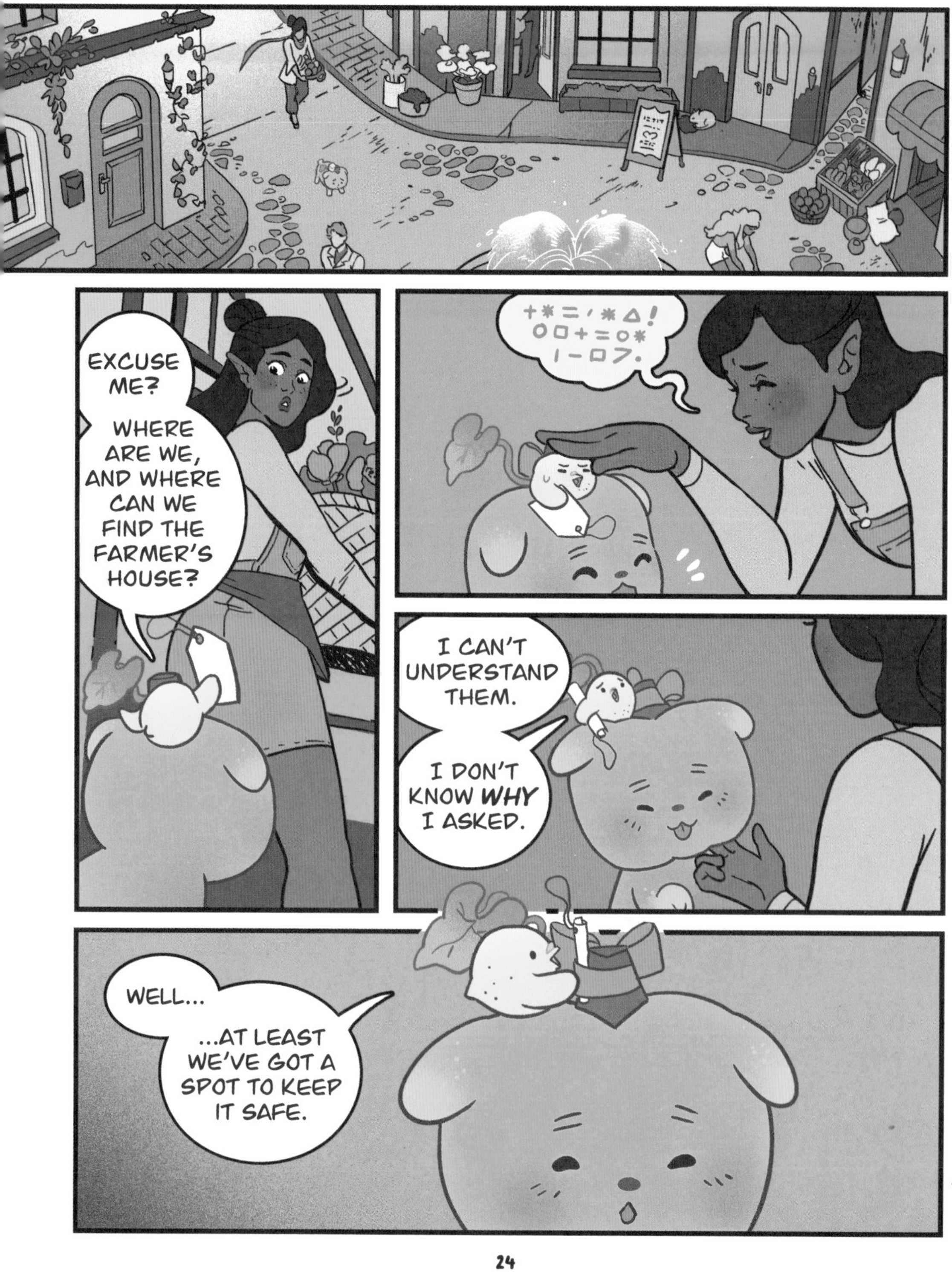
EXCUSE ME?
WHERE ARE WE, AND WHERE CAN WE FIND THE FARMER'S HOUSE?
I CAN'T UNDERSTAND THEM.
I DON'T KNOW **WHY** I ASKED.
WELL...
...AT LEAST WE'VE GOT A SPOT TO KEEP IT SAFE.

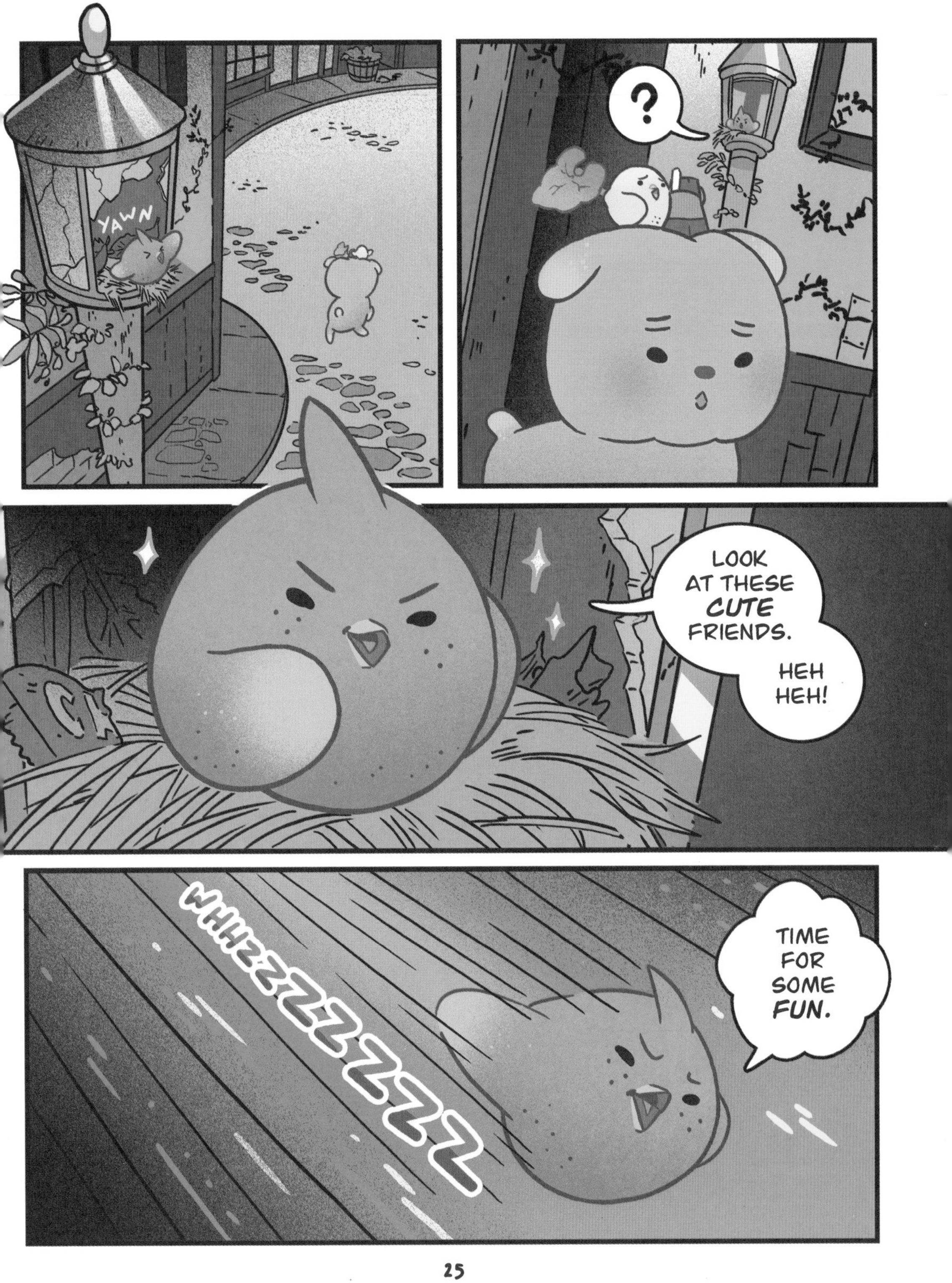
YAWN
?
LOOK AT THESE CUTE FRIENDS.
HEH HEH!
TIME FOR SOME FUN.
WHIZZZZZZZZ

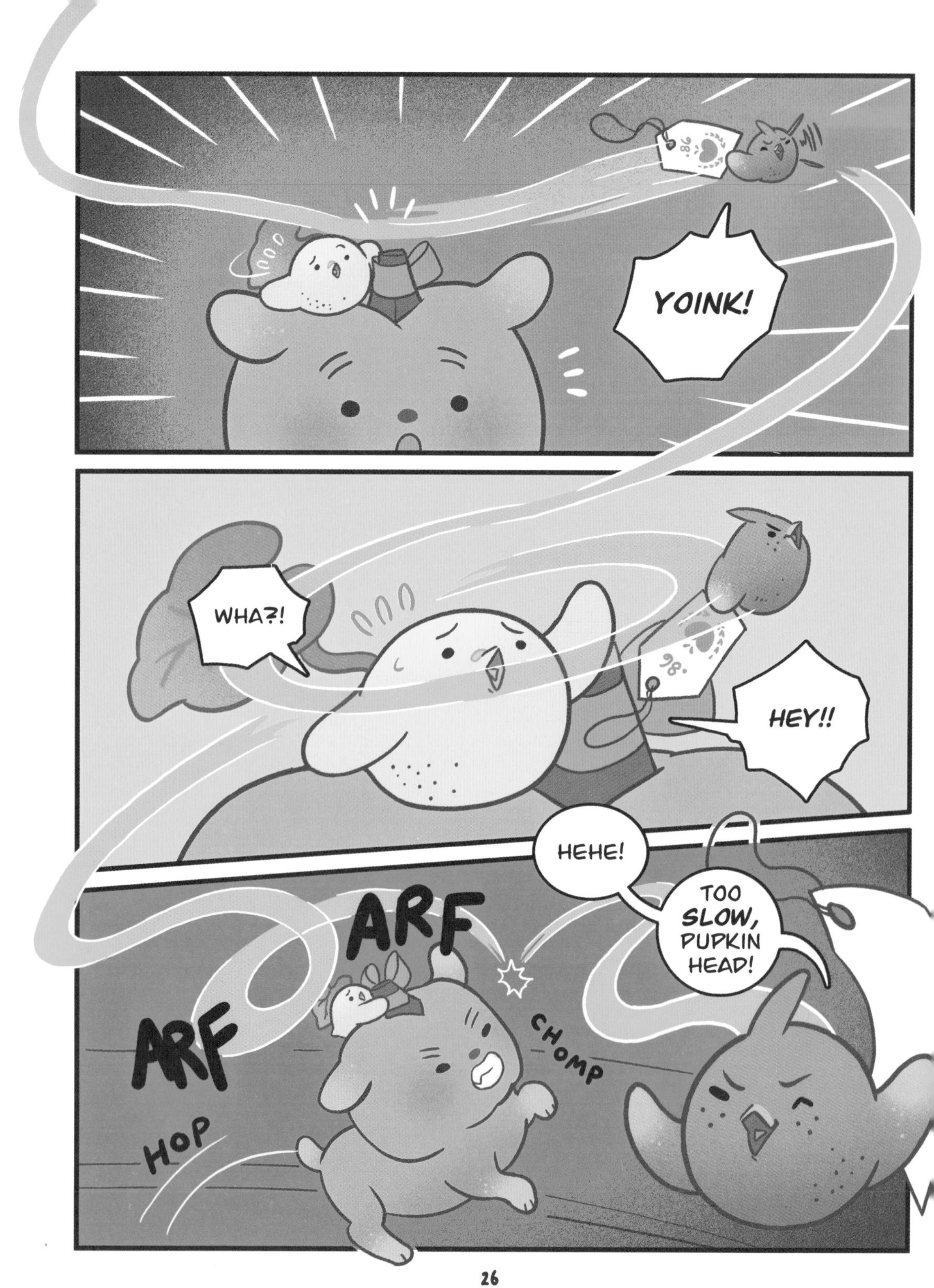

YOINK!
WHA?!
HEY!!
HEHE!
TOO SLOW, PUPKIN HEAD!
ARF
ARF
CHOMP
HOP

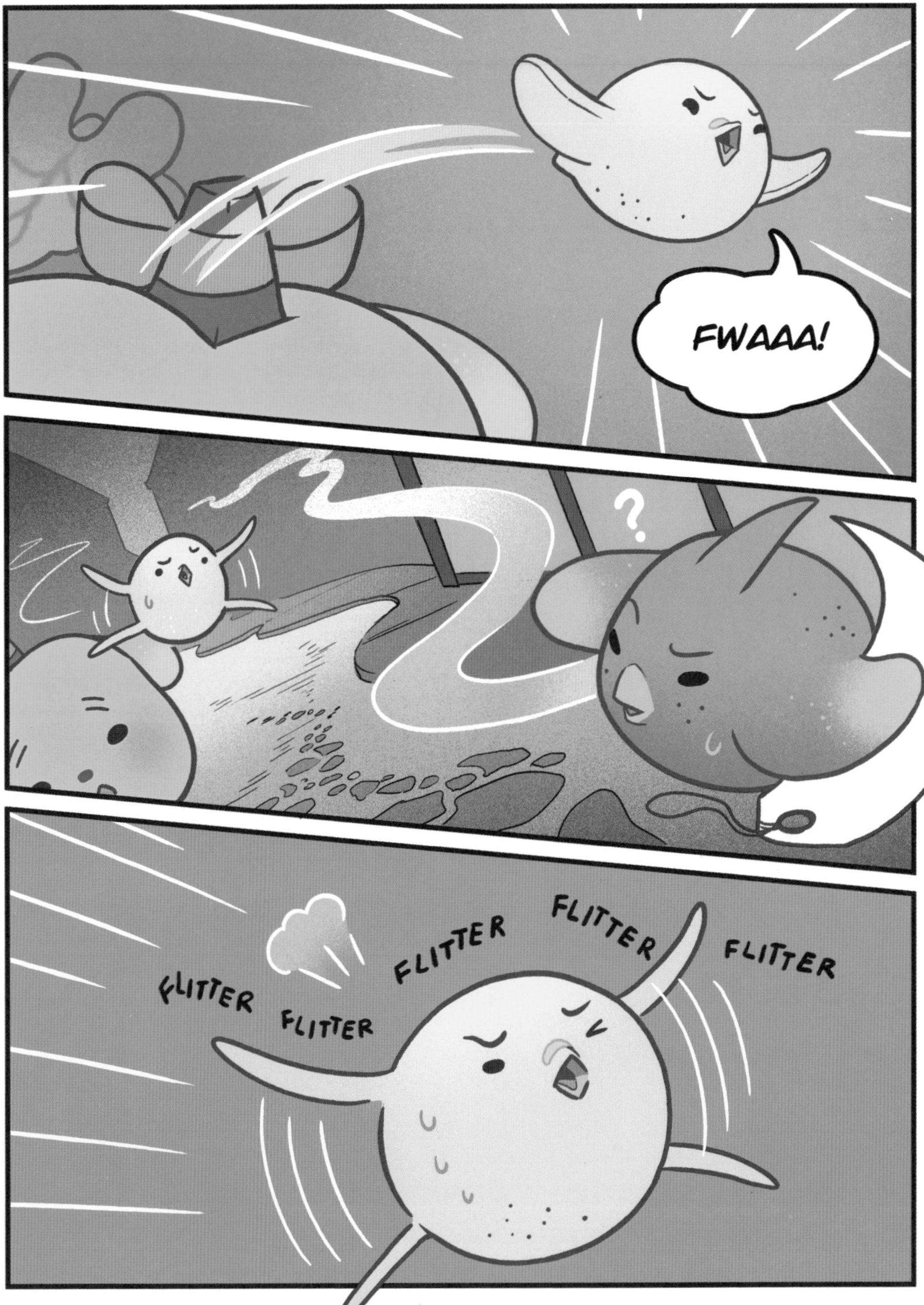
FWAAA!
?
FLITTER
FLITTER
FLITTER
FLITTER
FLITTER

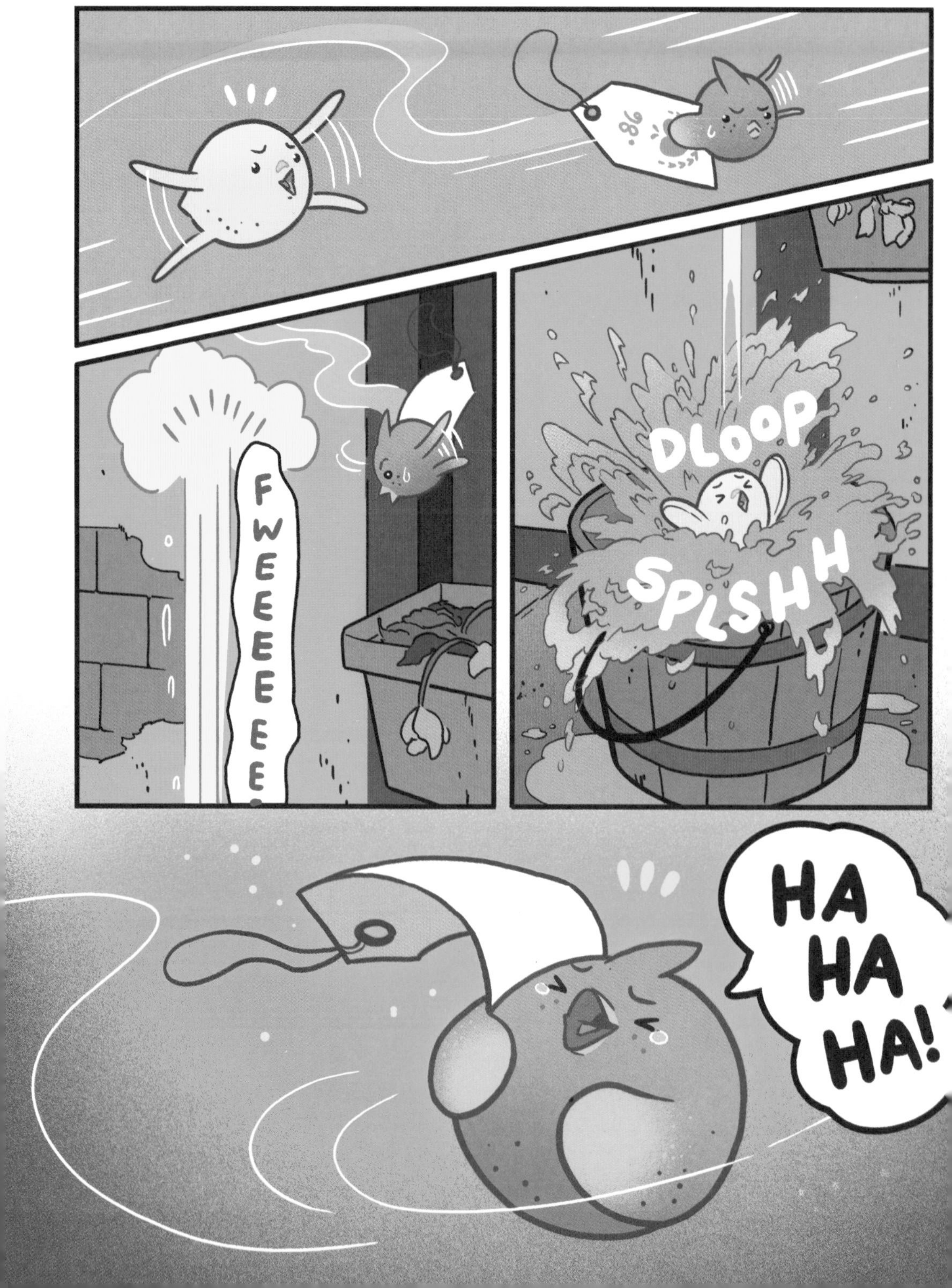
FWEEEEEEE
DLOOP
SPLSHH
HA HA HA!

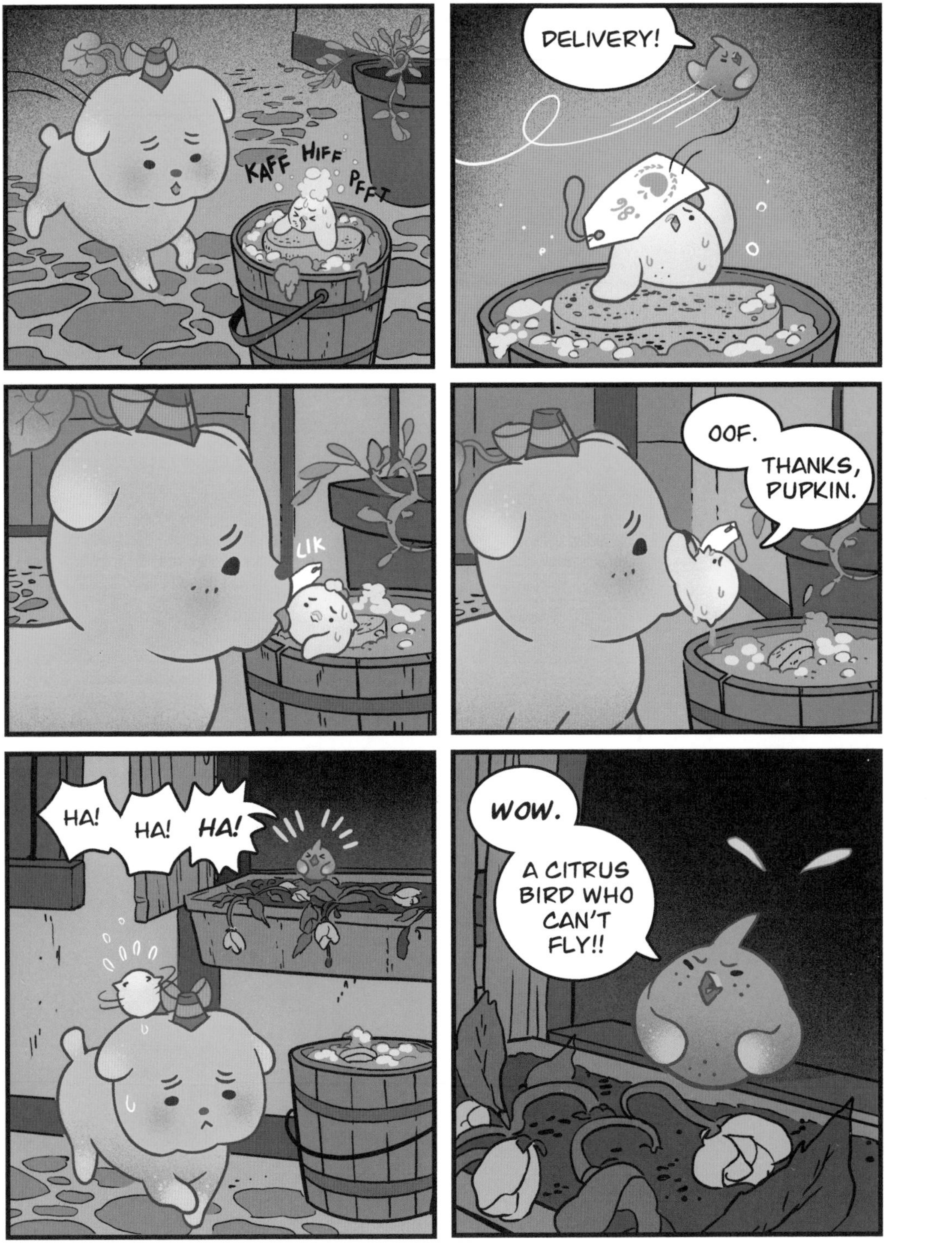
KAFF
HIFF
PFFT
DELIVERY!
LIK
OOF.
THANKS, PUPKIN.
HA!
HA!
HA!
WOW.
A CITRUS BIRD WHO CAN'T FLY!!

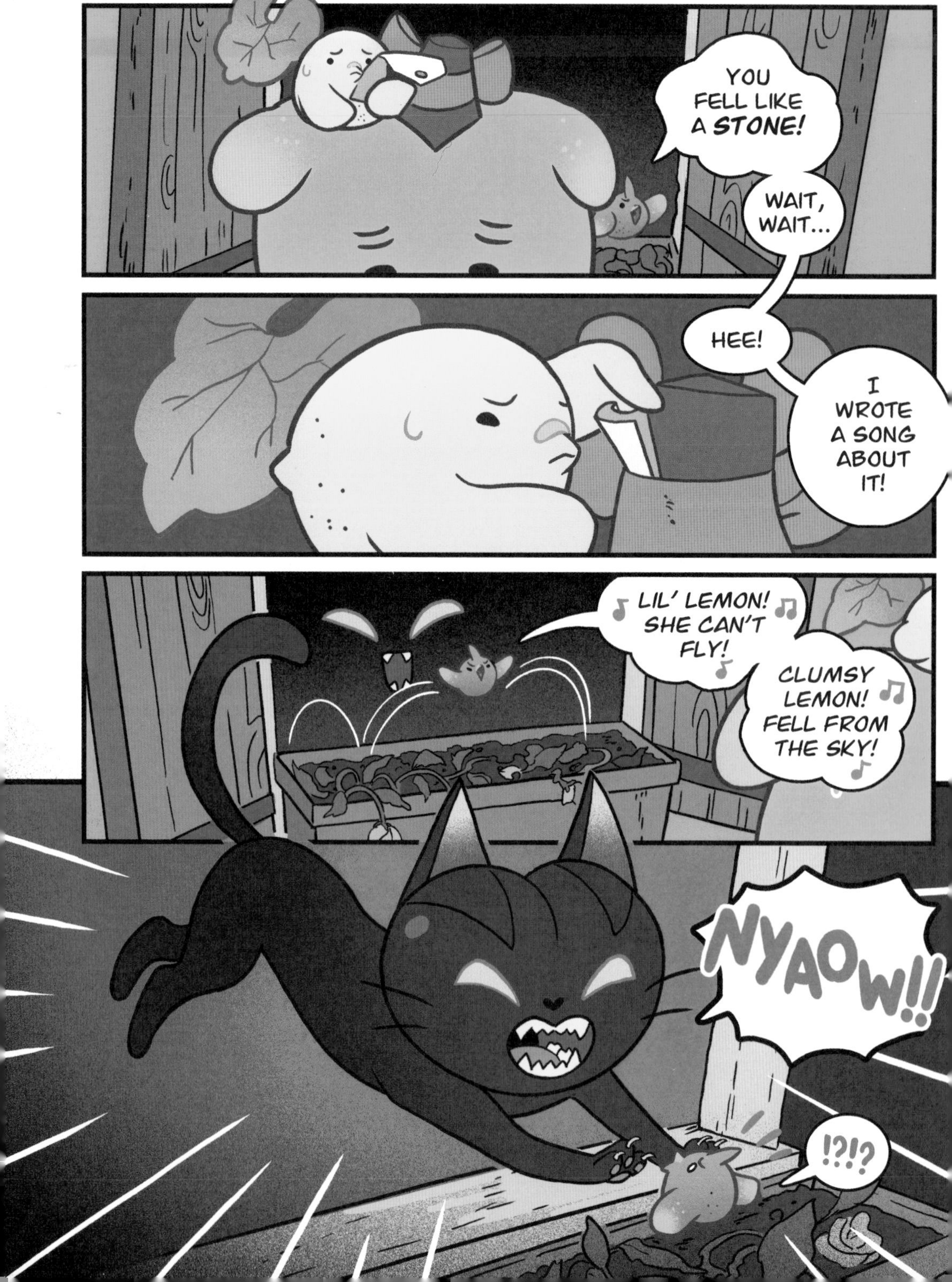
YOU FELL LIKE A STONE!
WAIT, WAIT...
HEE!
I WROTE A SONG ABOUT IT!
LIL' LEMON! SHE CAN'T FLY!
CLUMSY LEMON! FELL FROM THE SKY!
NYAOW!!
!?!?

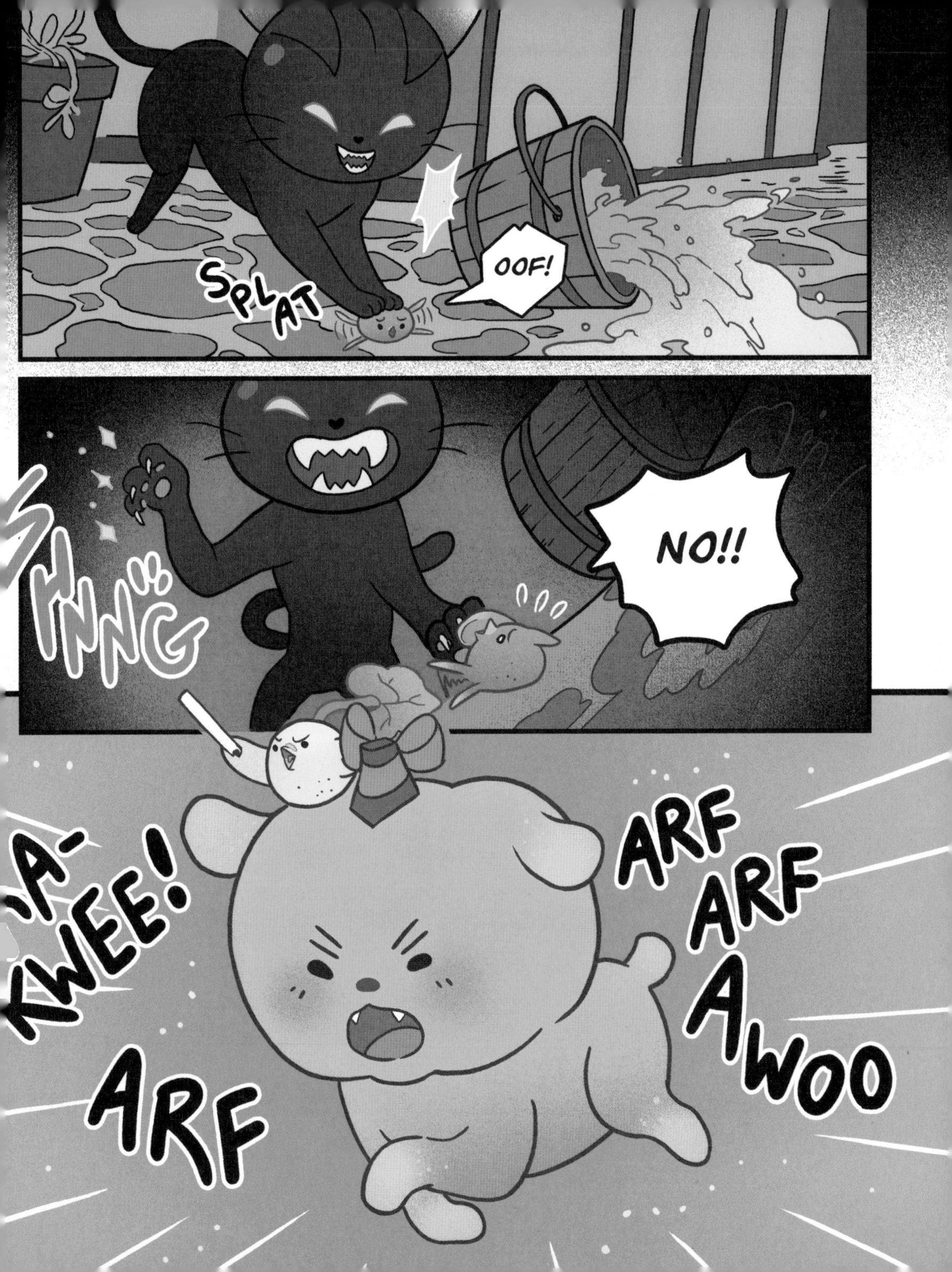
SPLAT
OOF!
SHHNNG!!
NO!!
'A-KWEE!
ARF
ARF
ARF
AWOO

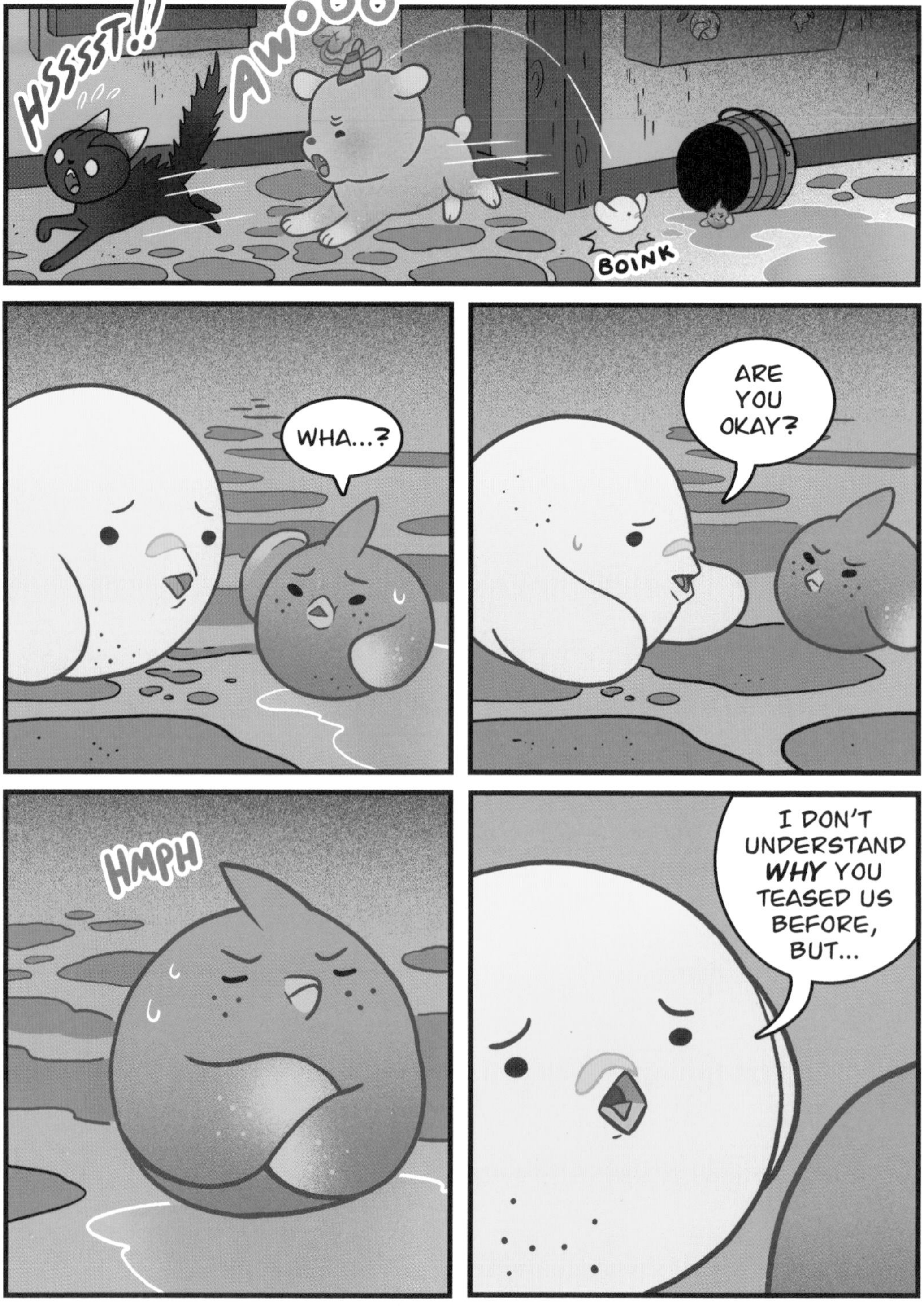
HSSSST!!
AWOOO
BOINK
WHA...?
ARE YOU OKAY?
HMPH
I DON'T UNDERSTAND **WHY** YOU TEASED US BEFORE, BUT...

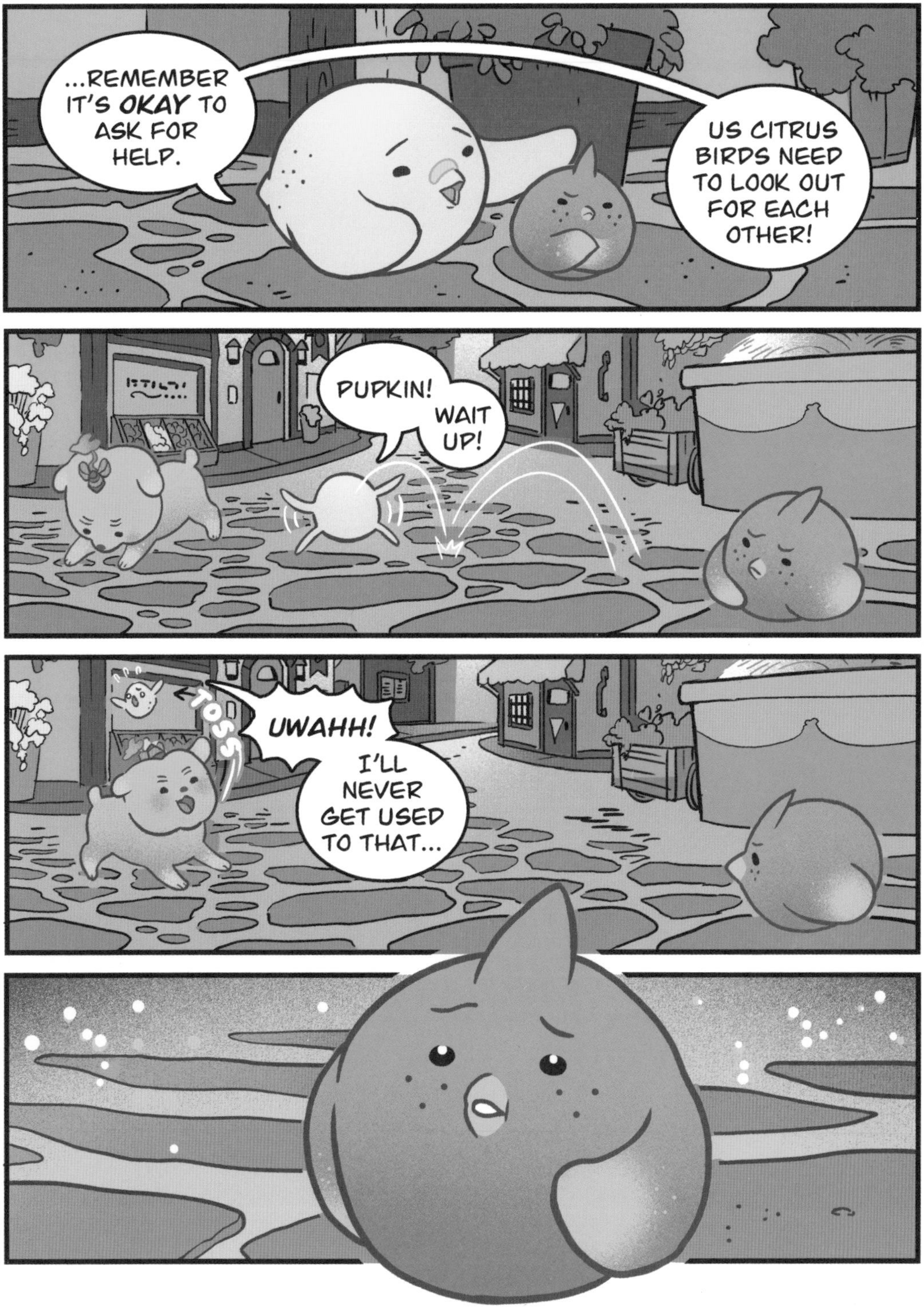
...REMEMBER IT'S OKAY TO ASK FOR HELP.
US CITRUS BIRDS NEED TO LOOK OUT FOR EACH OTHER!
PUPKIN!
WAIT UP!
TOSS
UWAHH!
I'LL NEVER GET USED TO THAT...

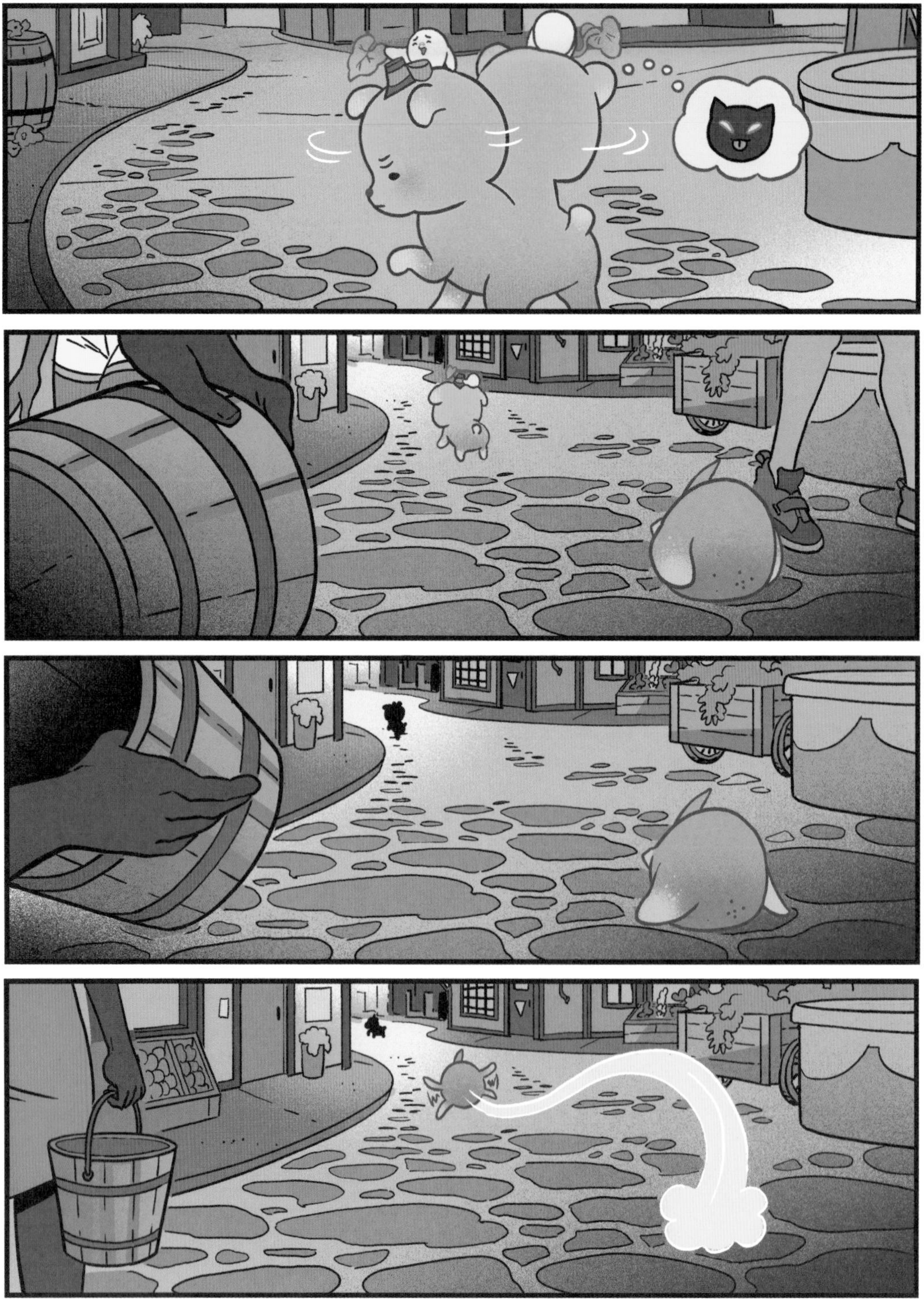

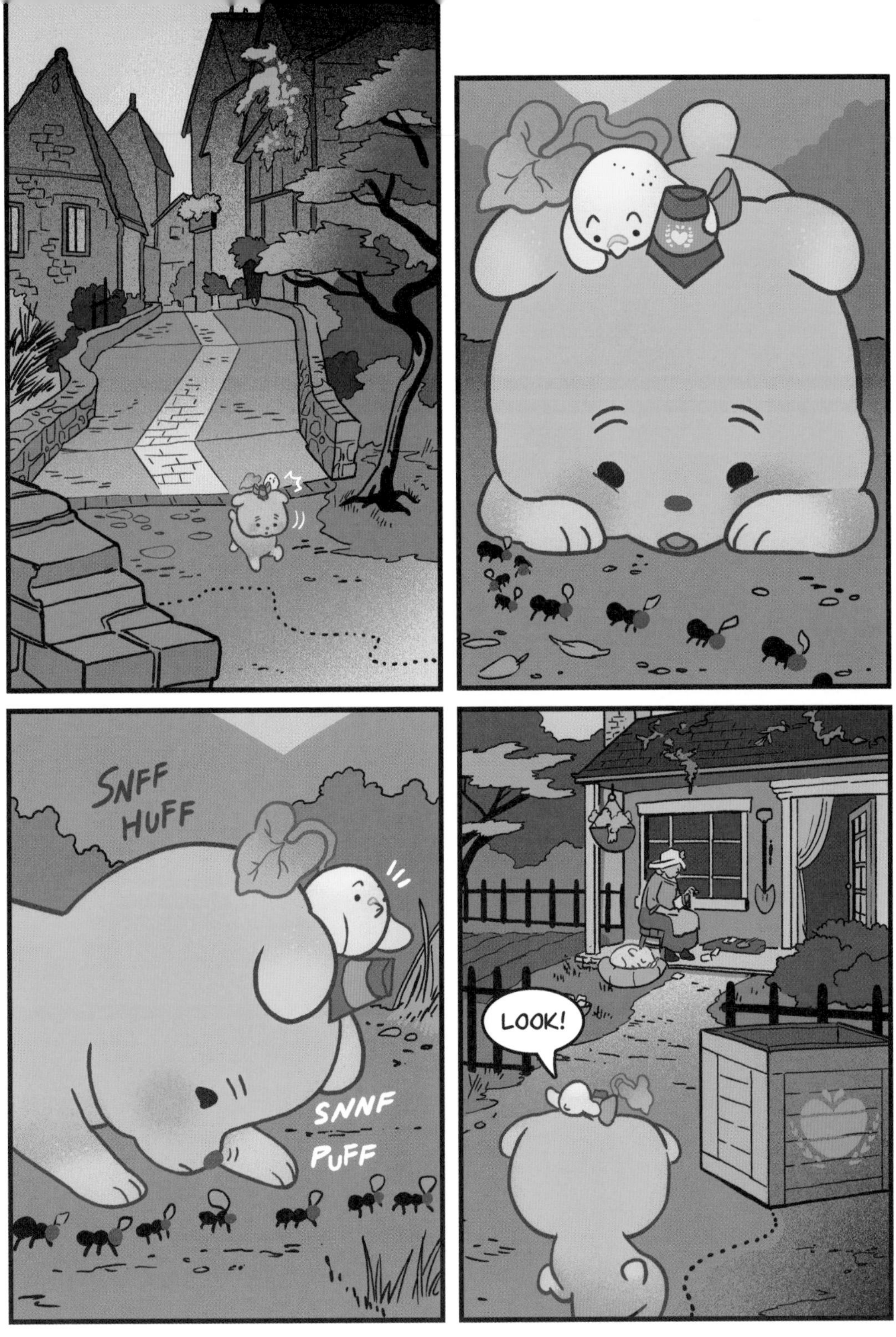
SNFF
HUFF
SNNF
PUFF
LOOK!

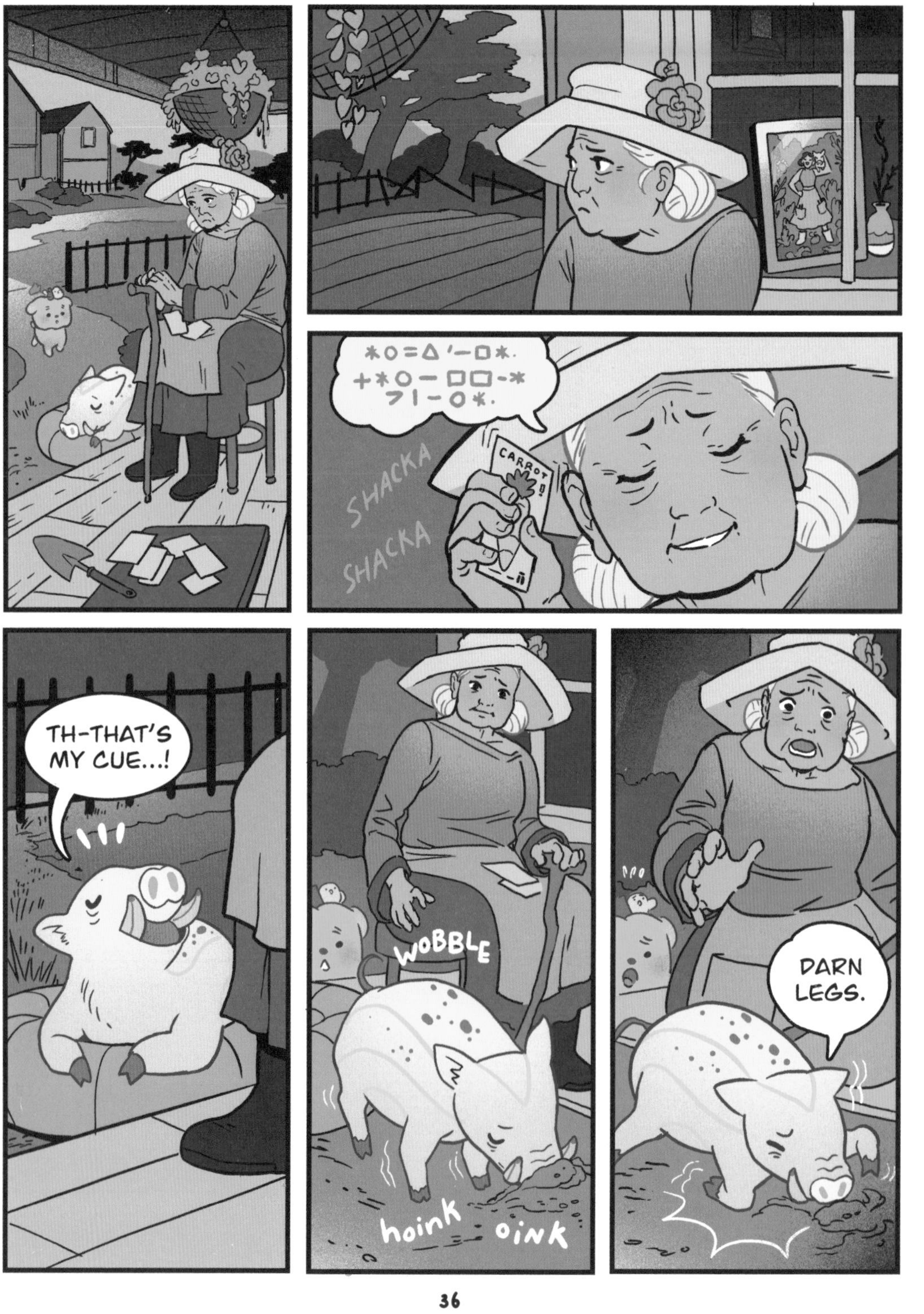
CARROT
SHACKA
SHACKA
TH-THAT'S MY CUE...!
WOBBLE
hoink oink
DARN LEGS.

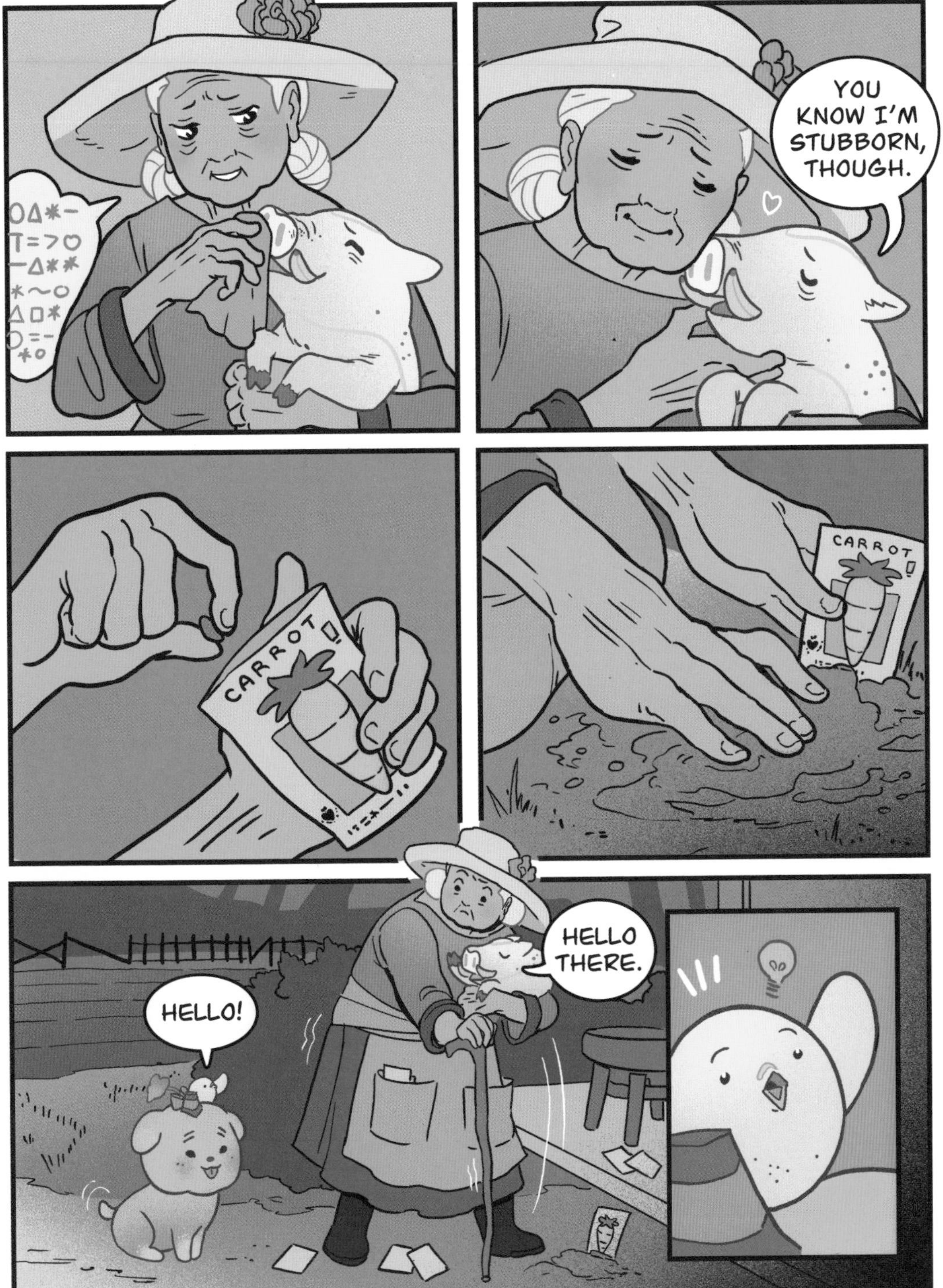
YOU KNOW I'M STUBBORN, THOUGH.
CARROT
CARROT
HELLO!
HELLO THERE.

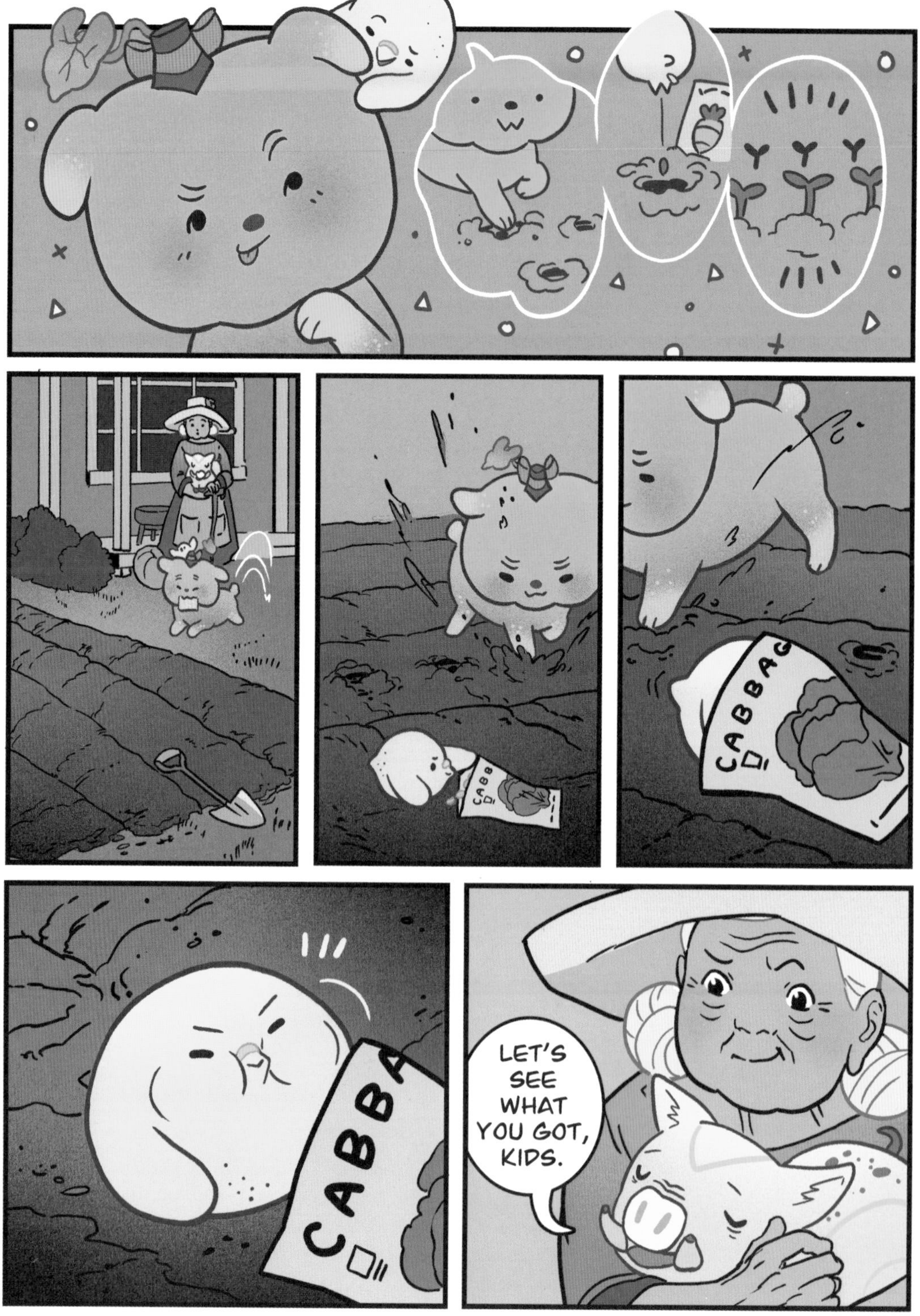

CABBAG
CABB
CABBA
LET'S SEE WHAT YOU GOT, KIDS.

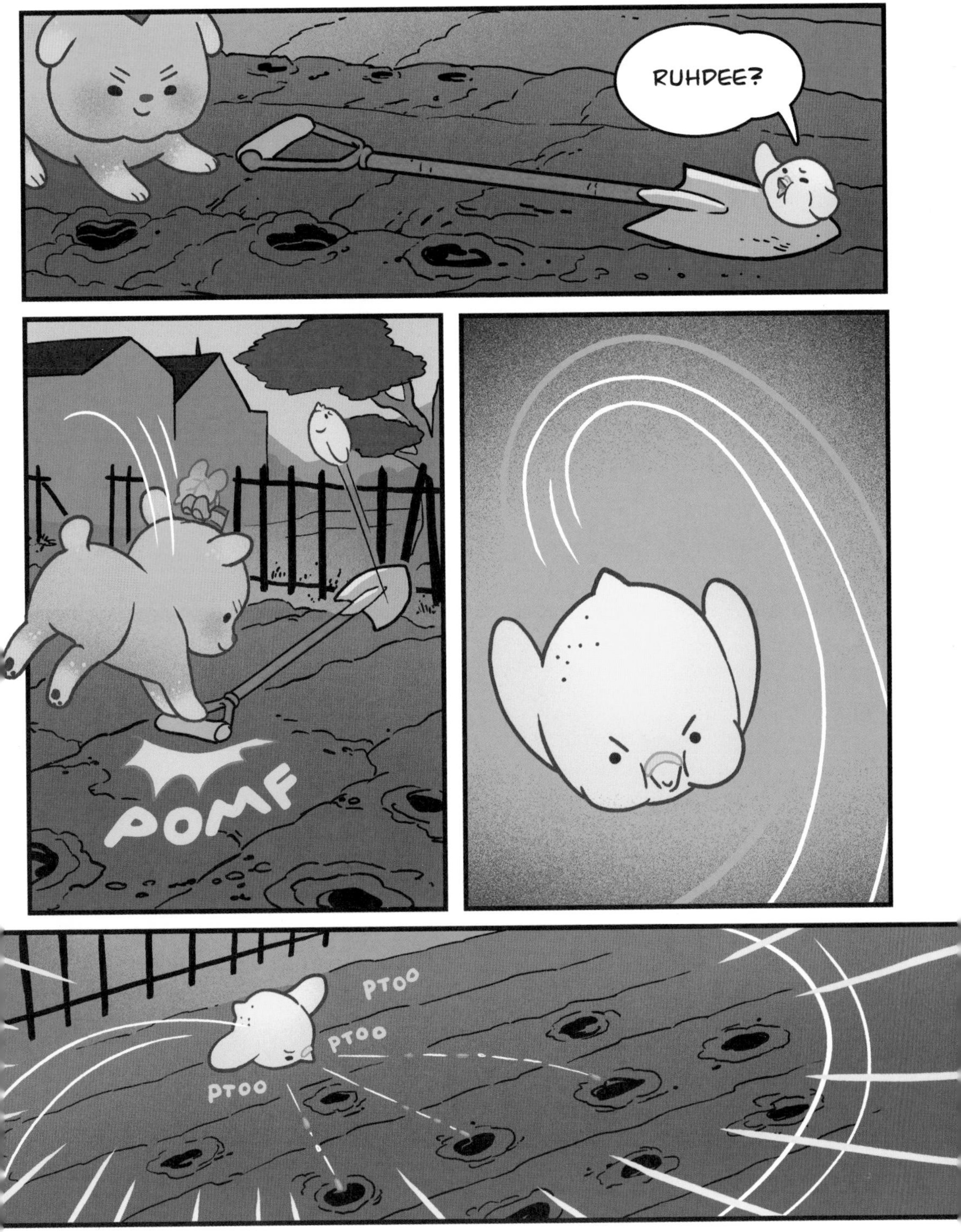
RUHDEE?
POMF
PTOO
PTOO
PTOO

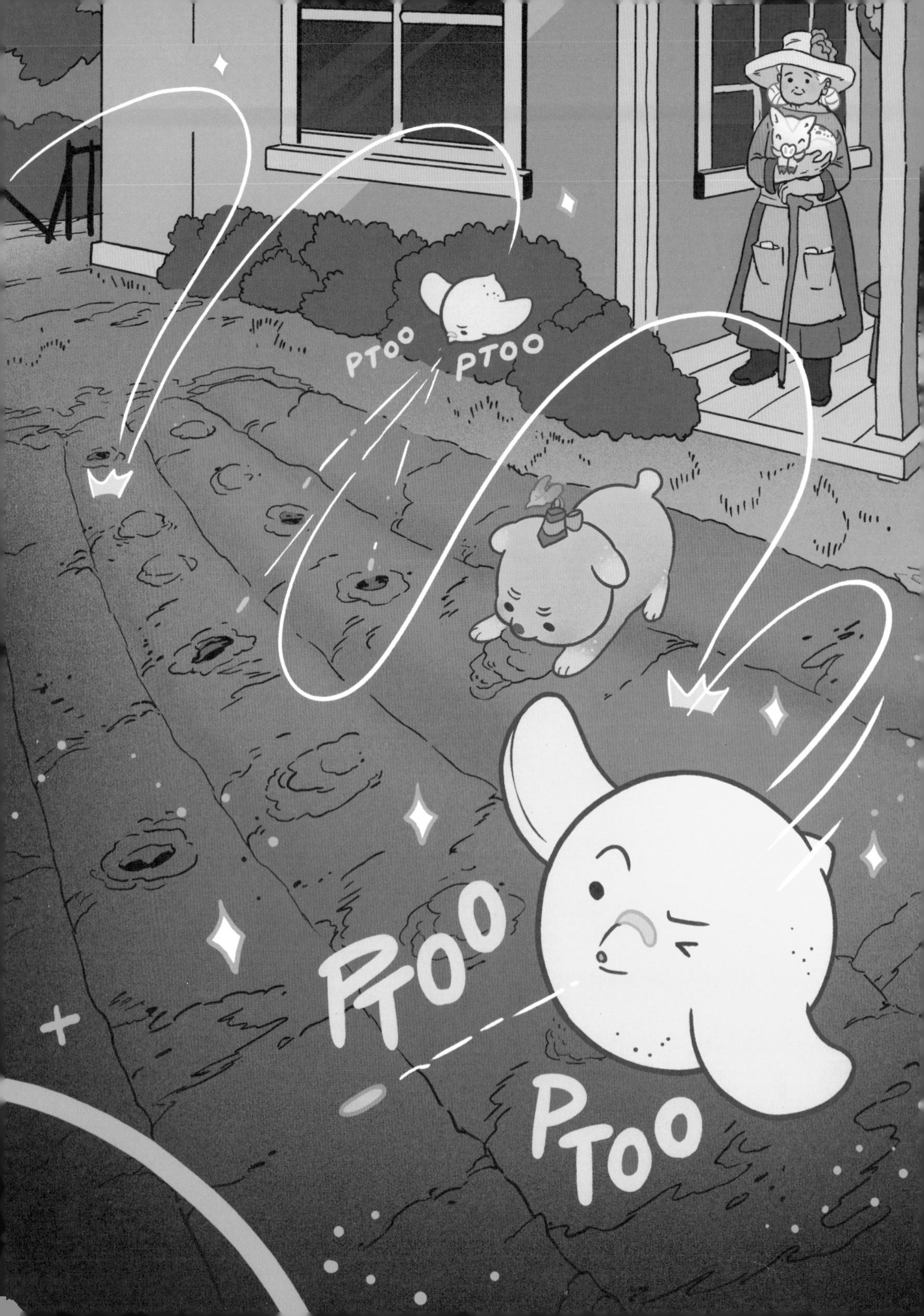
PTOO
PTOO
PTOO
PTOO

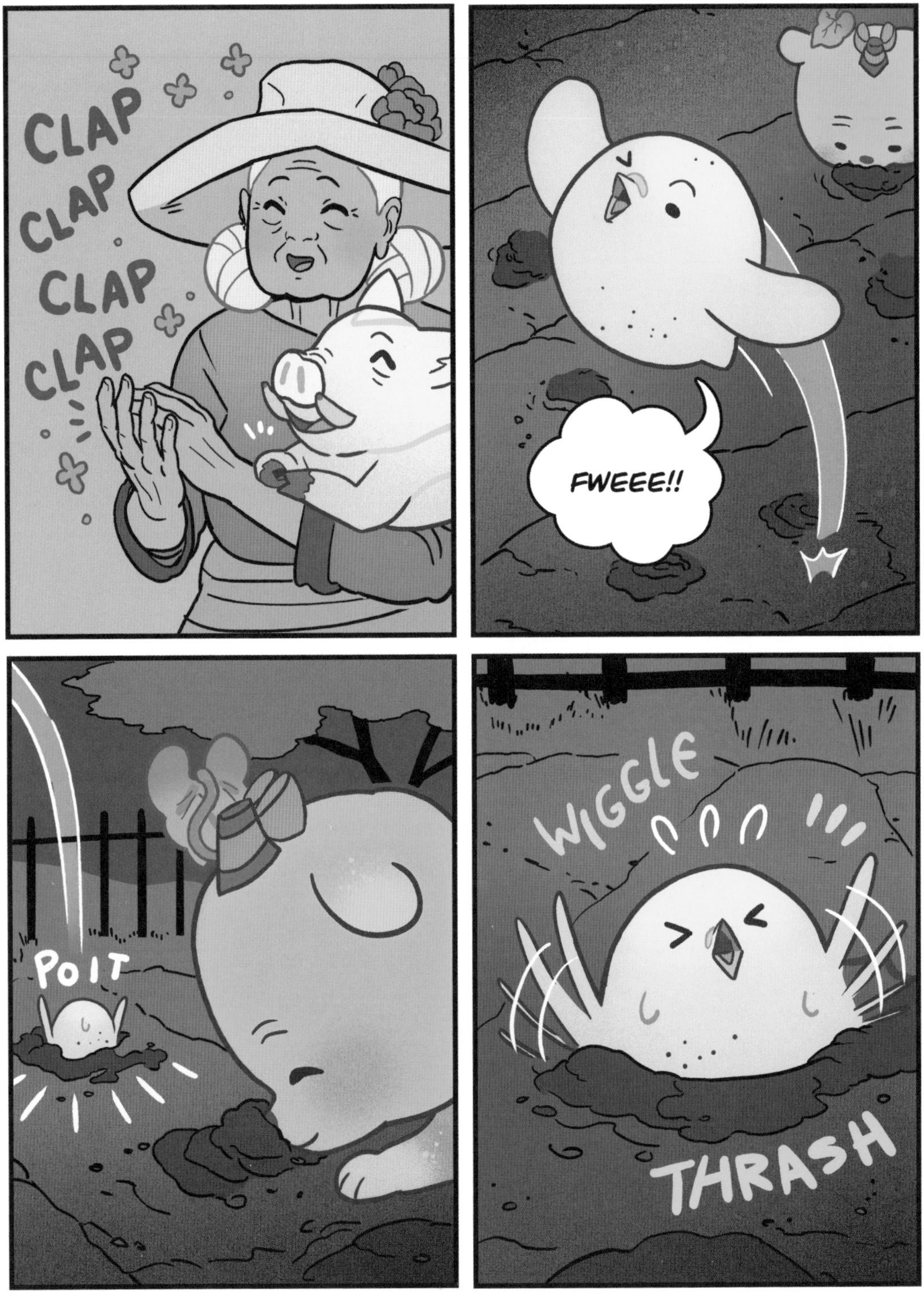
CLAP
CLAP
CLAP
CLAP
FWEEE!!
POIT
WIGGLE
THRASH

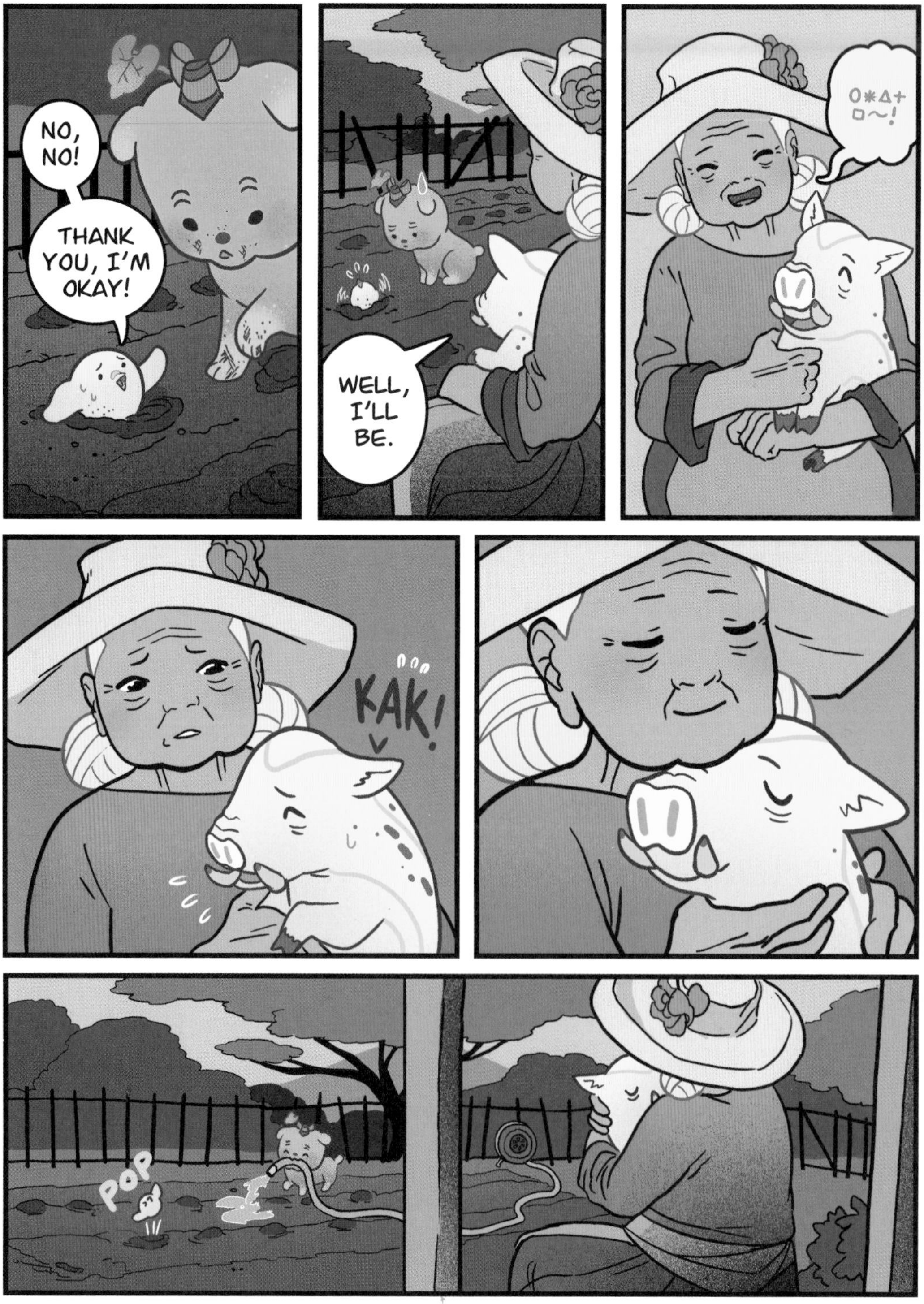
NO, NO!
THANK YOU, I'M OKAY!
WELL, I'LL BE.
KAK!
POP

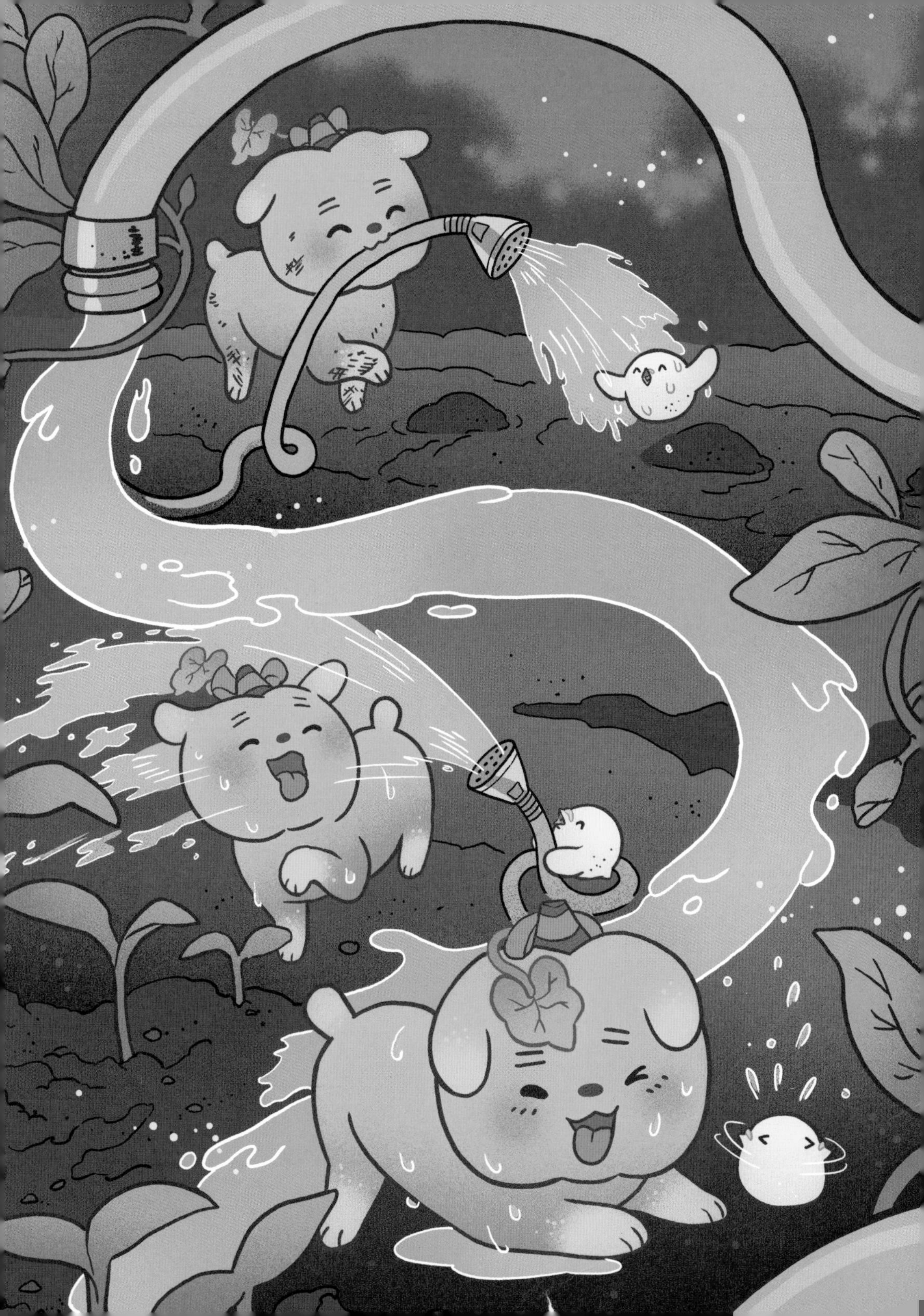

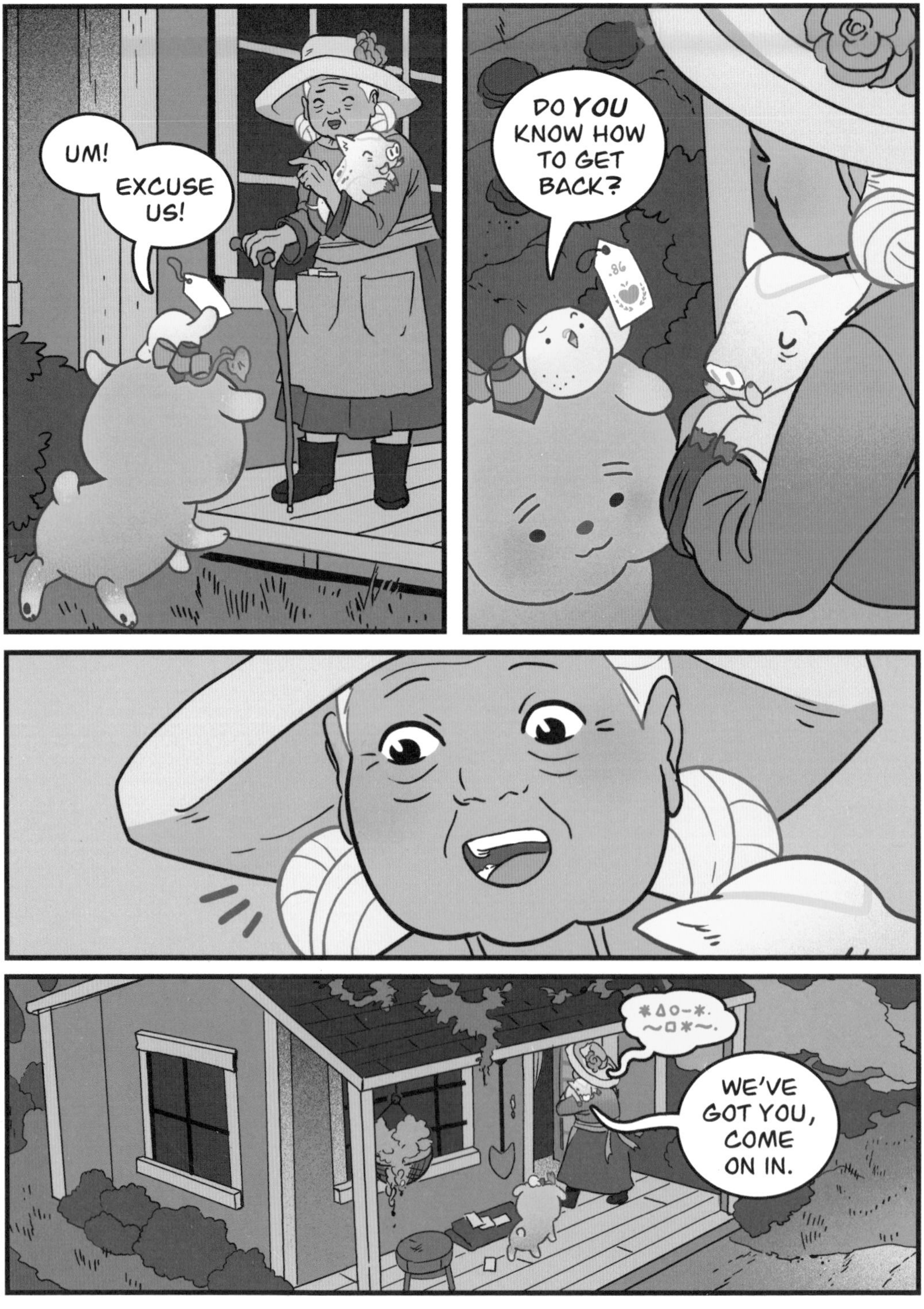
UM!
EXCUSE US!
DO YOU KNOW HOW TO GET BACK?
WE'VE GOT YOU, COME ON IN.

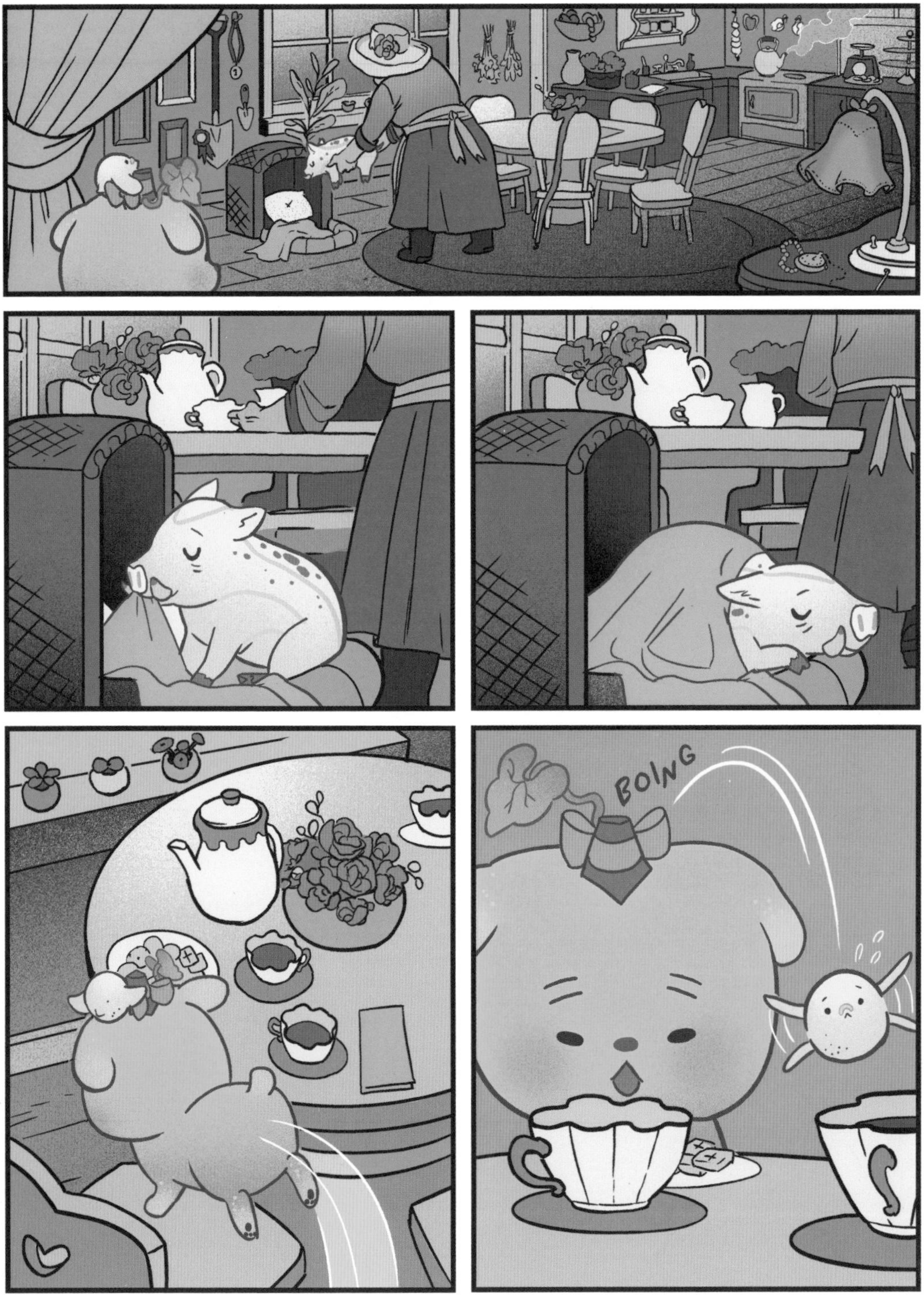
BOING

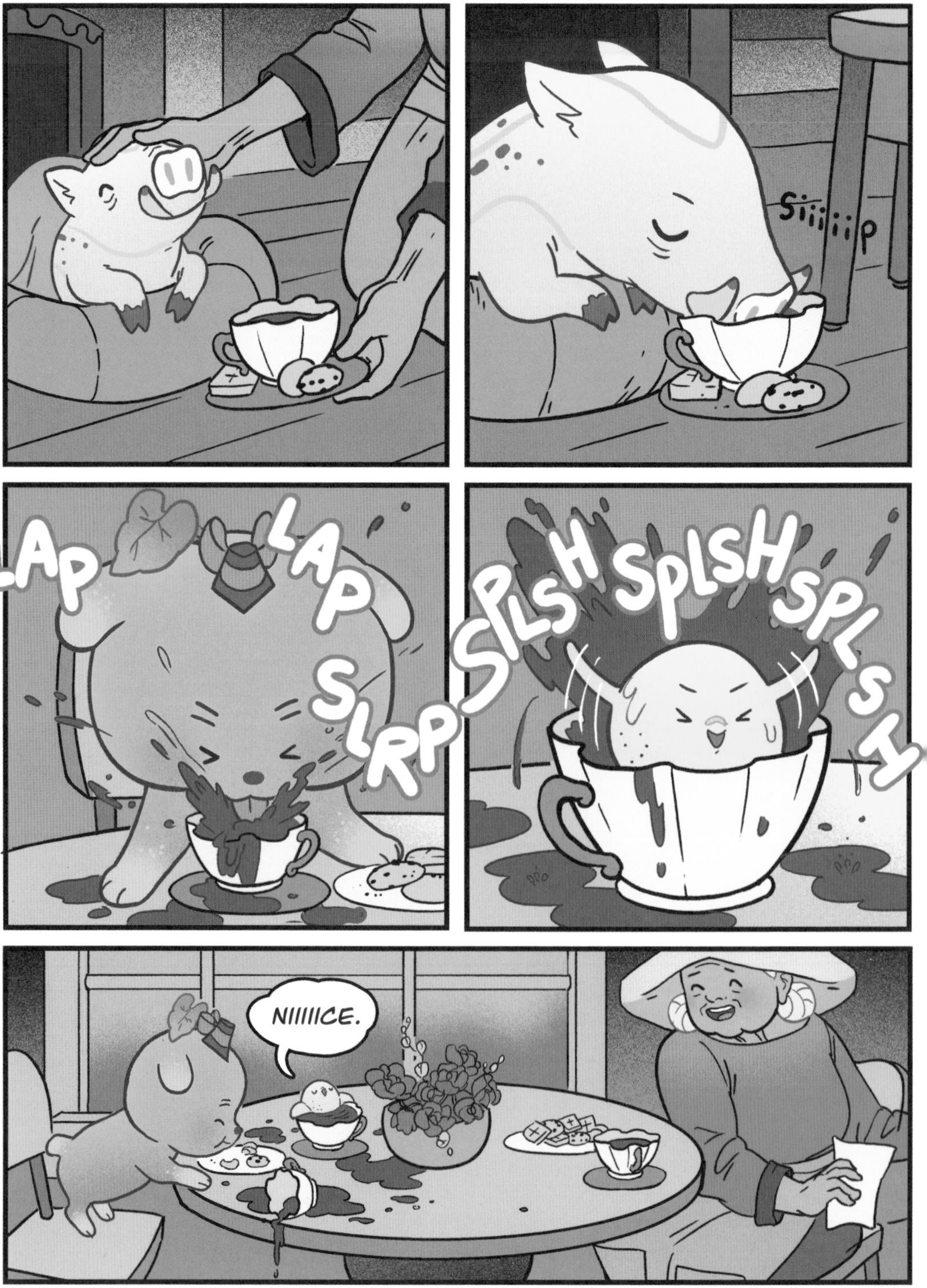
Siiiiiip
LAP
LAP
SLRP
SPLSH
SPLSH
SPLSH
NIIIIICE.

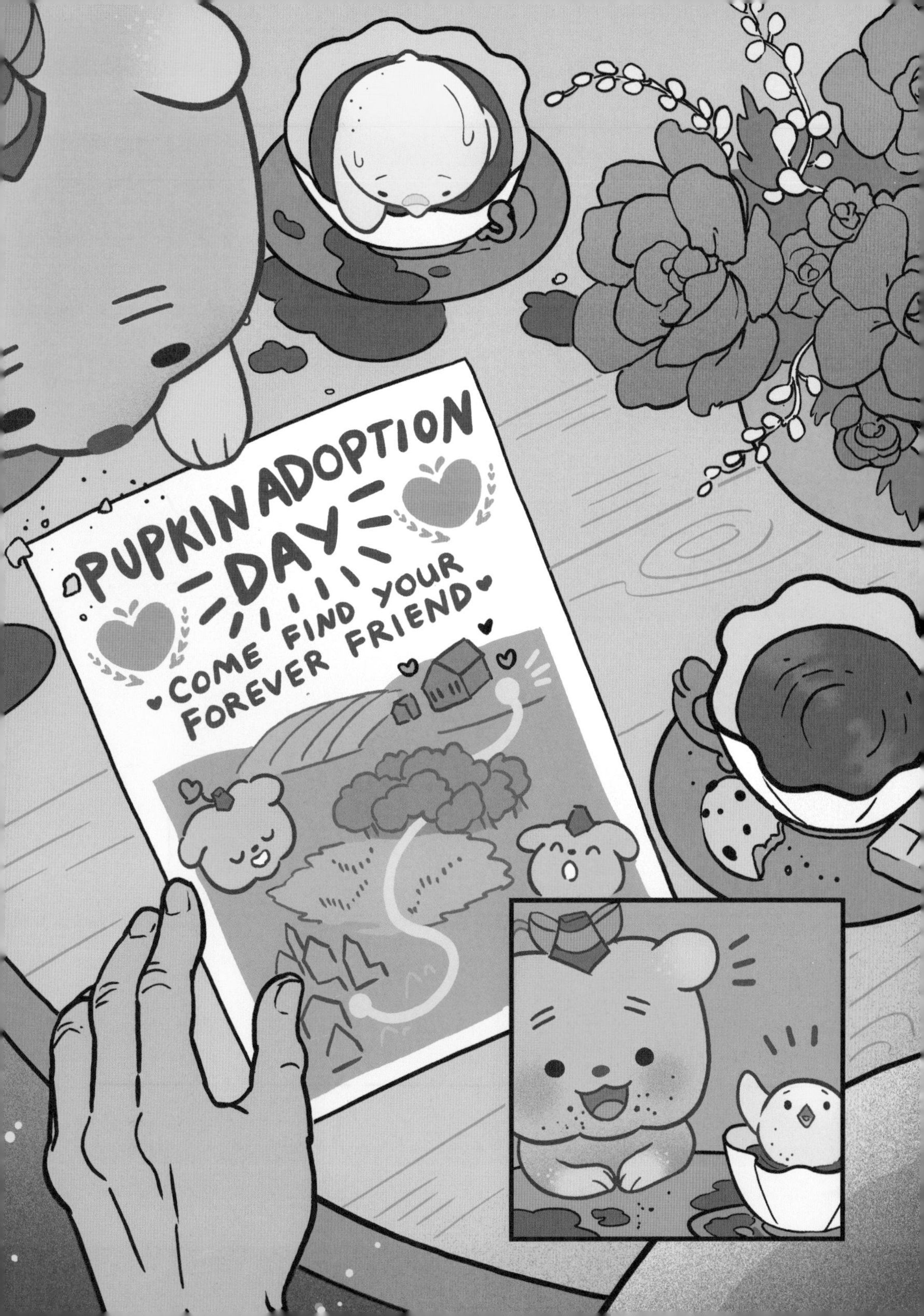
PUPKIN ADOPTION DAY
COME FIND YOUR FOREVER FRIEND

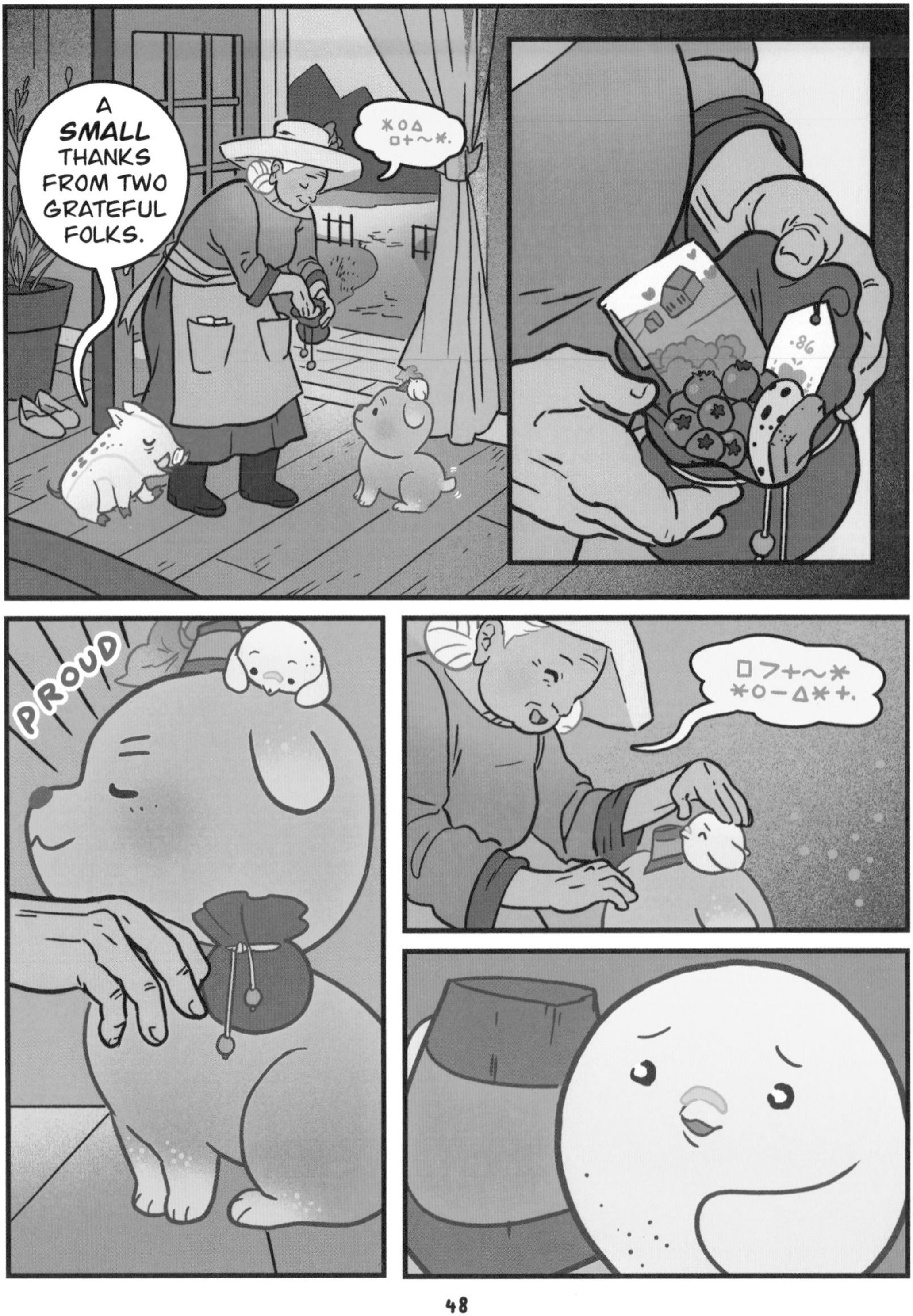
A SMALL THANKS FROM TWO GRATEFUL FOLKS.
PROUD

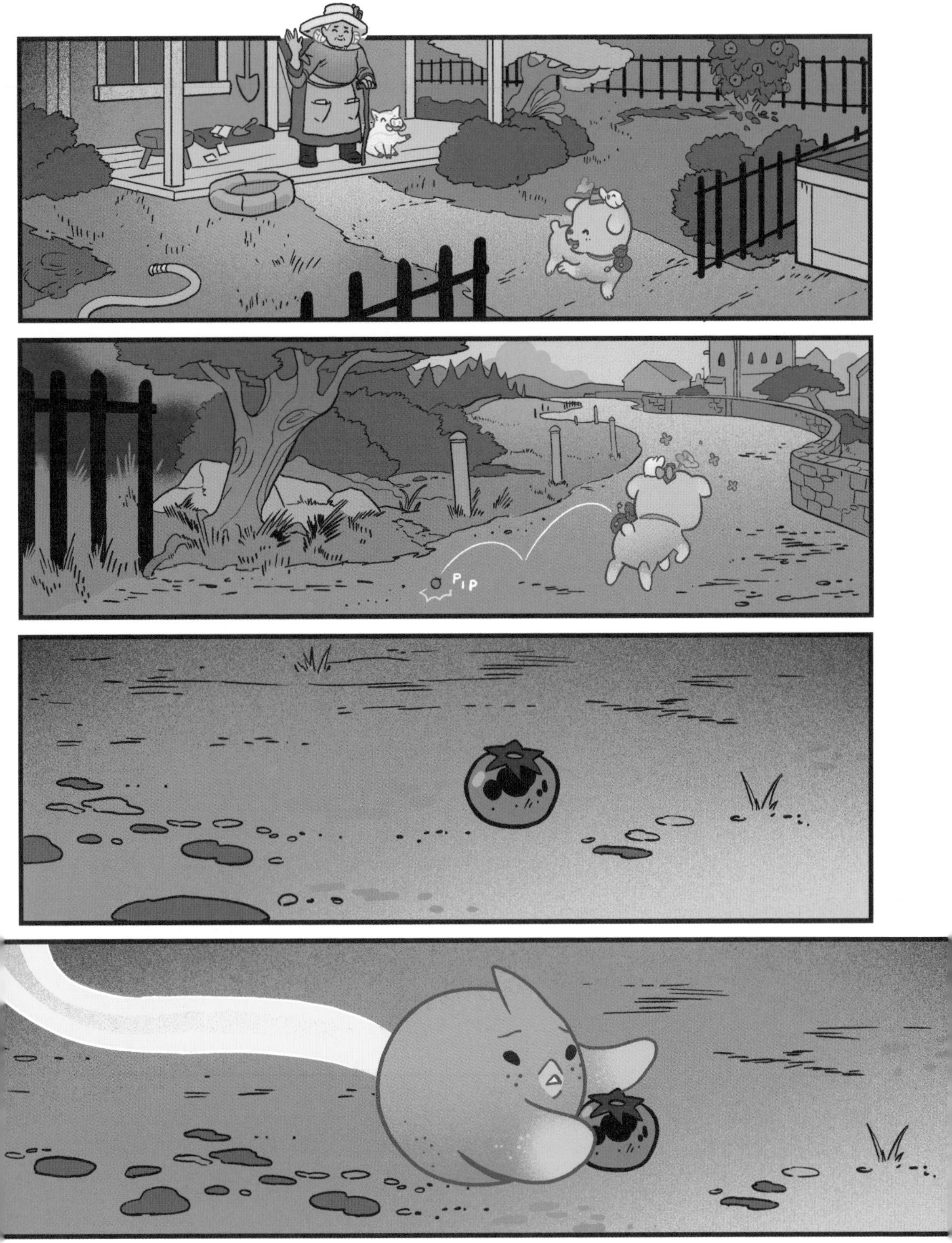
PIP

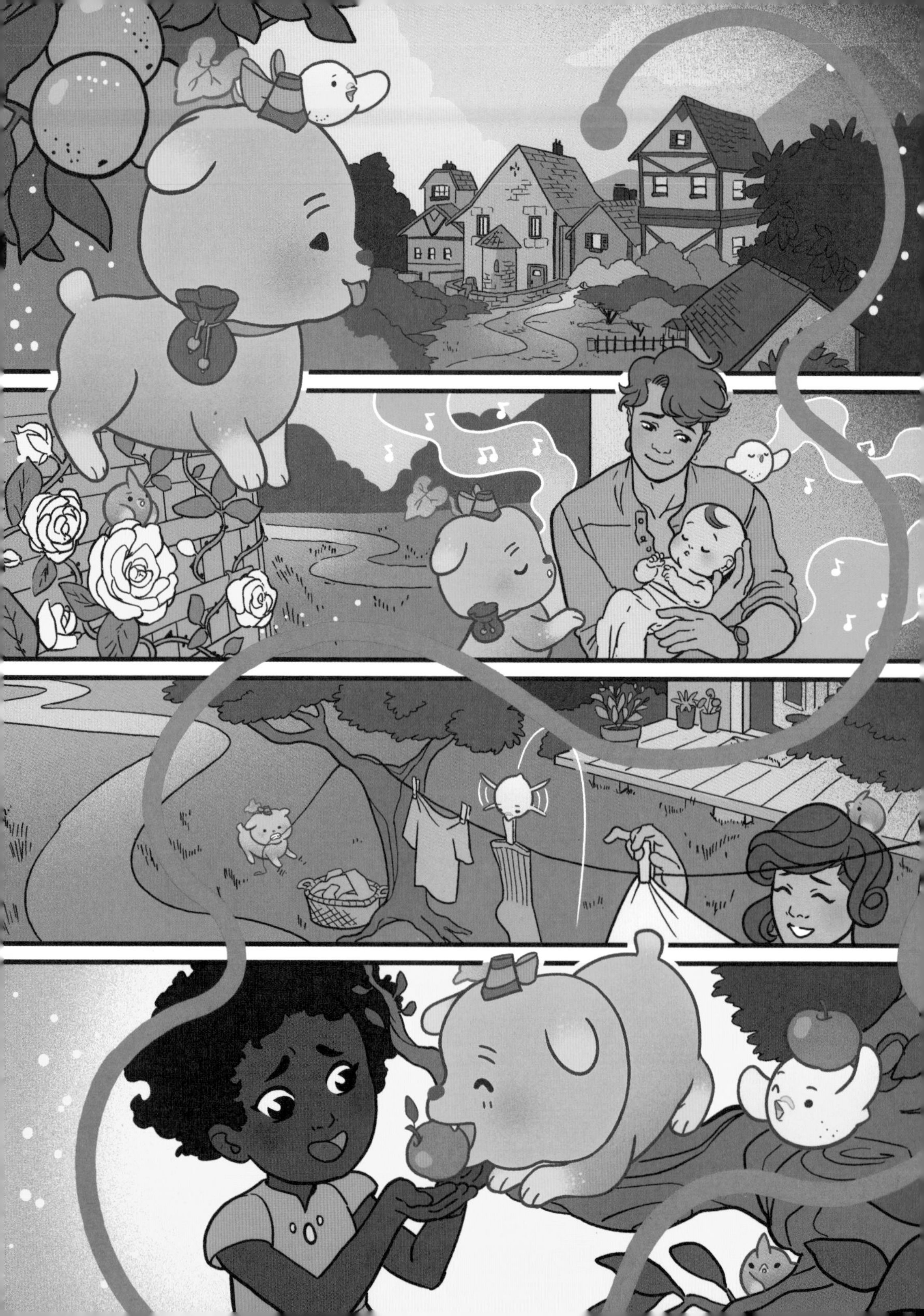

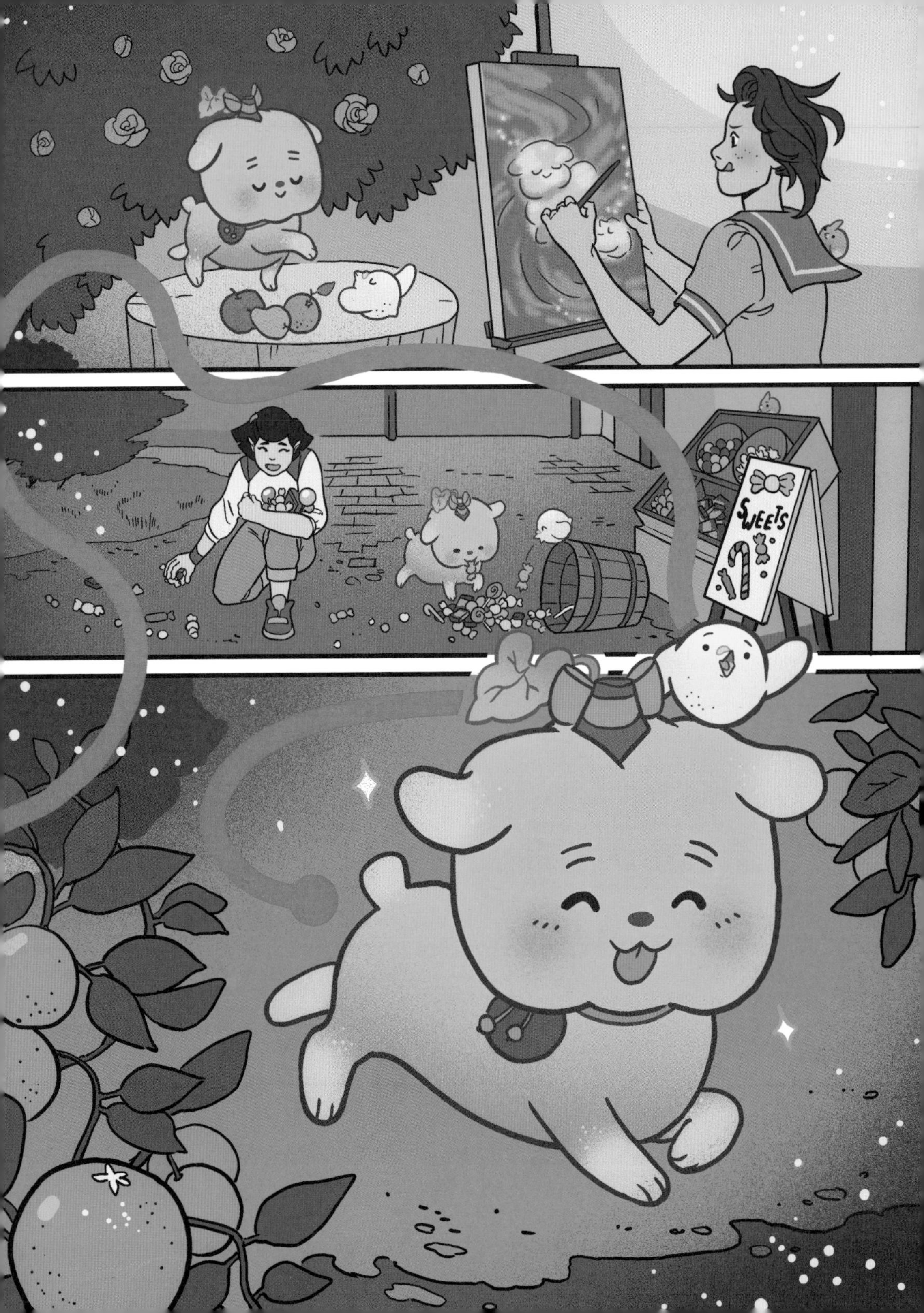
SWEETS

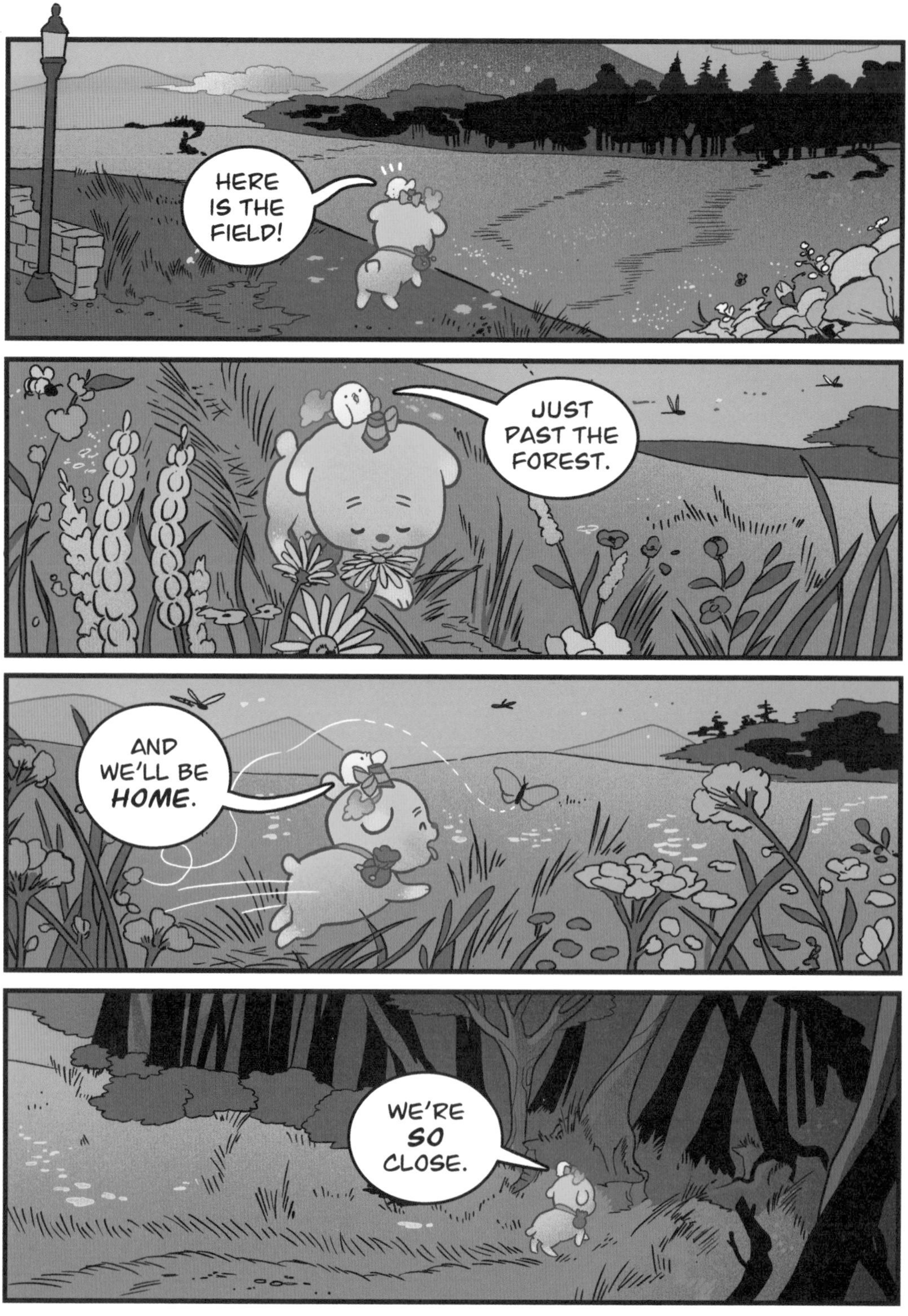
HERE IS THE FIELD!
JUST PAST THE FOREST.
AND WE'LL BE **HOME**.
WE'RE **SO** CLOSE.

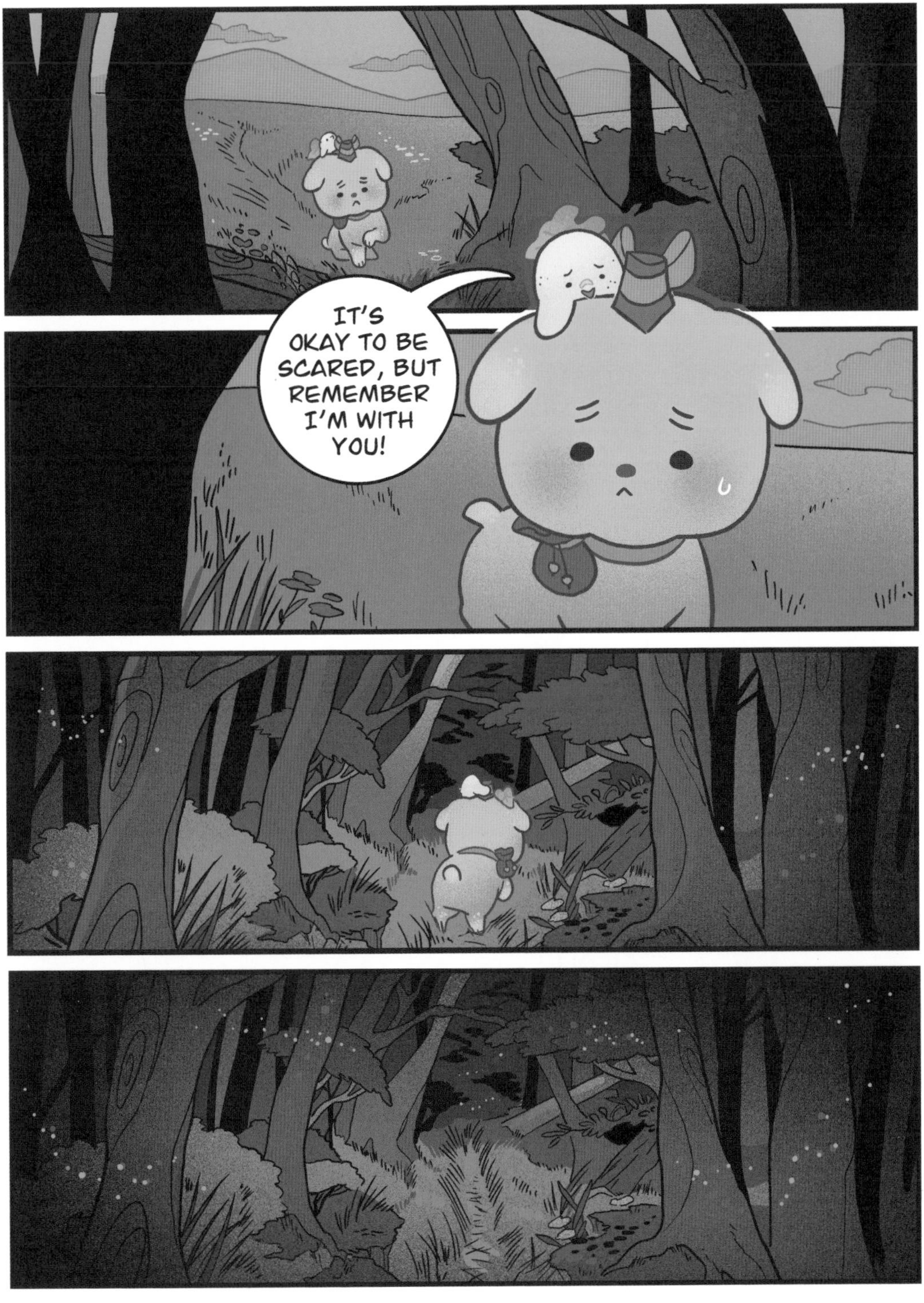
IT'S OKAY TO BE SCARED, BUT REMEMBER I'M WITH YOU!

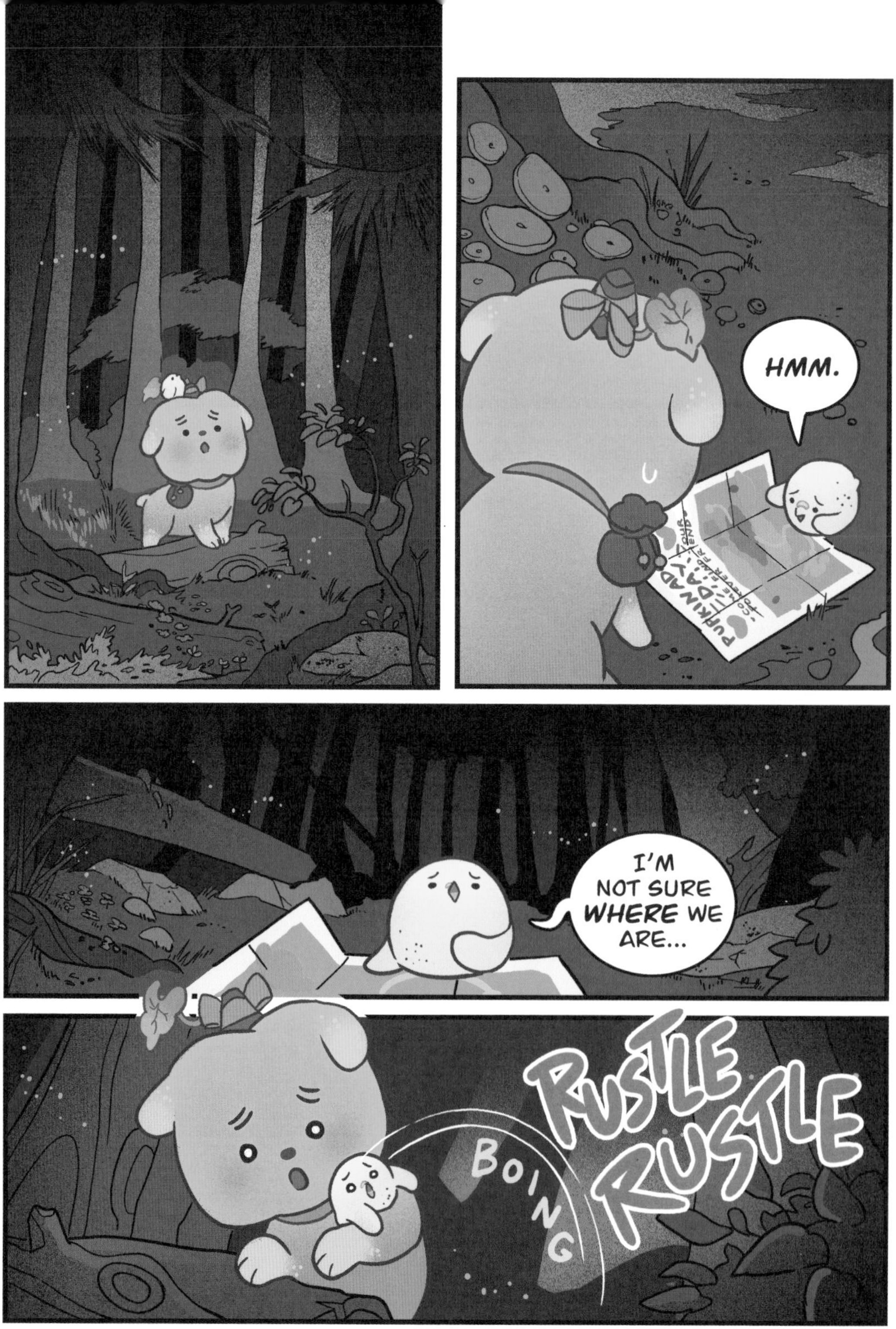
HMM.
I'M NOT SURE WHERE WE ARE...
RUSTLE RUSTLE
BOING

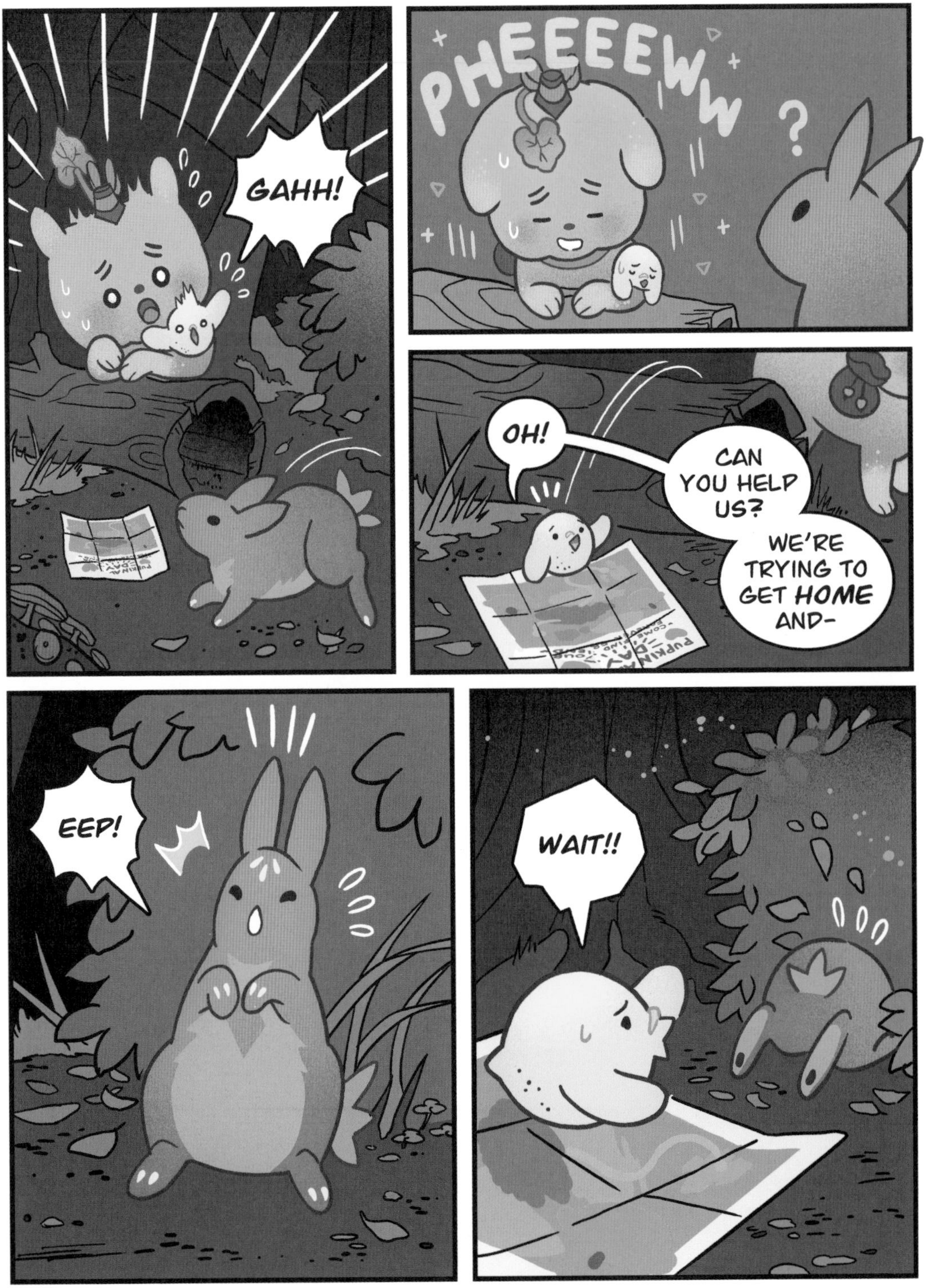
GAHH!
PHEEEEWW
?
OH!
CAN YOU HELP US?
WE'RE TRYING TO GET **HOME** AND-
EEP!
WAIT!!

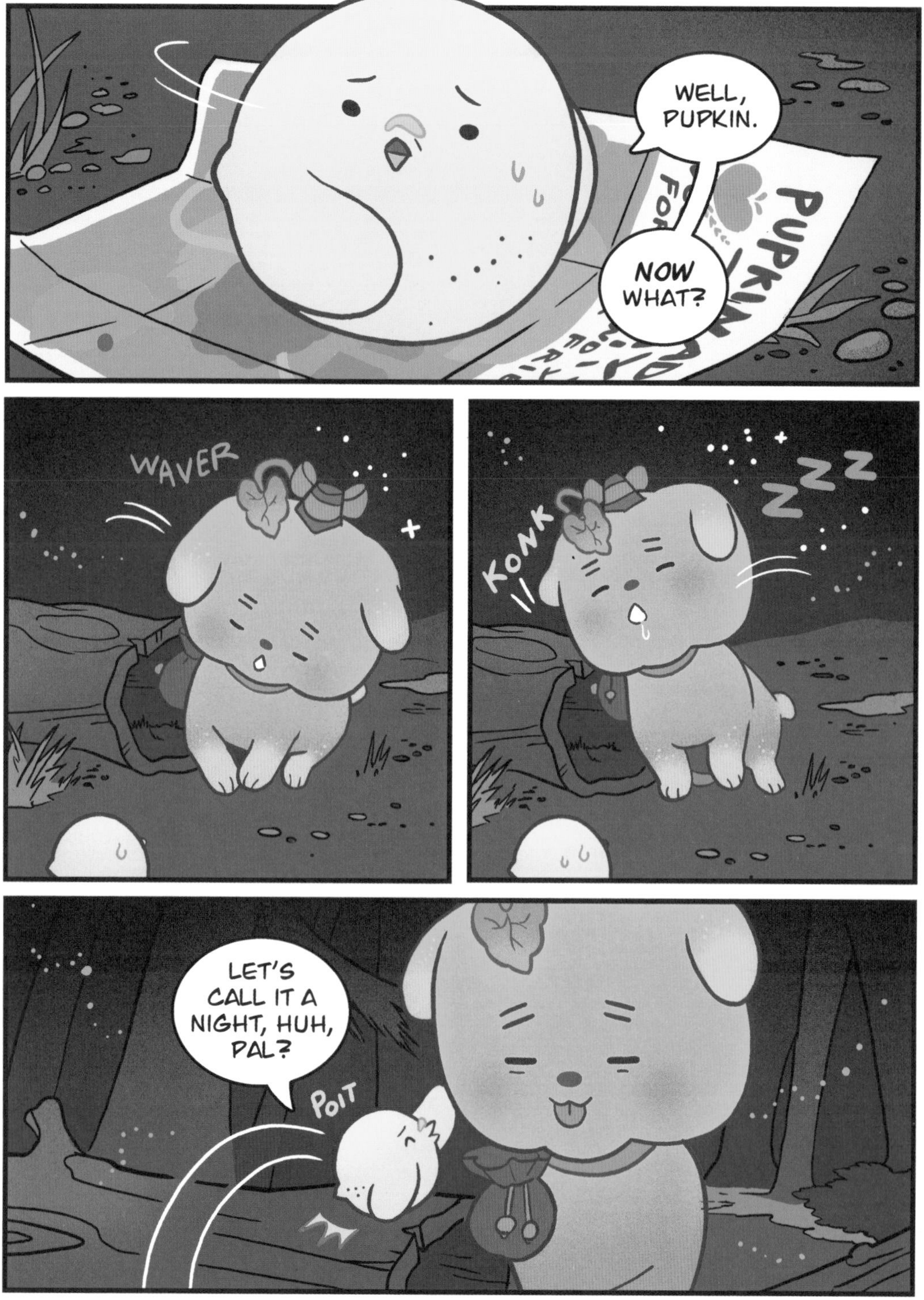
WELL, PUPKIN.
NOW WHAT?
WAVER
KONK
ZZZ
LET'S CALL IT A NIGHT, HUH, PAL?
POIT

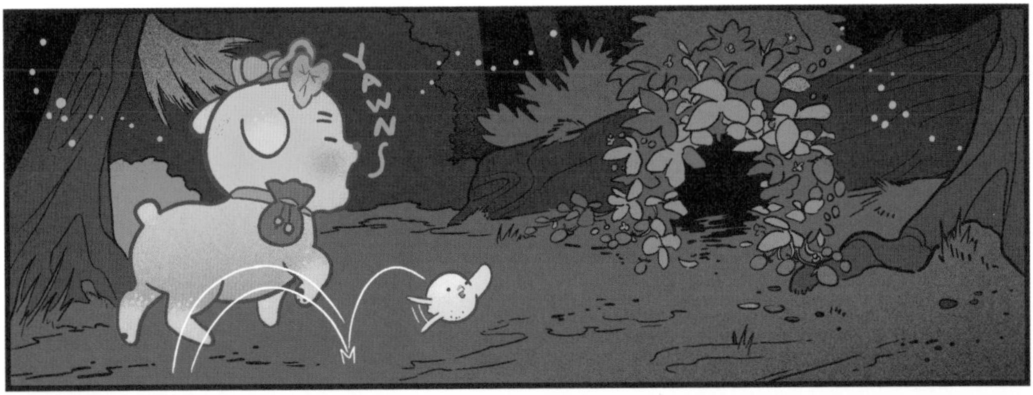
YAWNS

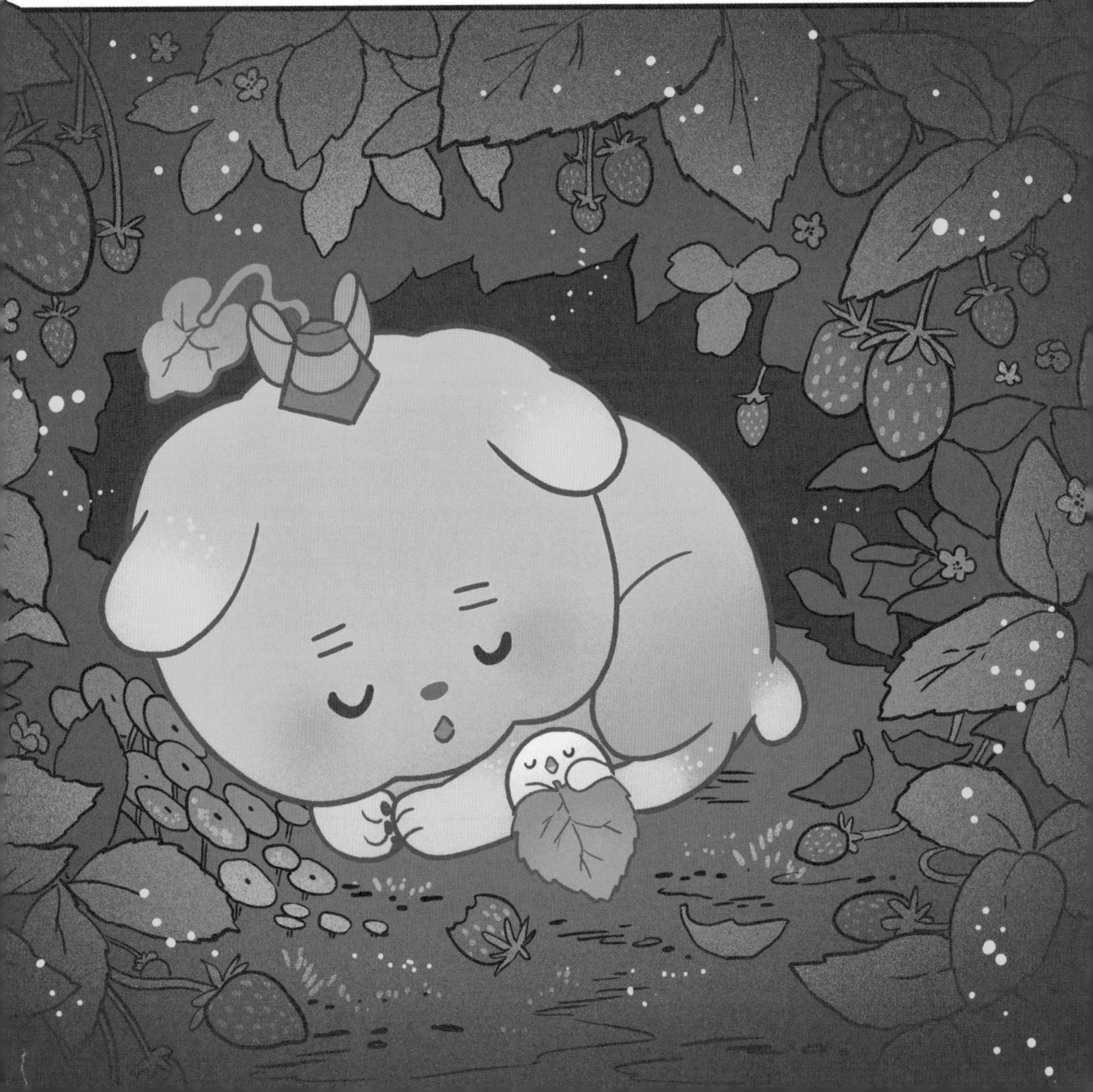

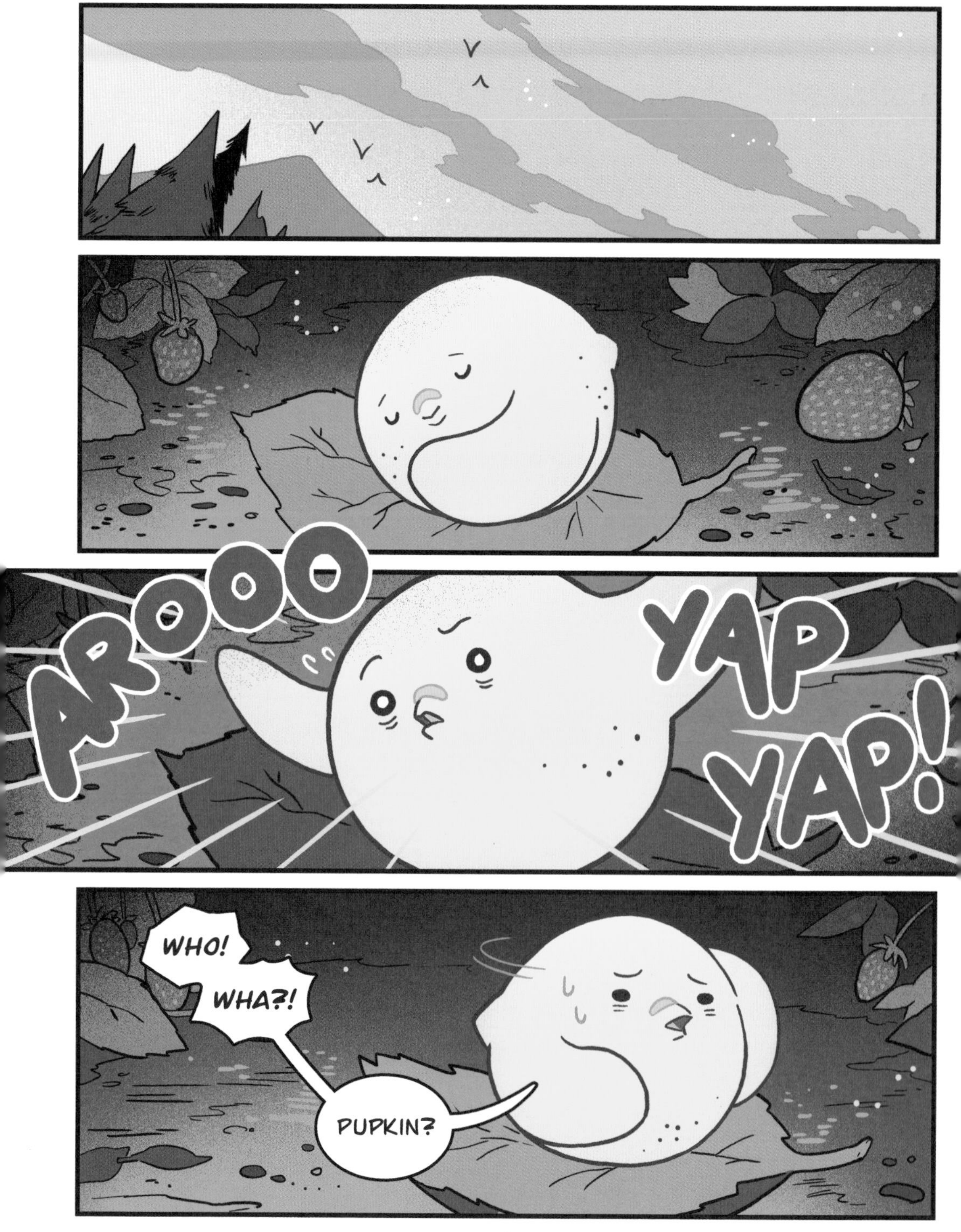
AROOO
YAP YAP!
WHO!
WHA?!
PUPKIN?

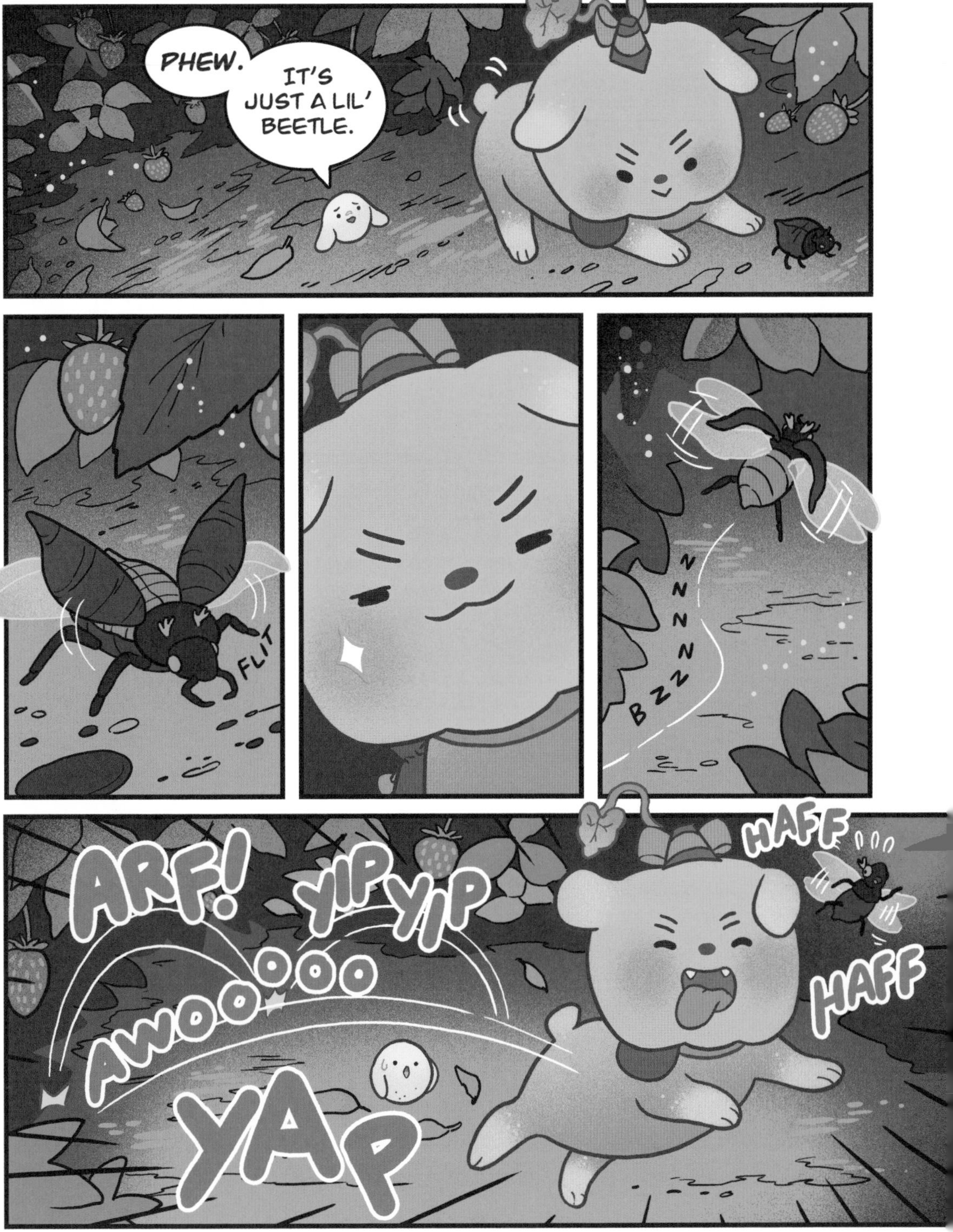
PHEW.
IT'S JUST A LIL' BEETLE.
FLIT
BZZNNNNN
ARF!
YIP YIP
AWOOOOOO
YAP
HAFF
HAFF

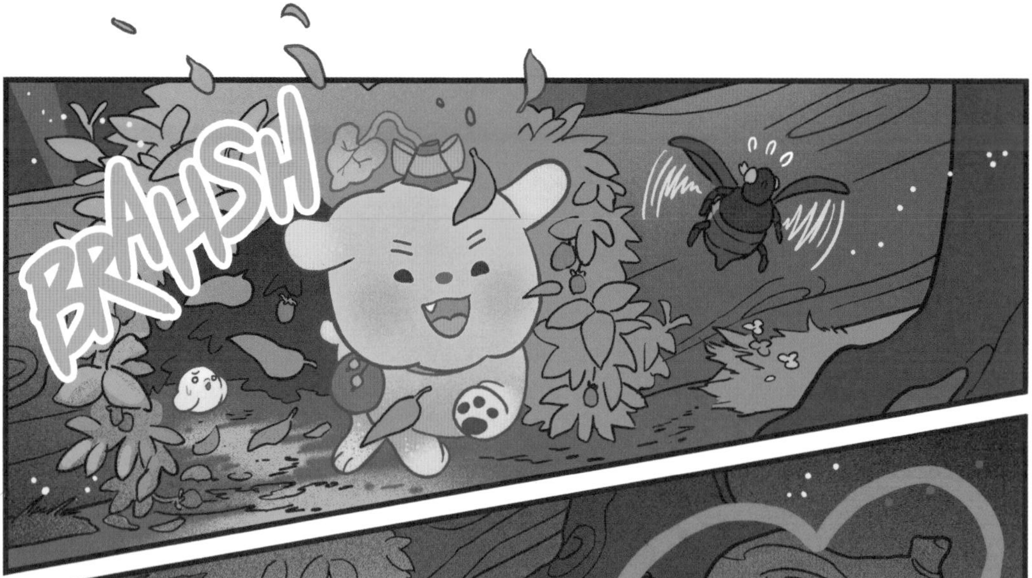
BRAHSH

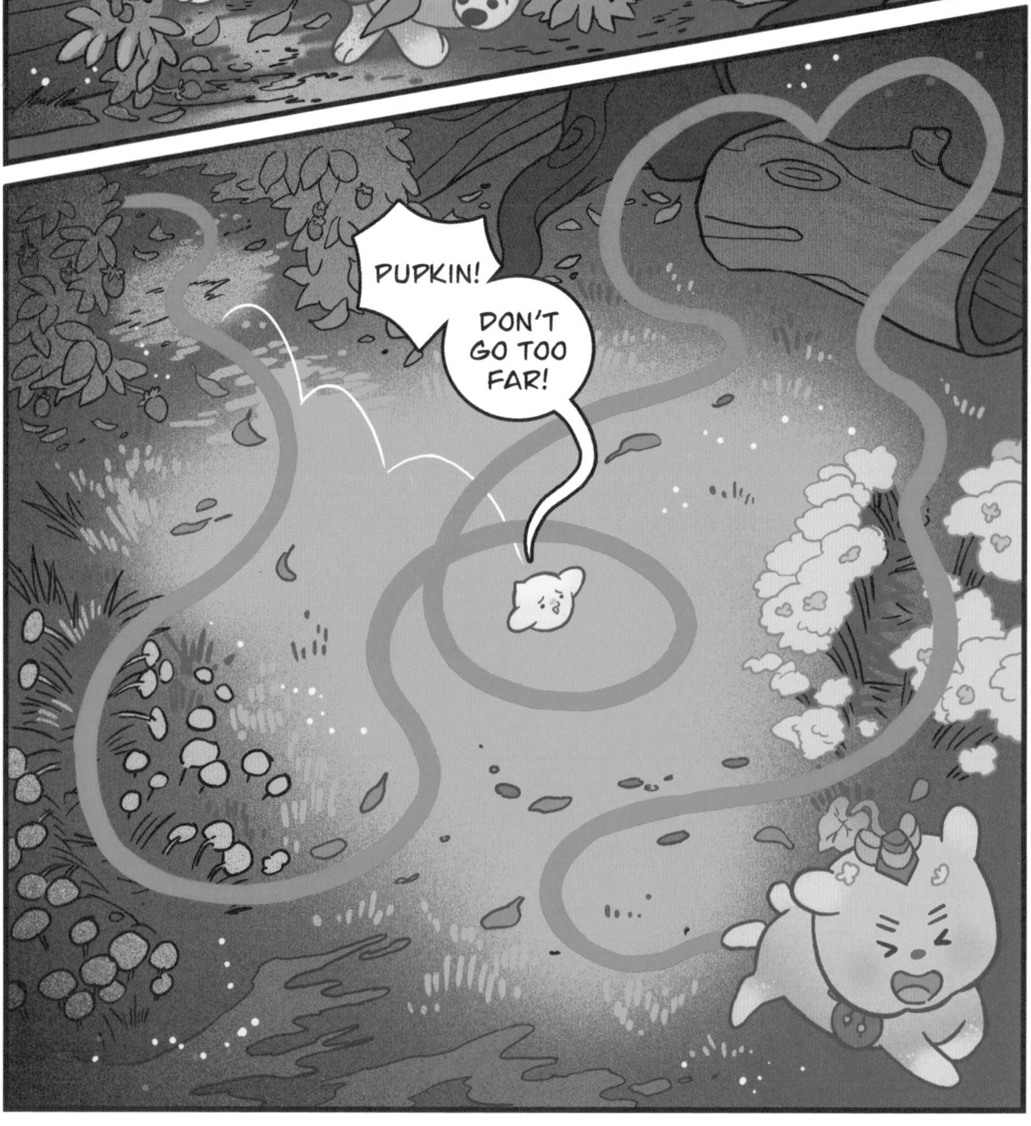
PUPKIN!
DON'T GO TOO FAR!

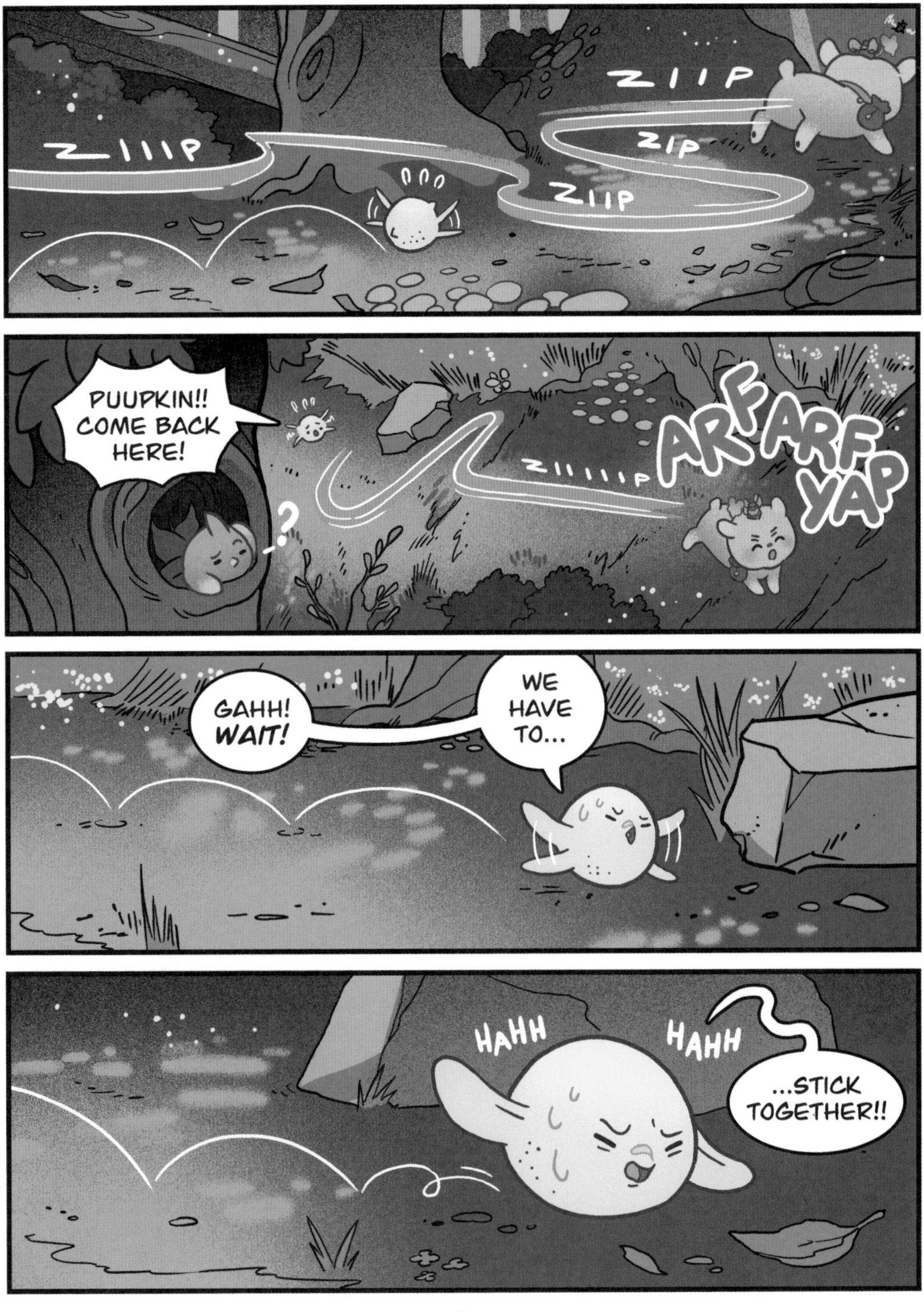
ZIIIP
ZIIP
ZIP
ZIIP
PUUPKIN!! COME BACK HERE!
?
ZIIIIIP
ARF ARF YAP
GAHH! WAIT!
WE HAVE TO...
HAHH
HAHH
...STICK TOGETHER!!

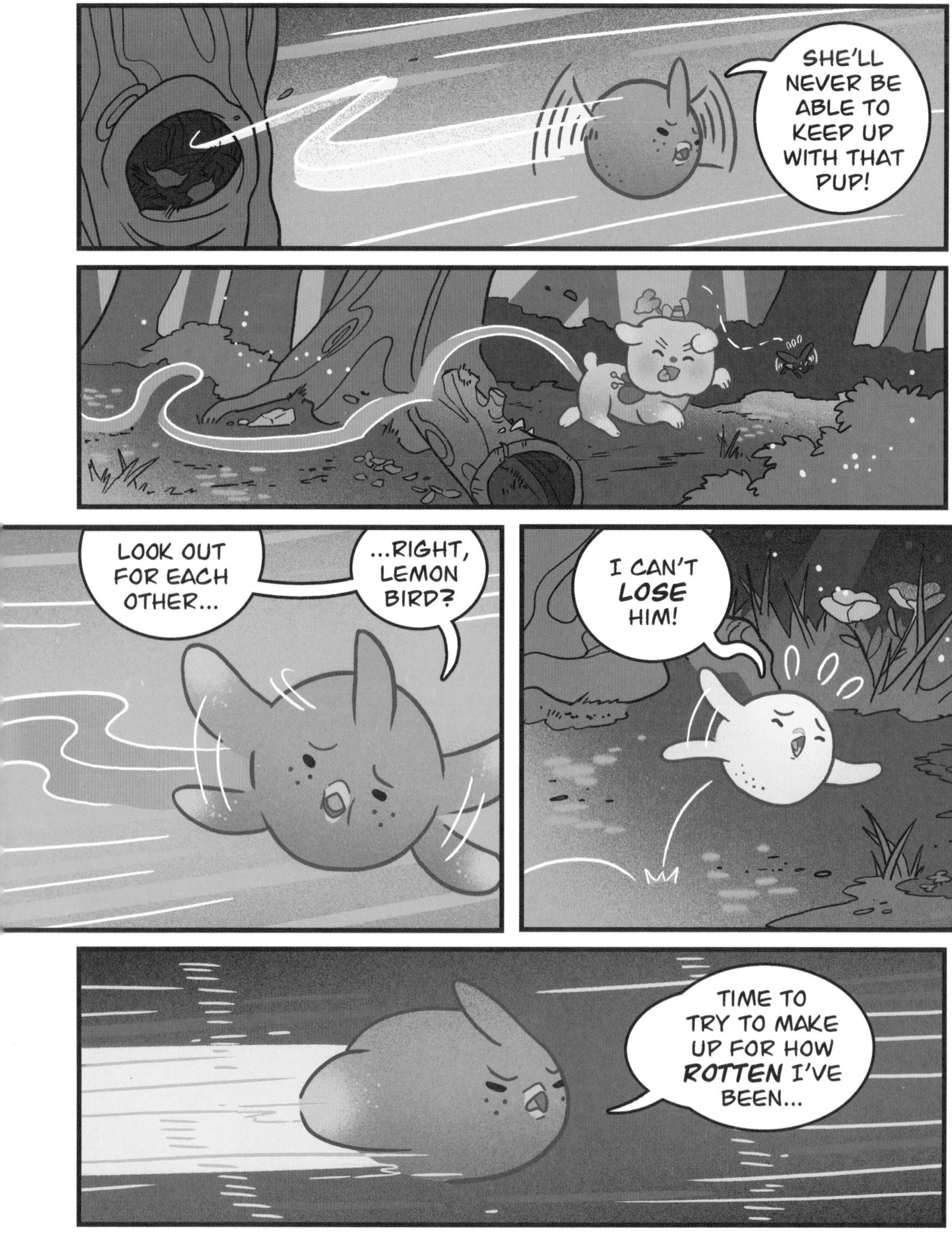

SHE'LL NEVER BE ABLE TO KEEP UP WITH THAT PUP!
LOOK OUT FOR EACH OTHER...
...RIGHT, LEMON BIRD?
I CAN'T **LOSE** HIM!
TIME TO TRY TO MAKE UP FOR HOW **ROTTEN** I'VE BEEN...

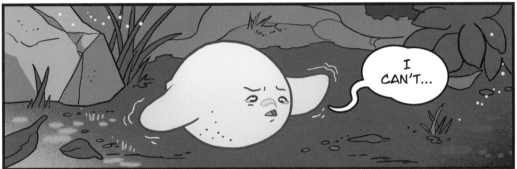

I CAN'T...

LEMON BIRD!

I'VE GOT THIS!!

PUPKIN! **STOP!**

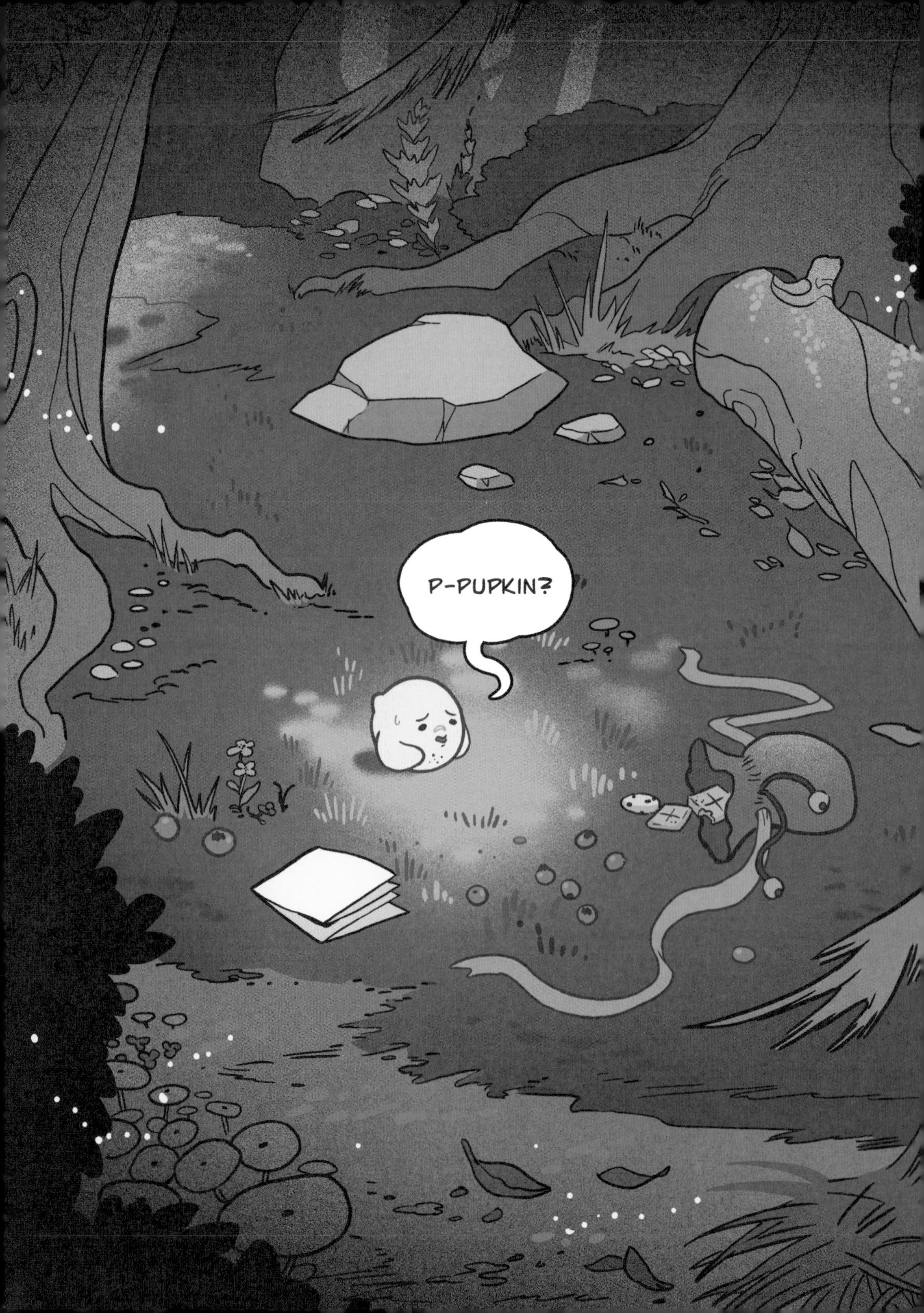
P-PUPKIN?

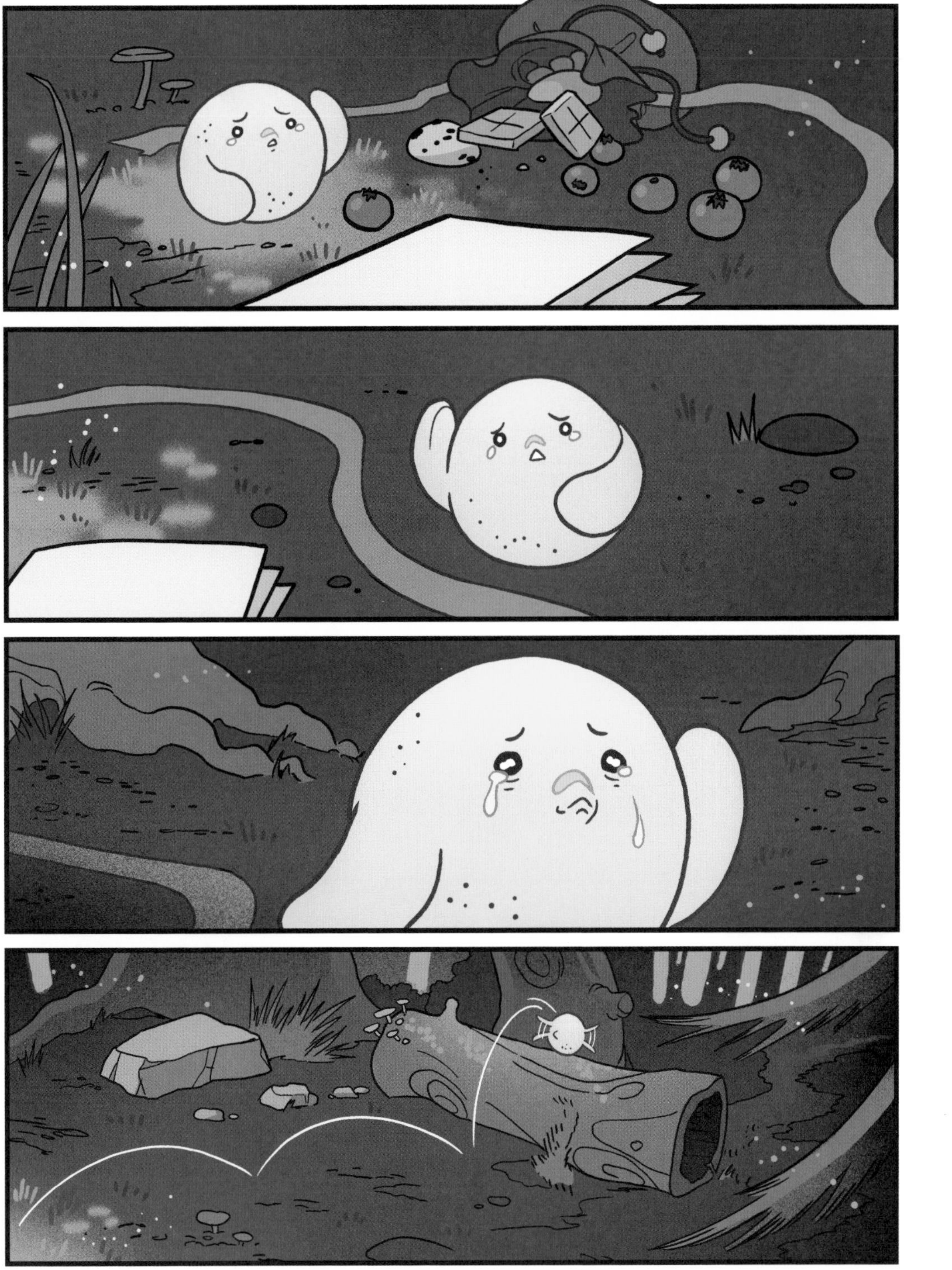

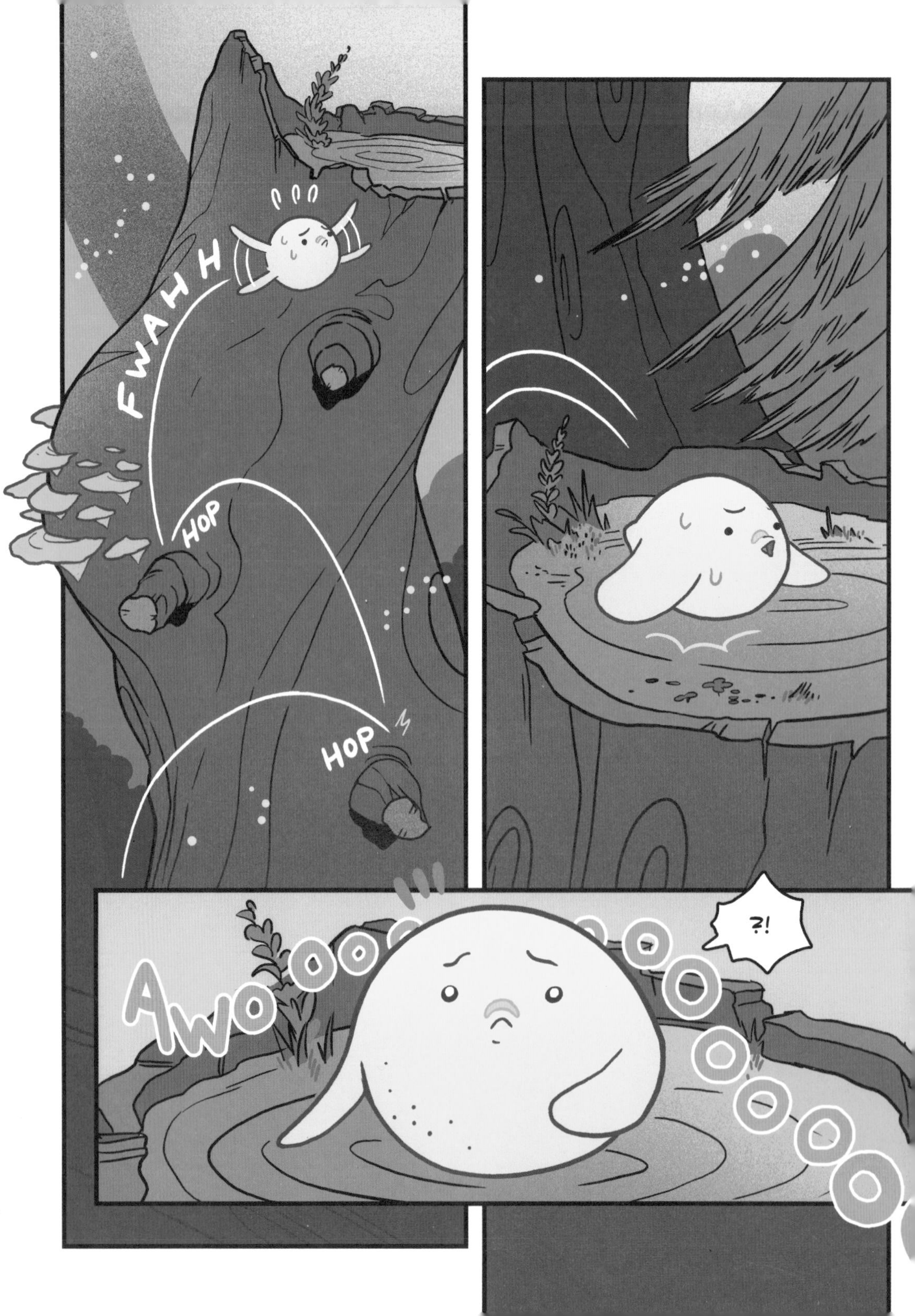
FWAHH
HOP
HOP
AWOOOOOOOOOOOOOOO
?!

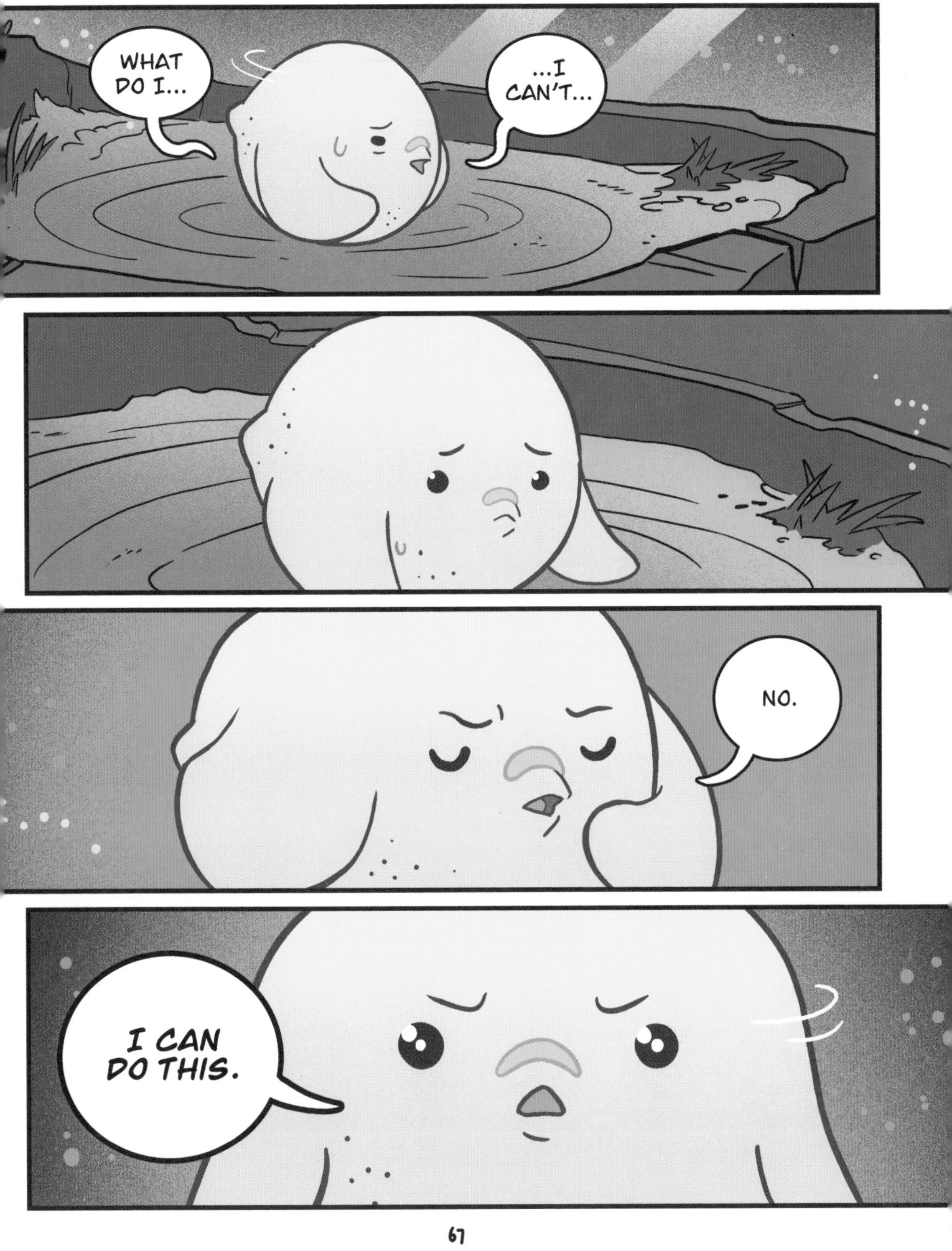
WHAT DO I...
...I CAN'T...
NO.
I CAN DO THIS.

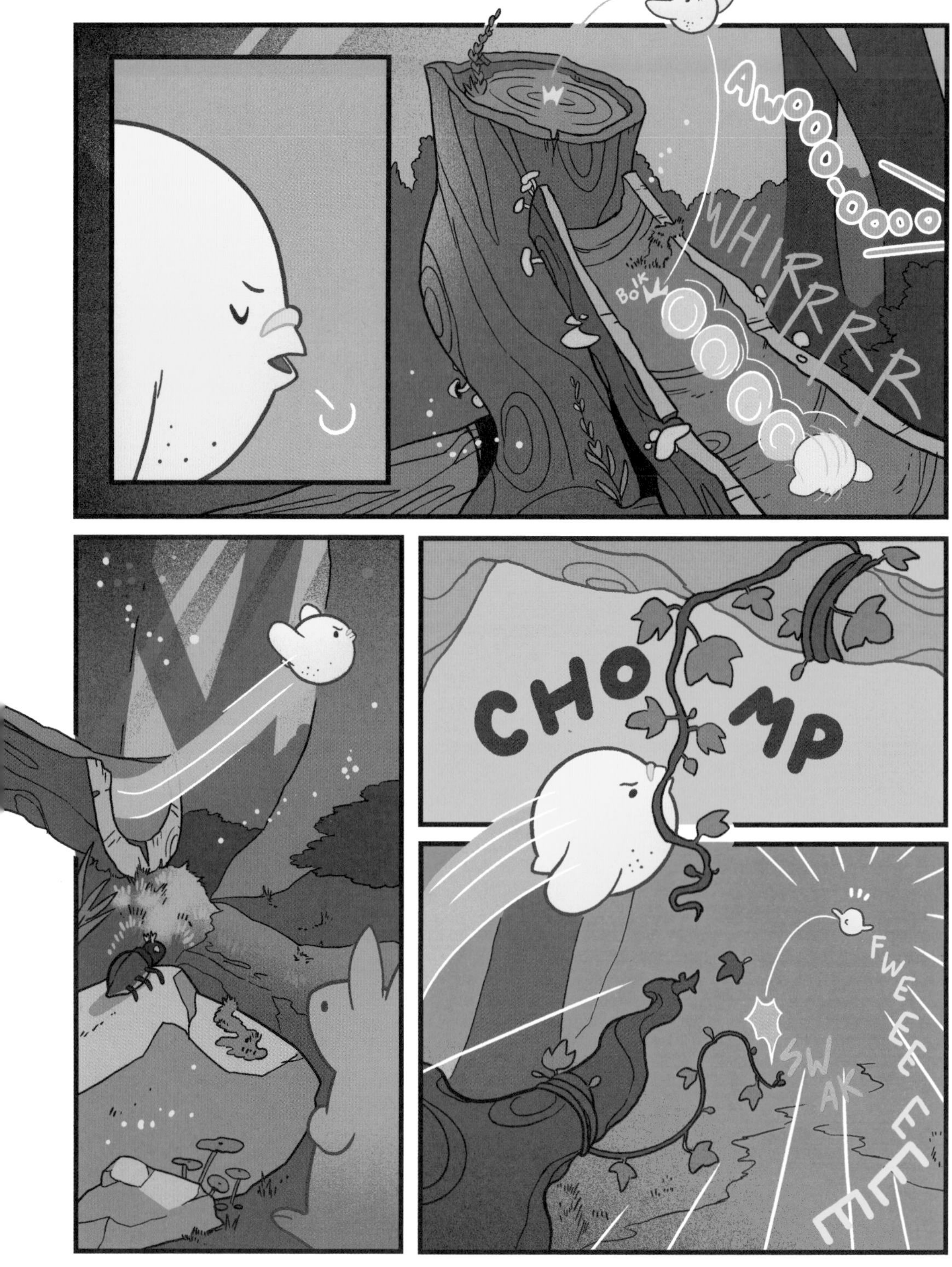
AWOOO-OOOO
WHIRRRRR
BOIK
CHOMP
FWEEEEE
SWAK

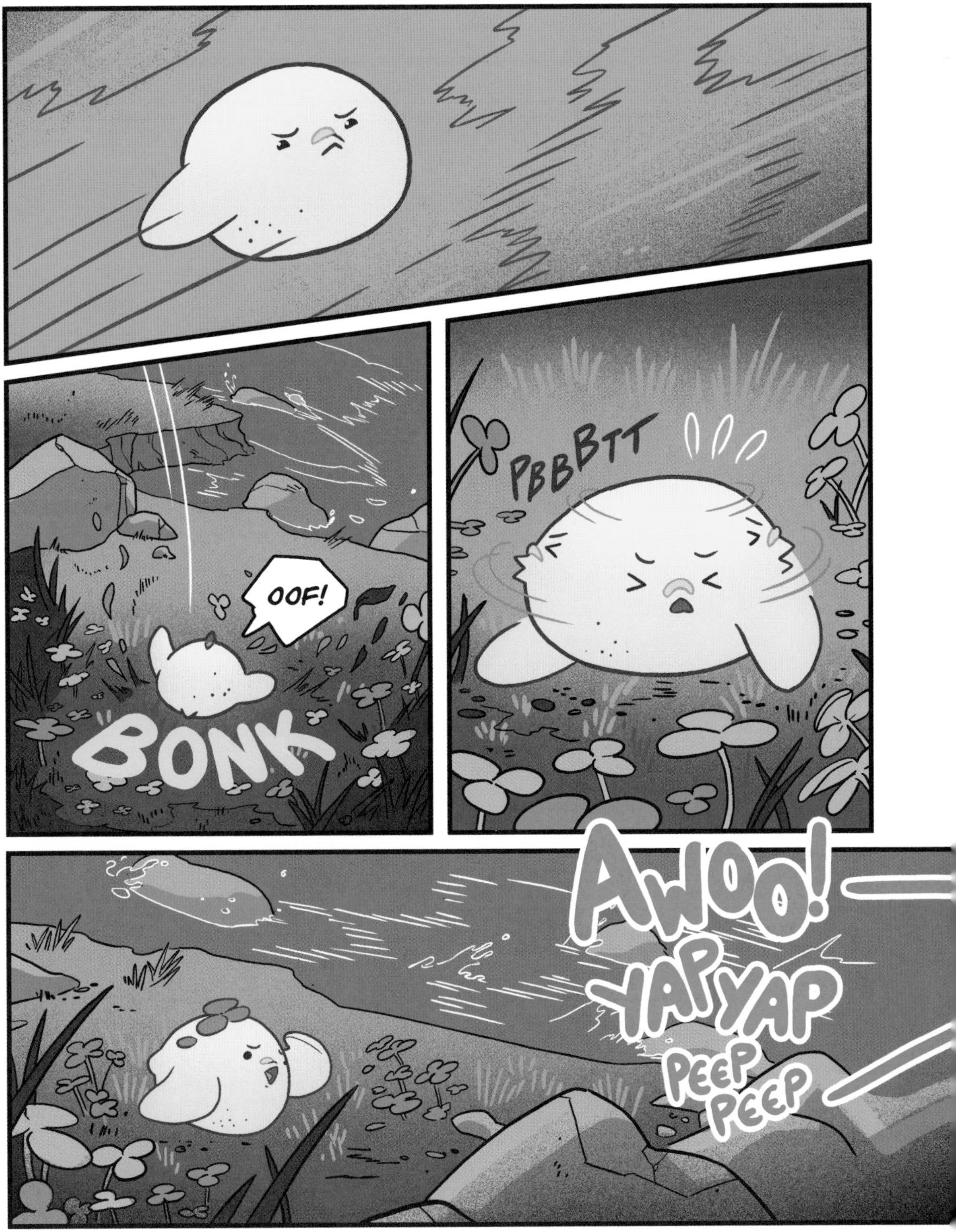
OOF!
BONK
PBBBTT
AWOO!
YAP YAP
PEEP
PEEP

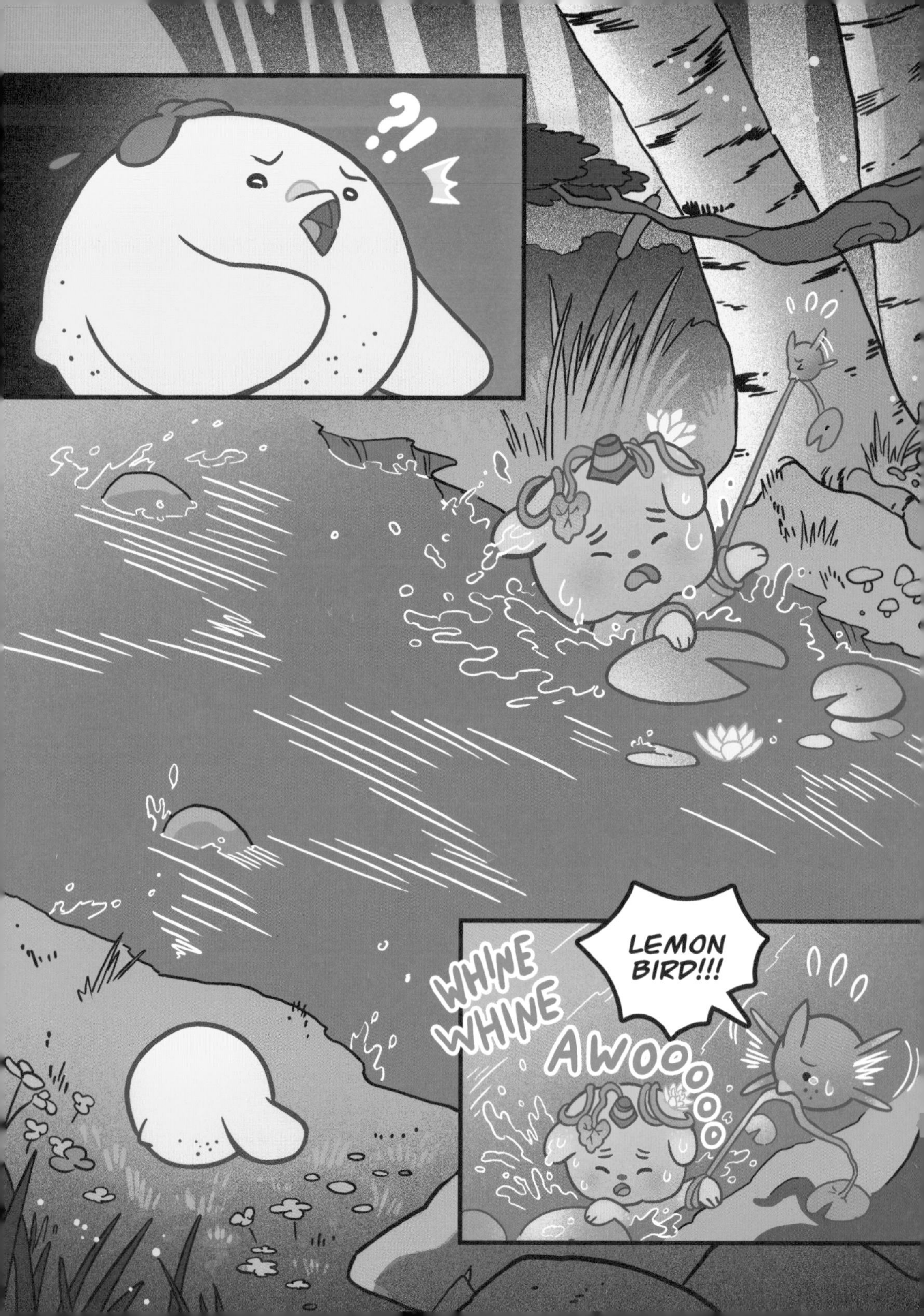
?!
LEMON BIRD!!!
WHINE WHINE
AWOOOOOOO

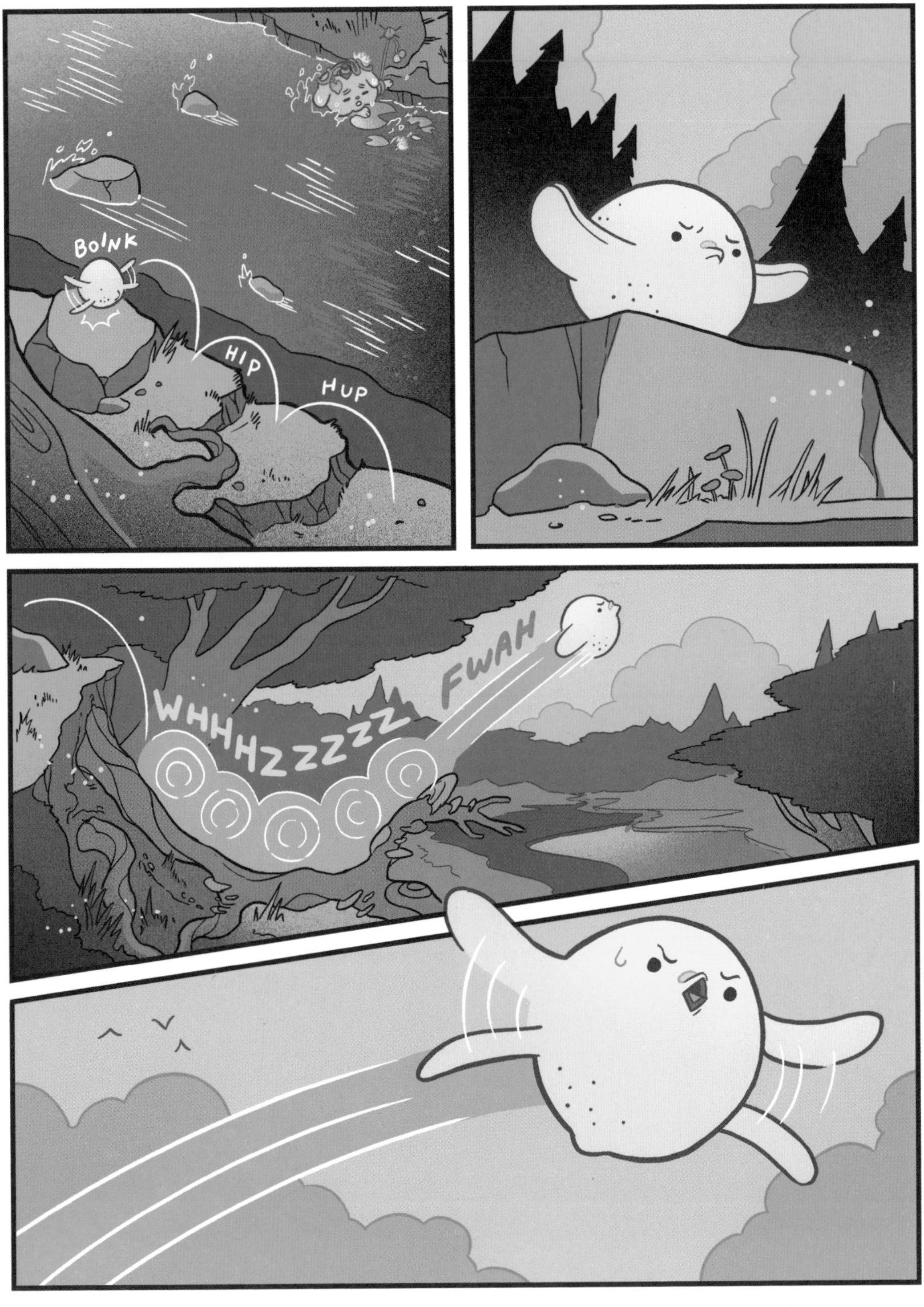
BOINK
HIP
HUP
WHHHZZZZZ
FWAH

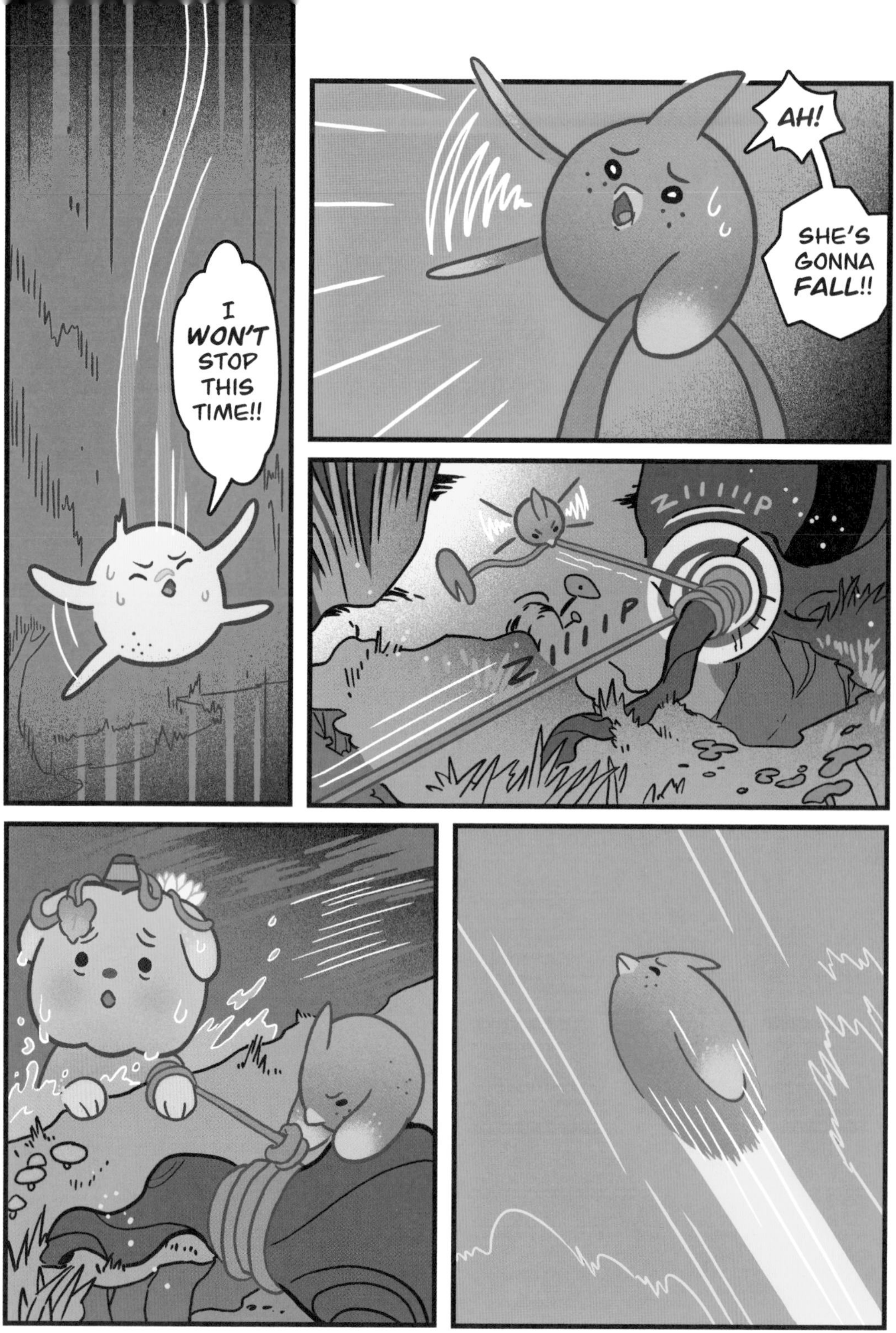
I WON'T STOP THIS TIME!!
AH!
SHE'S GONNA FALL!!
ZIIIIP
ZIIIIP

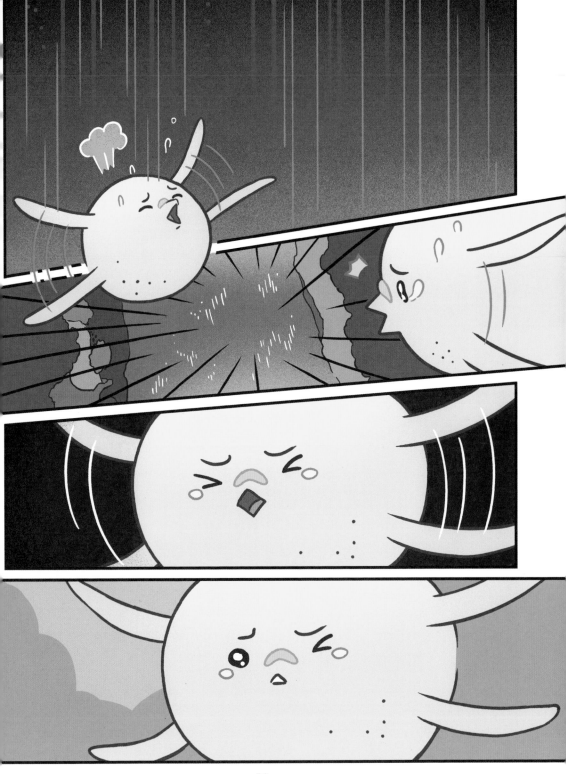

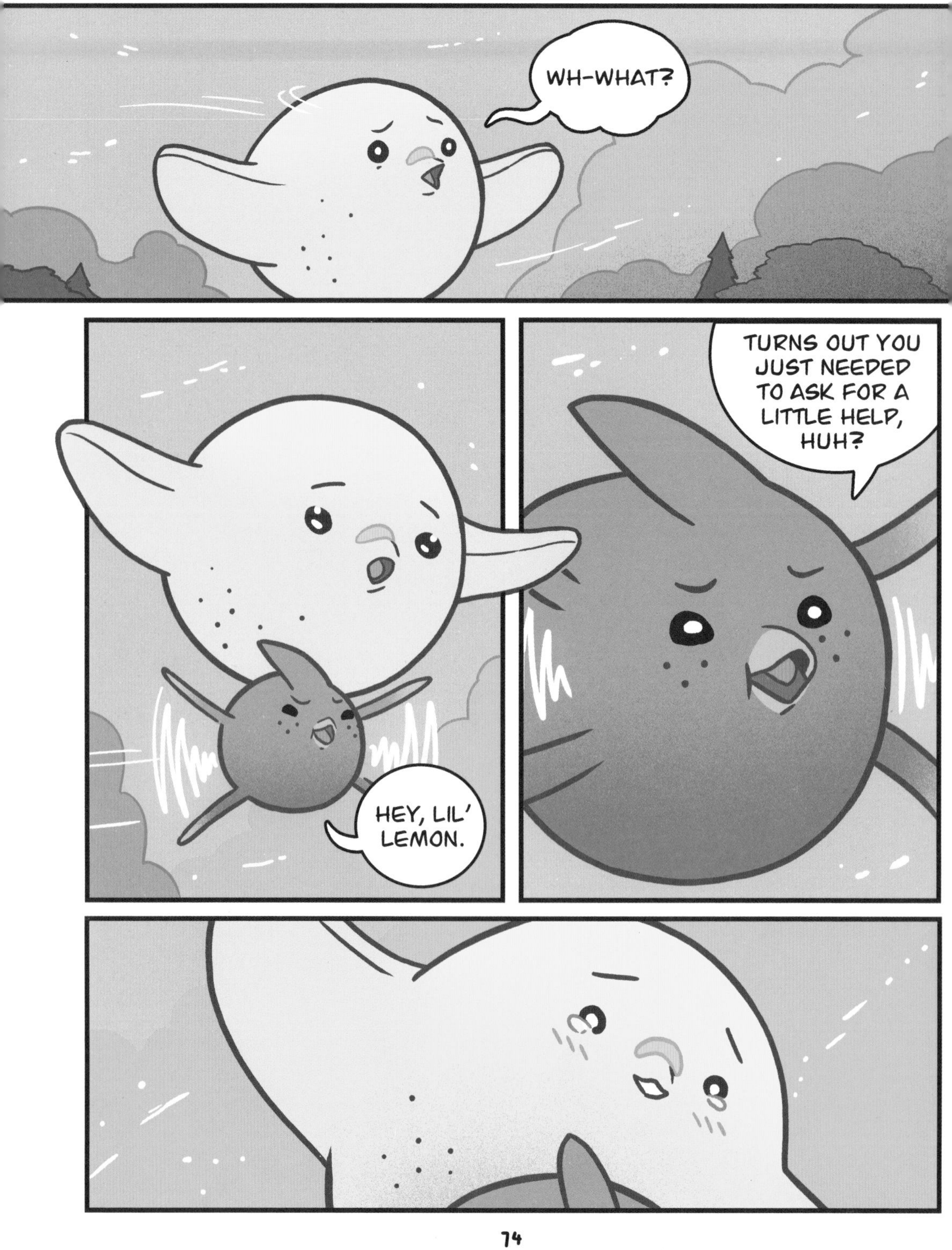
WH-WHAT?
HEY, LIL' LEMON.
TURNS OUT YOU JUST NEEDED TO ASK FOR A LITTLE HELP, HUH?

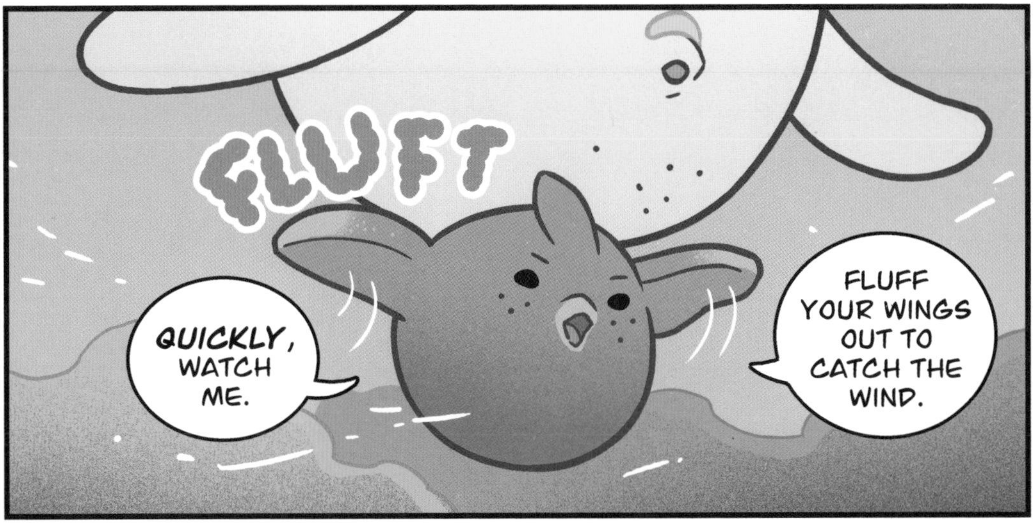
FLUFT
QUICKLY, WATCH ME.
FLUFF YOUR WINGS OUT TO CATCH THE WIND.

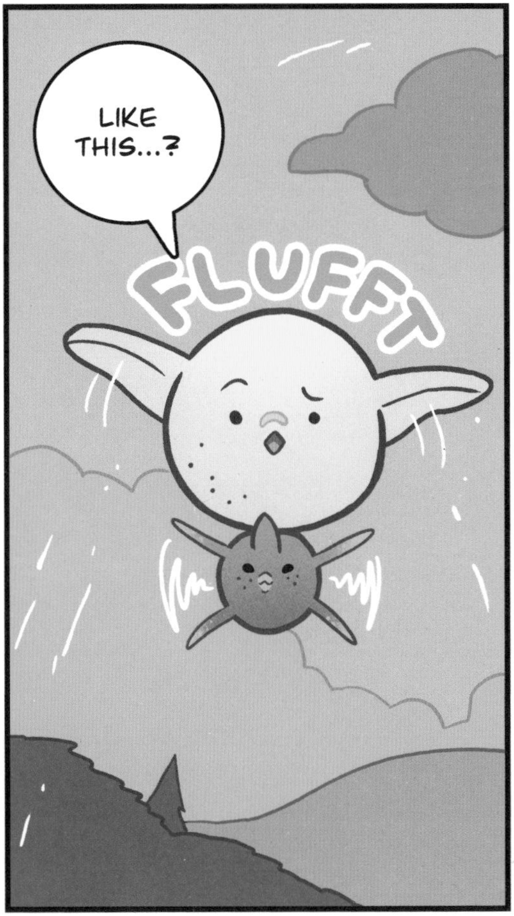
LIKE THIS...?
FLUFFT

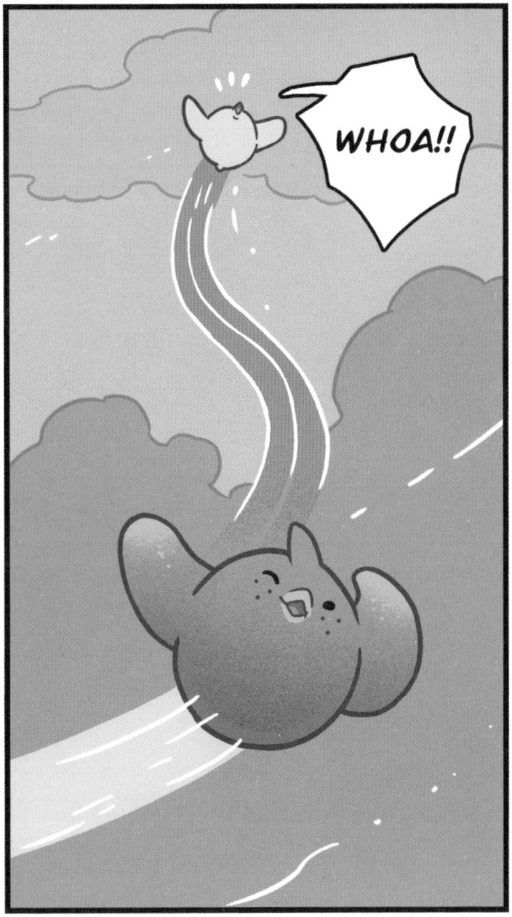
WHOA!!

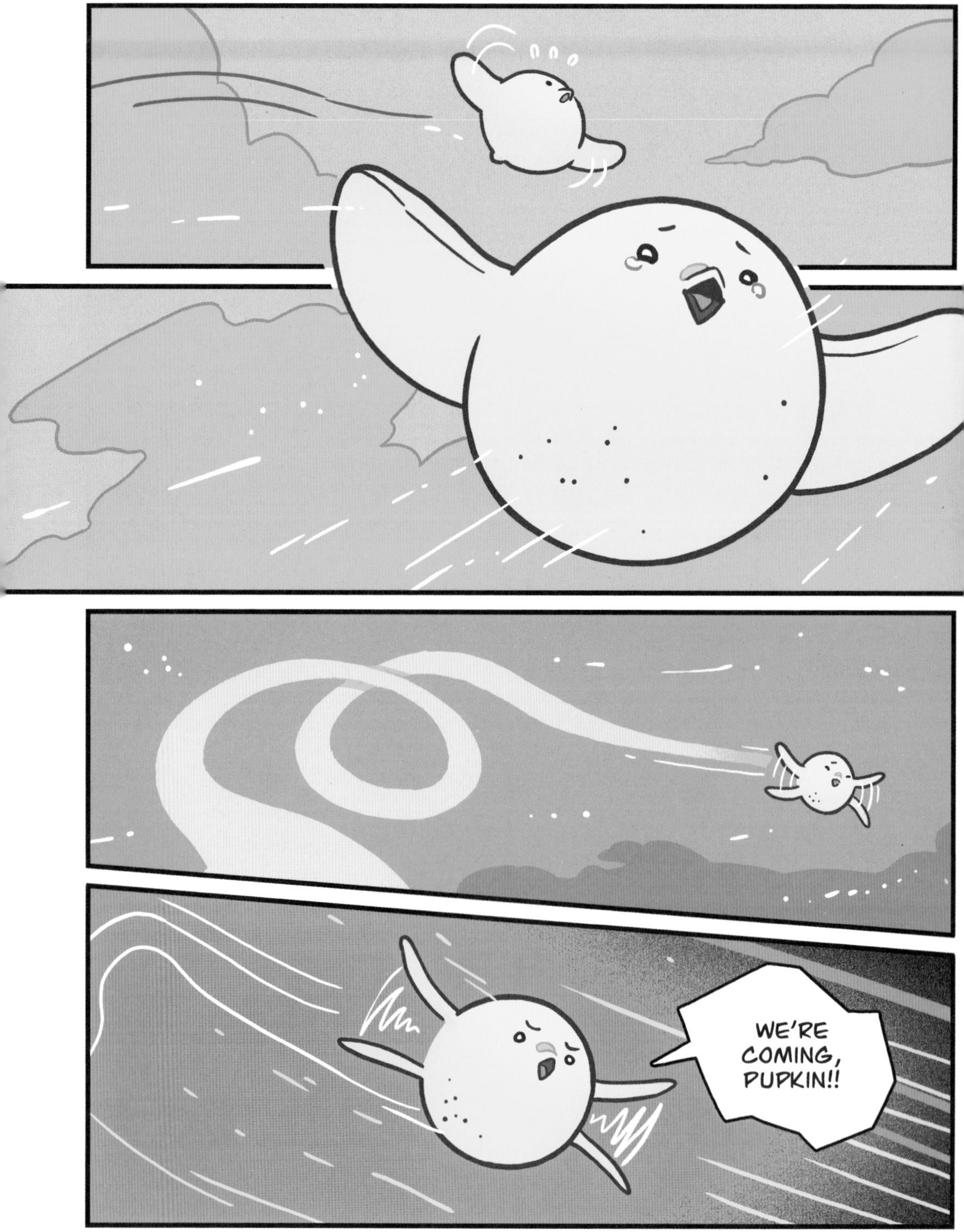
WE'RE COMING, PUPKIN!!

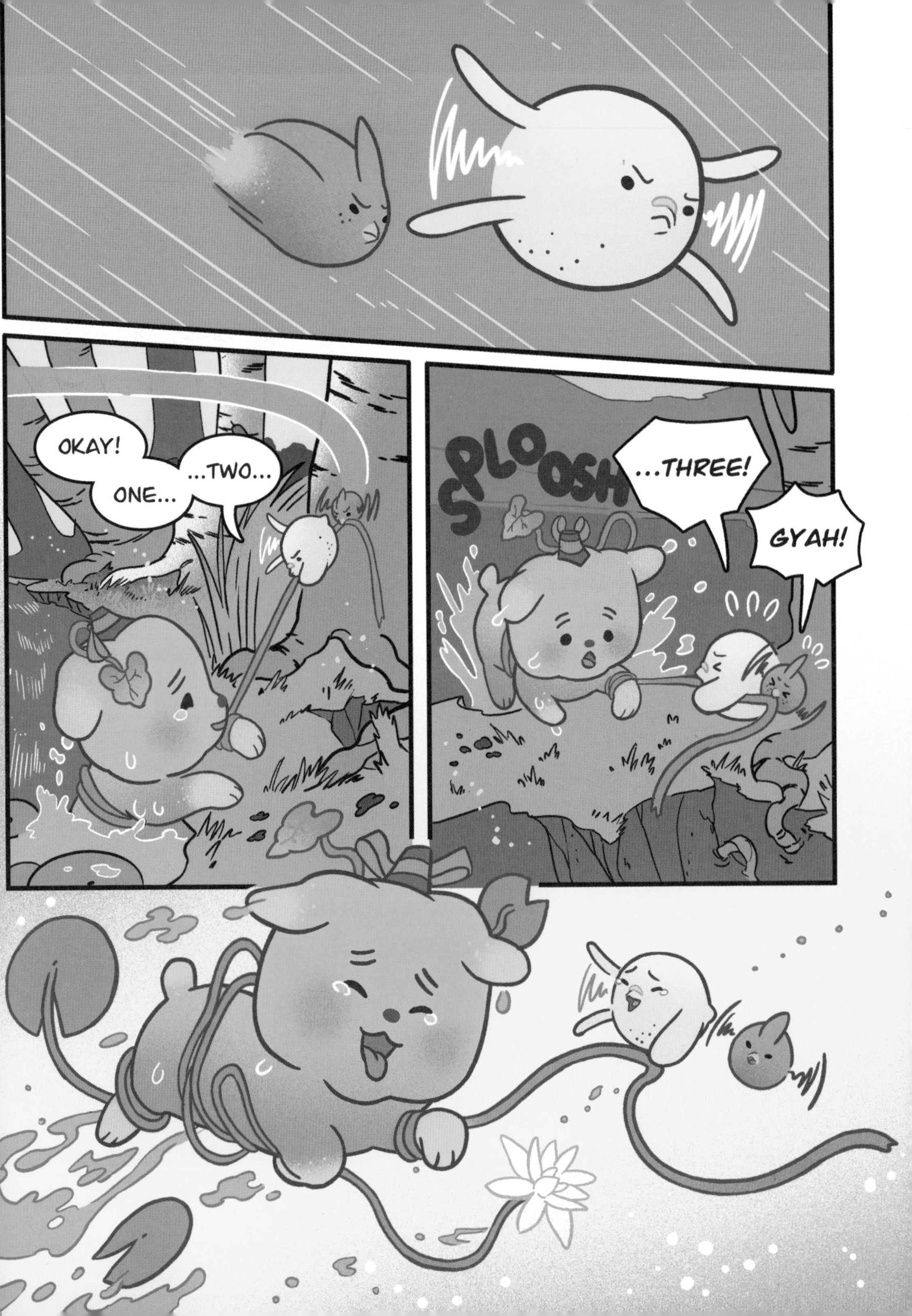
OKAY!
ONE...
...TWO...
SPLOOSH
...THREE!
GYAH!

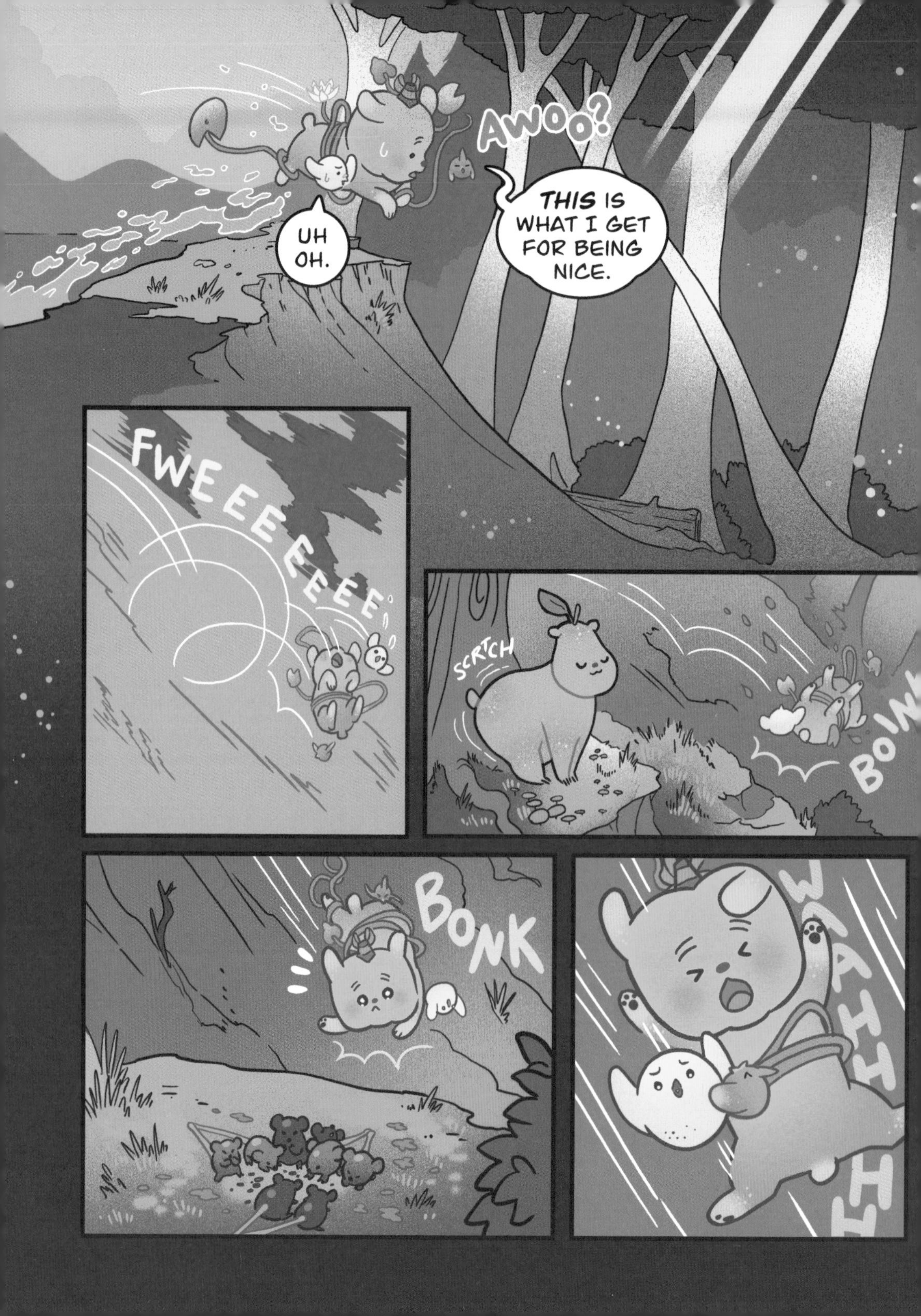
AWOO?
UH OH.
THIS IS WHAT I GET FOR BEING NICE.
FWEEEEEEEE
SCRTCH
BOIN
BONK
WAAHHHH

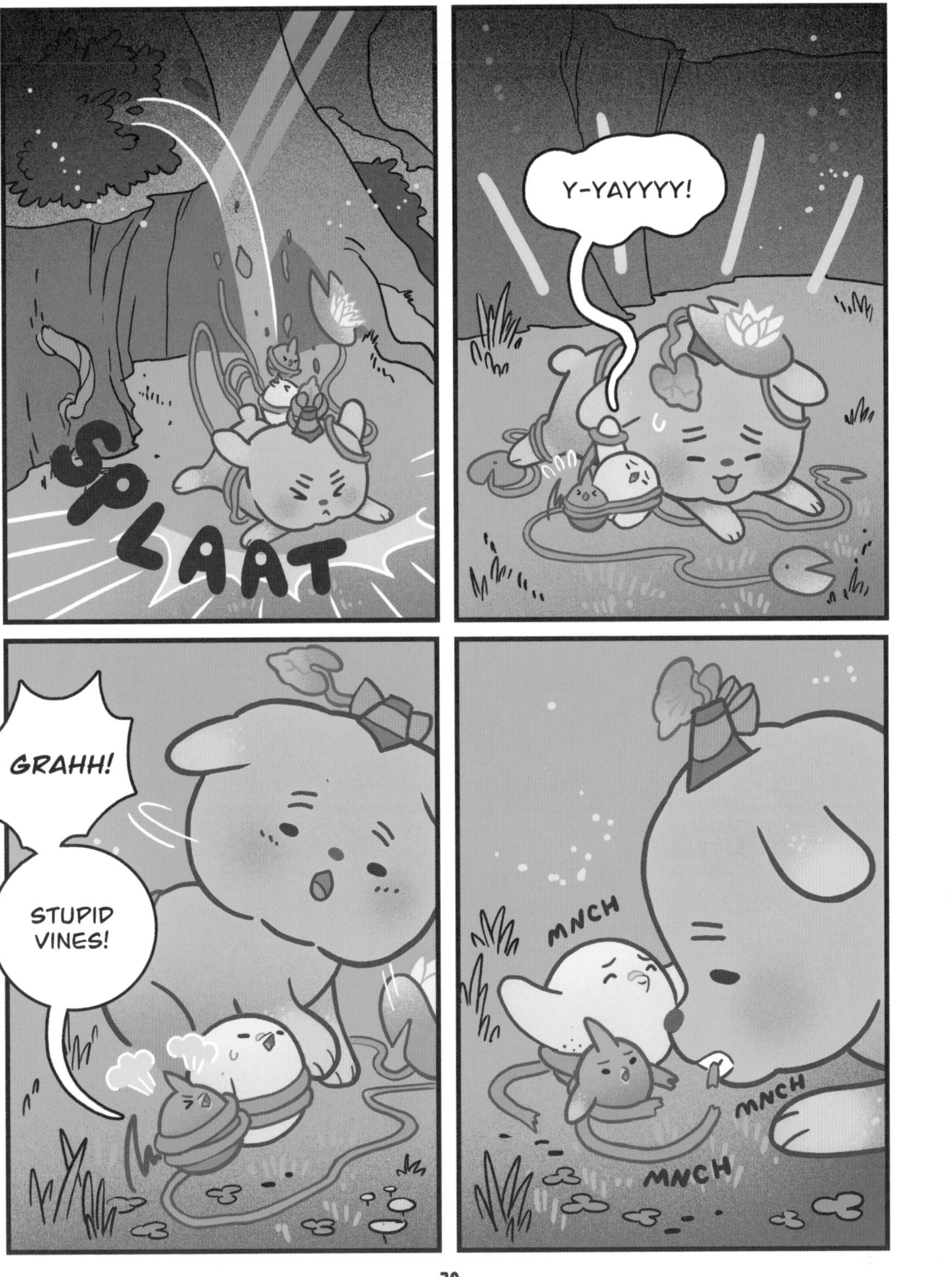
SPLAAT
Y-YAYYYY!
GRAHH!
STUPID VINES!
MNCH
MNCH
MNCH

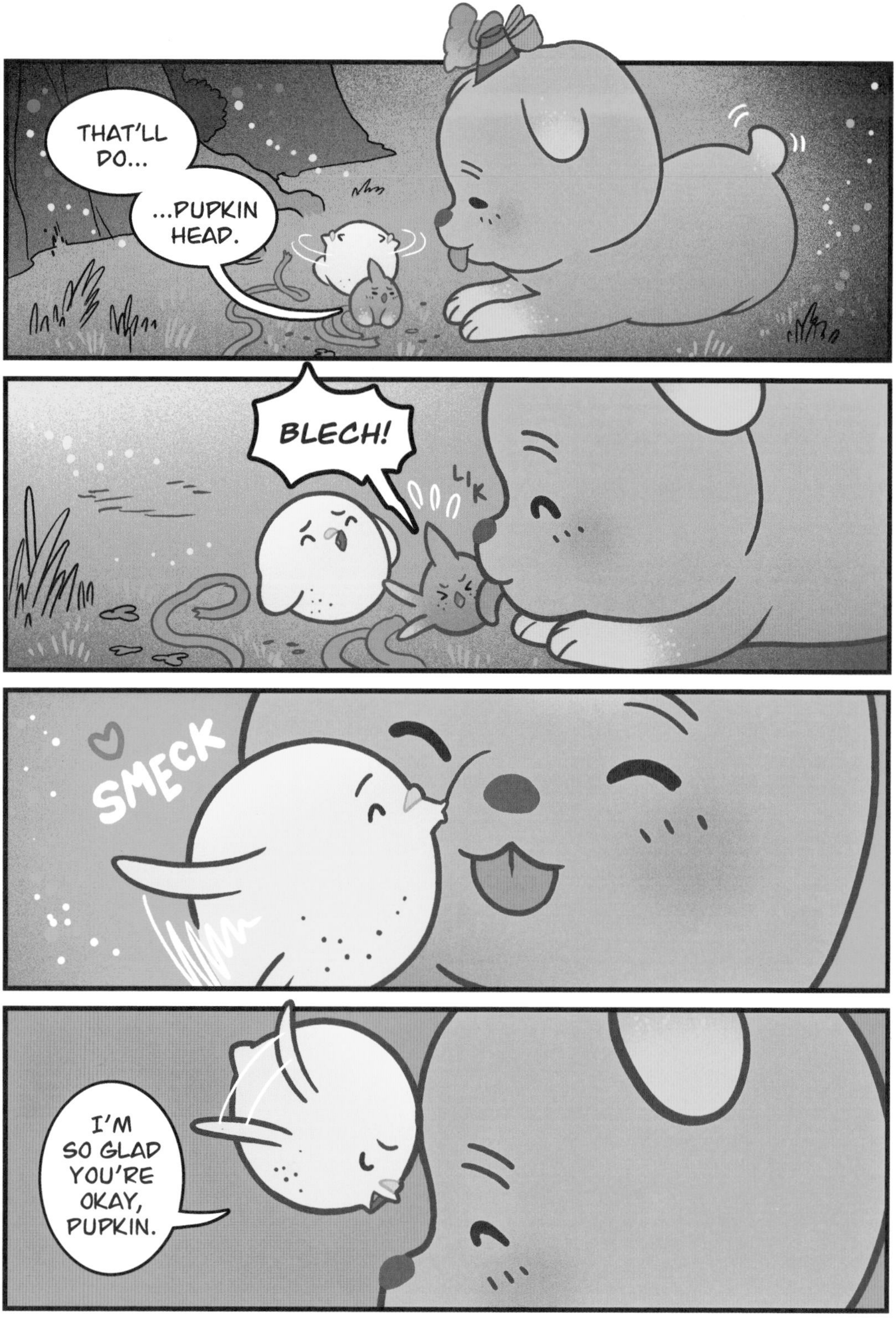
THAT'LL DO...
...PUPKIN HEAD.
BLECH!
LIK
SMECK
I'M SO GLAD YOU'RE OKAY, PUPKIN.

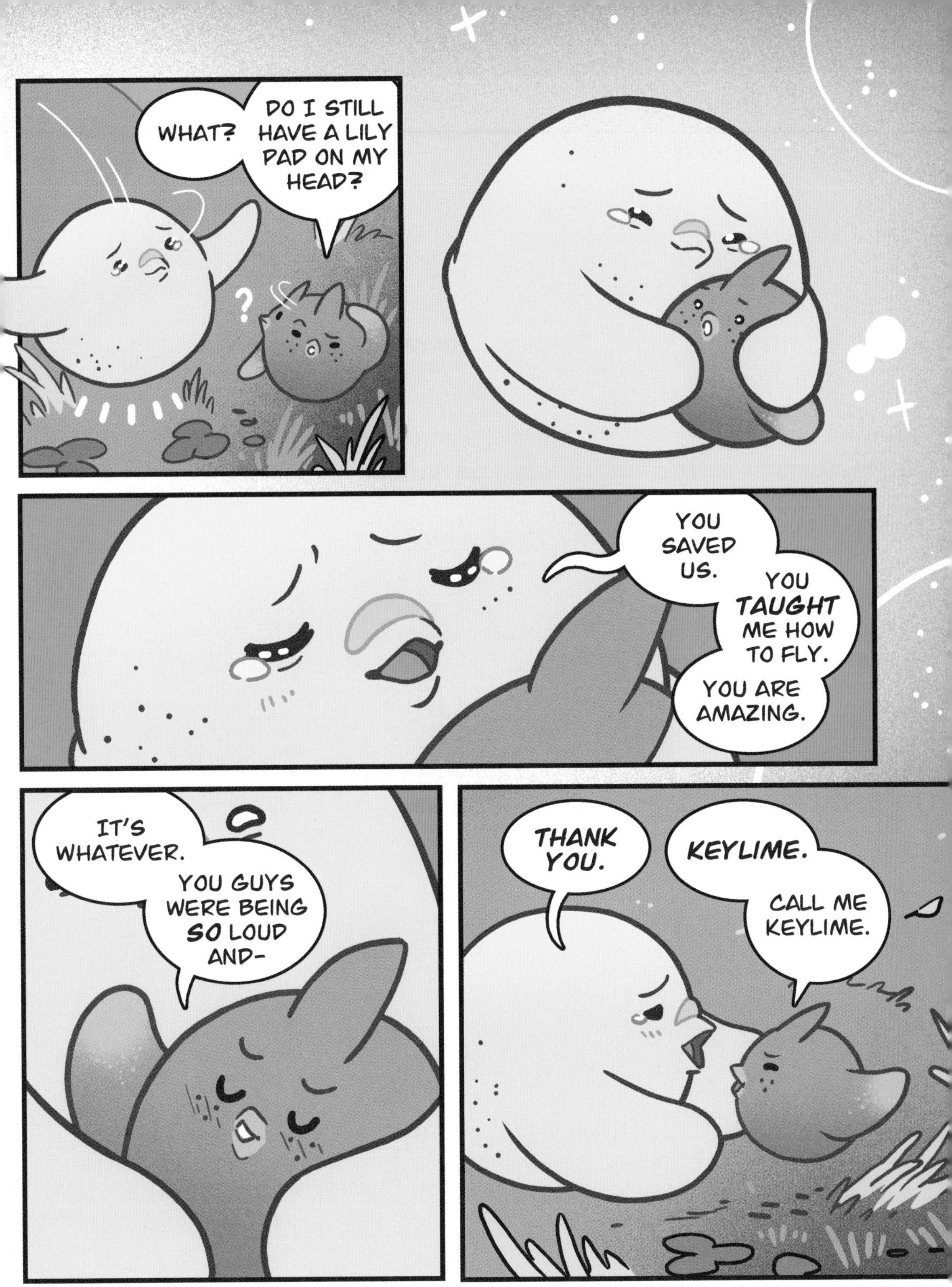
WHAT?
DO I STILL HAVE A LILY PAD ON MY HEAD?
?
YOU SAVED US.
YOU TAUGHT ME HOW TO FLY.
YOU ARE AMAZING.
IT'S WHATEVER.
YOU GUYS WERE BEING SO LOUD AND-
THANK YOU.
KEYLIME.
CALL ME KEYLIME.

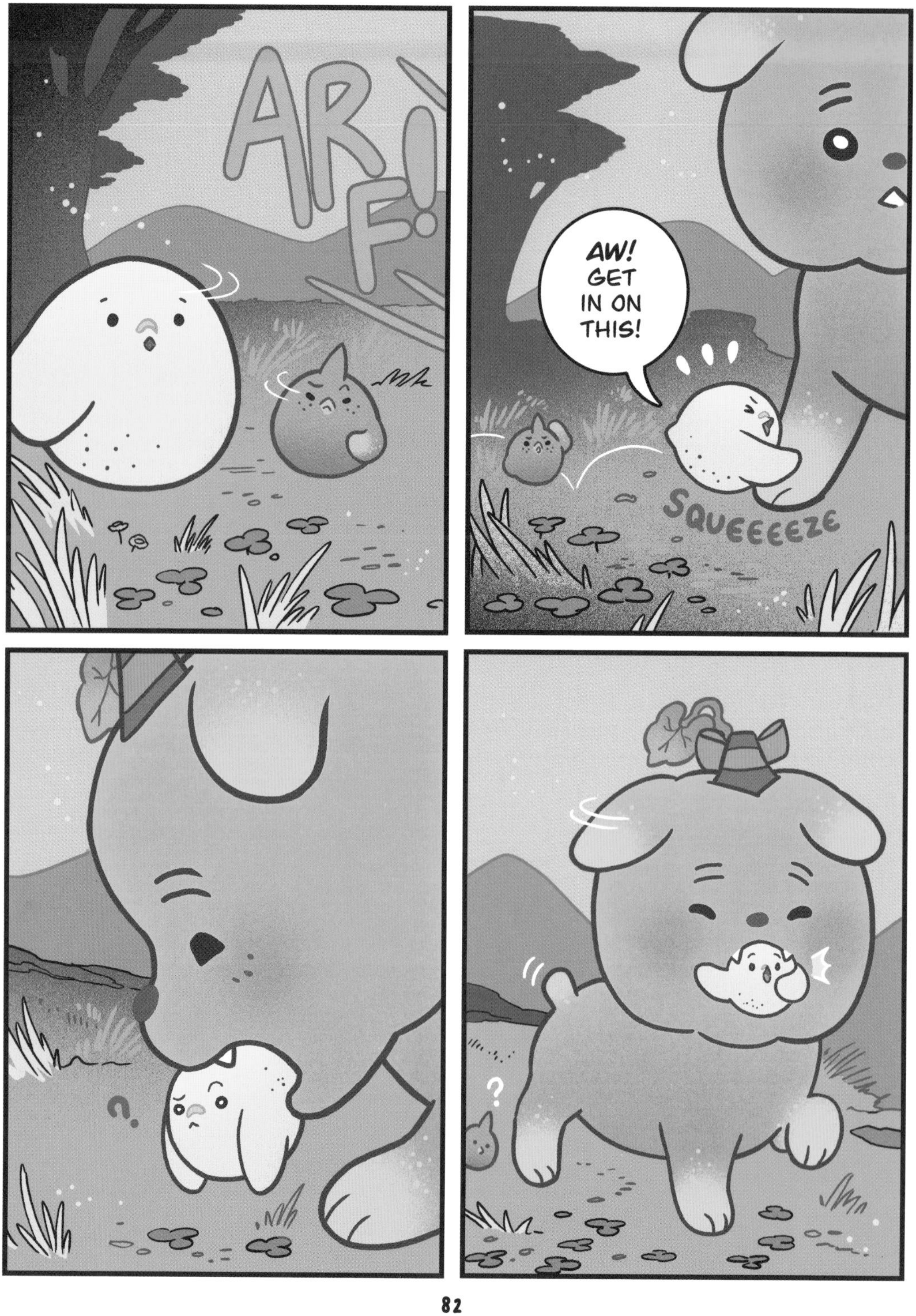
ARF!
AW! GET IN ON THIS!
SQUEEEEEZE

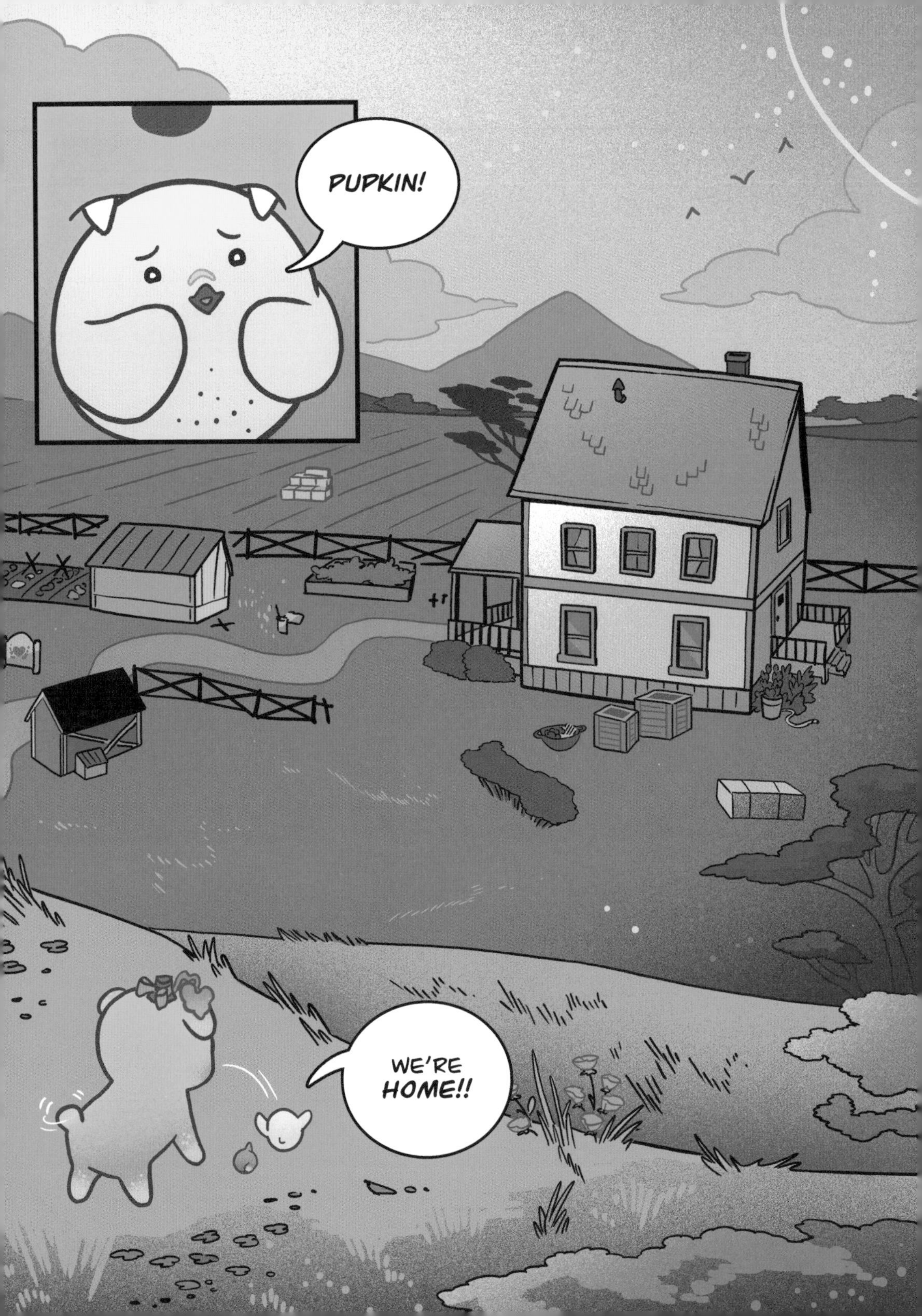
PUPKIN!
WE'RE HOME!!

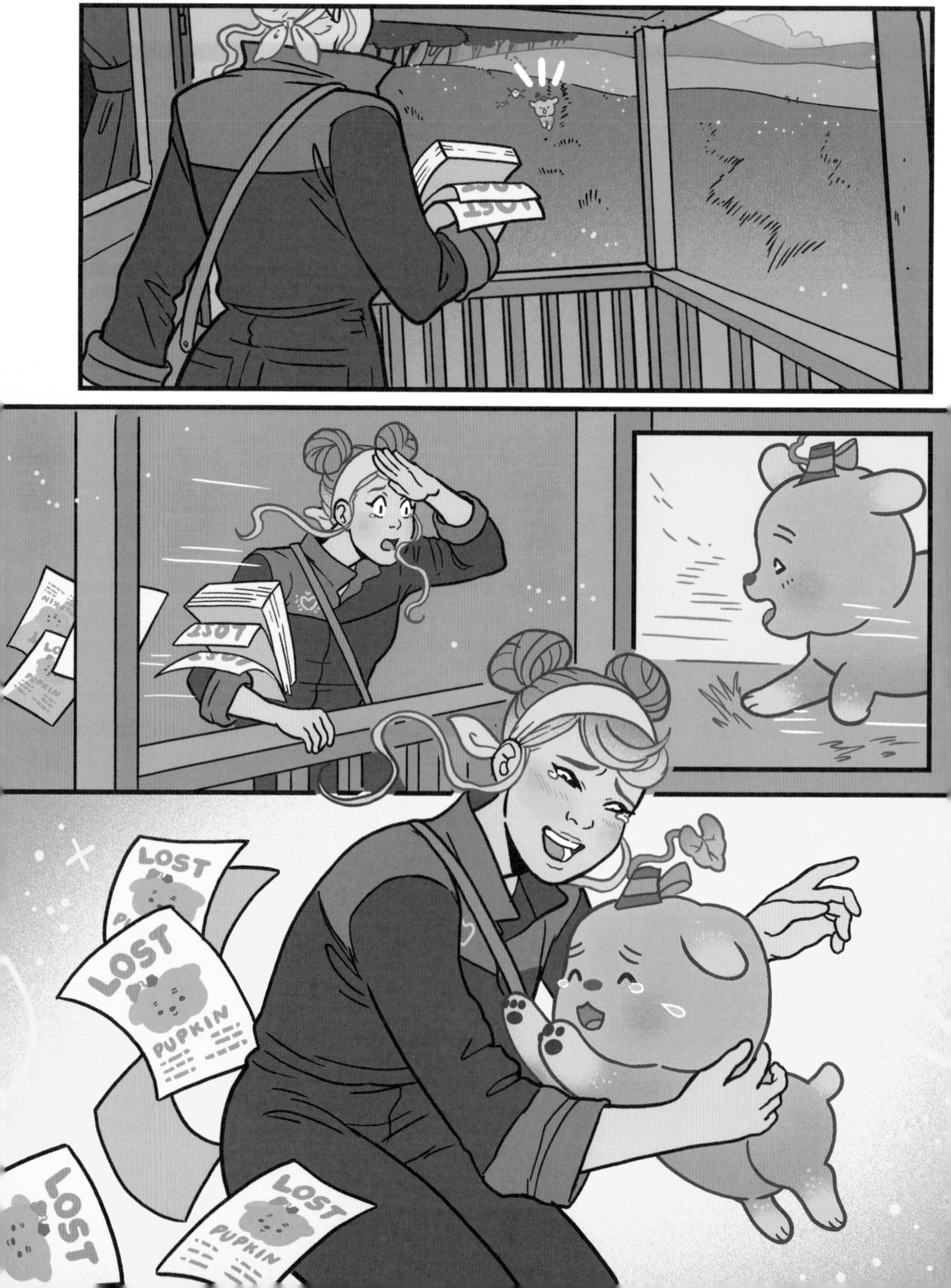
LOST
PUPKIN
LOST
PUPKIN
LOST
LOST
PUPKIN

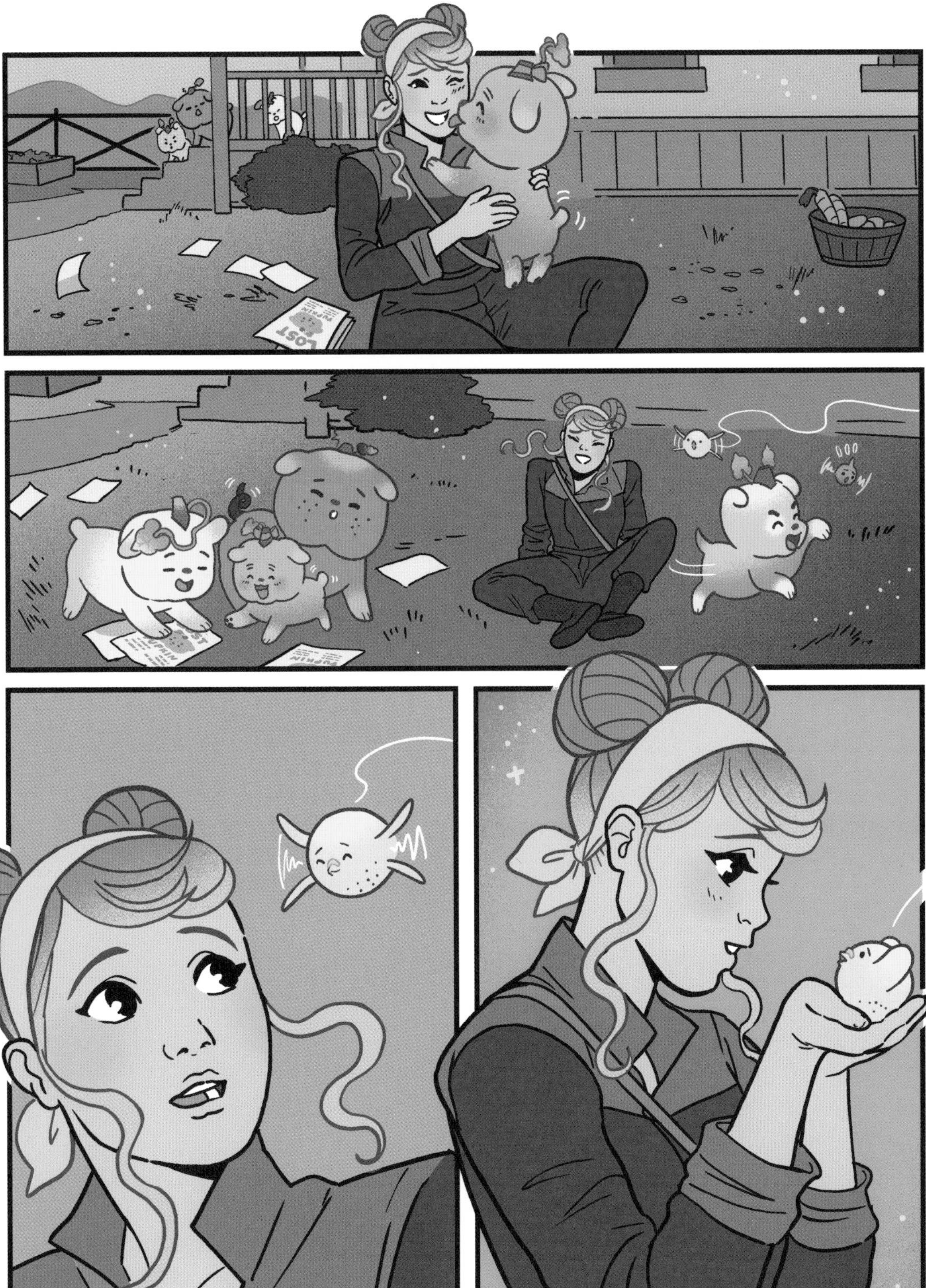
LOST
PUPKIN

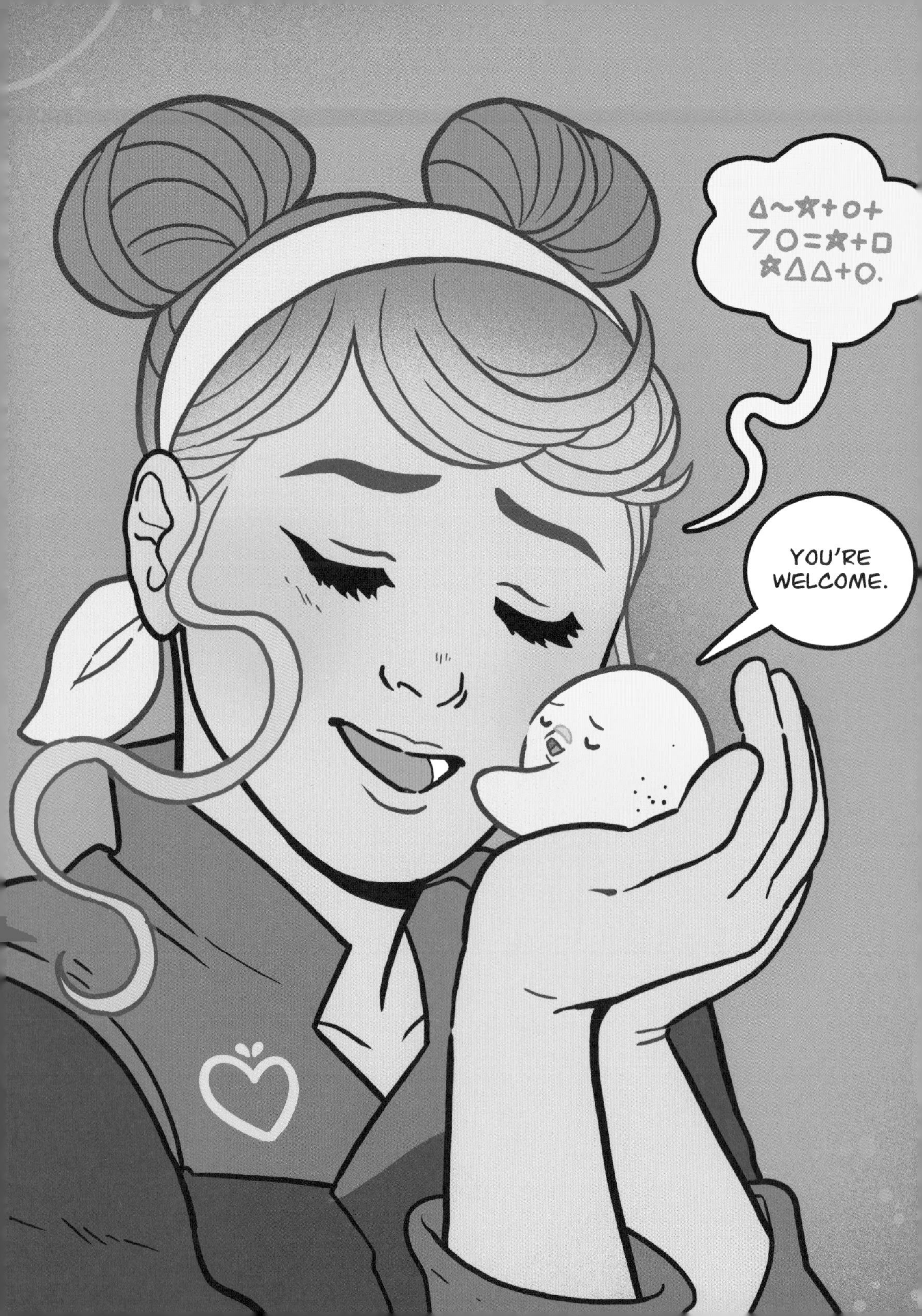
YOU'RE WELCOME.

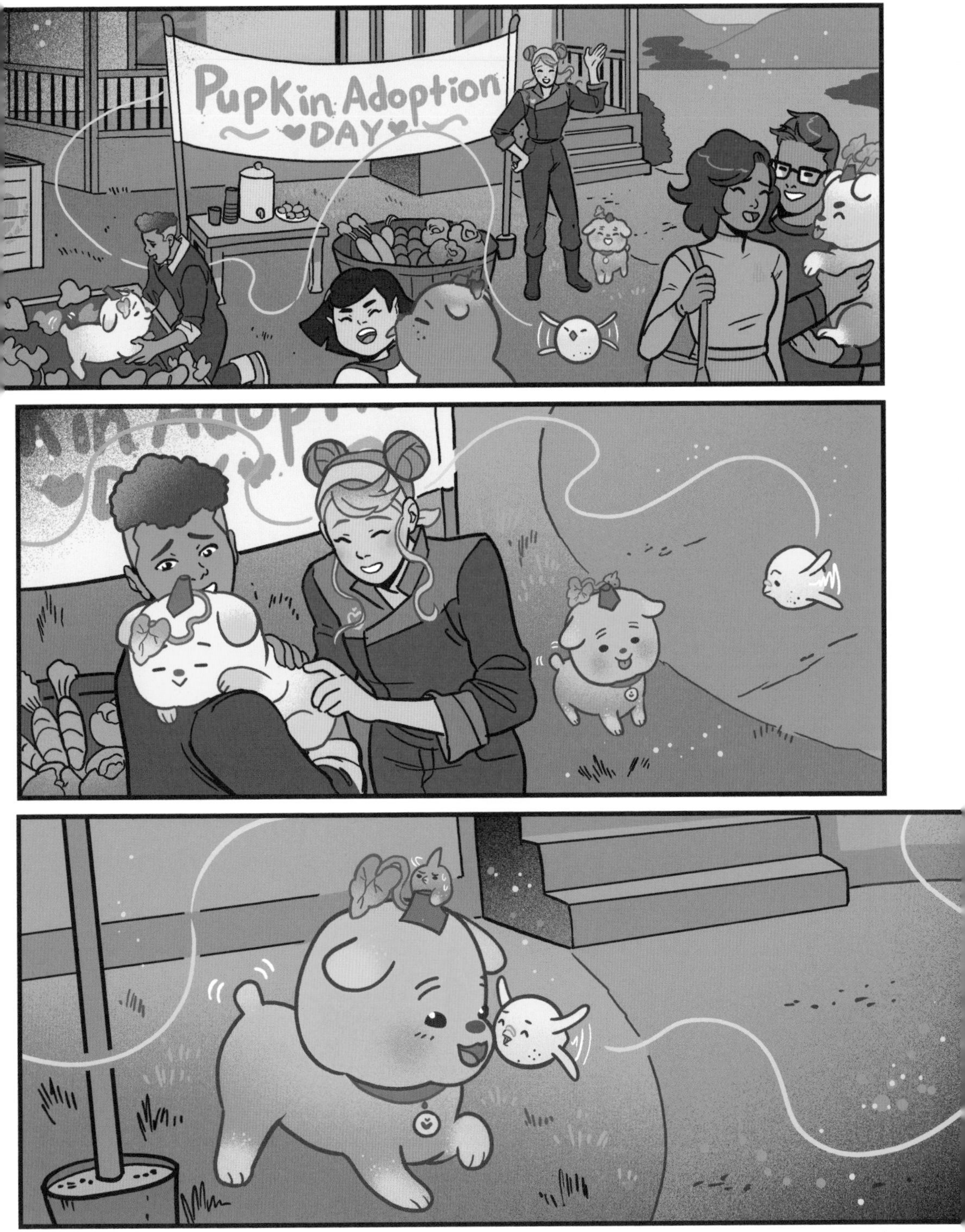
Pupkin Adoption
DAY

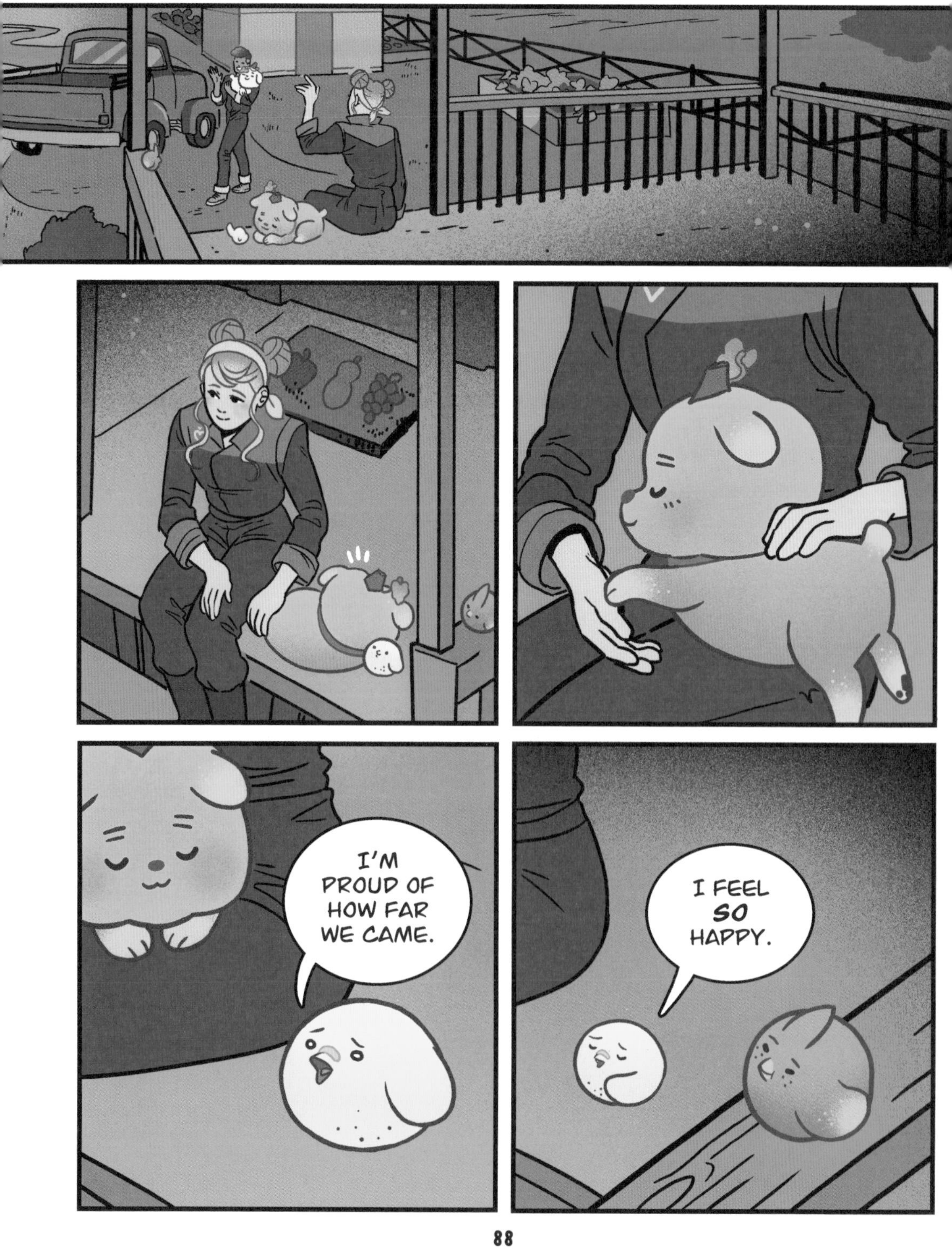
I'M PROUD OF HOW FAR WE CAME.
I FEEL SO HAPPY.

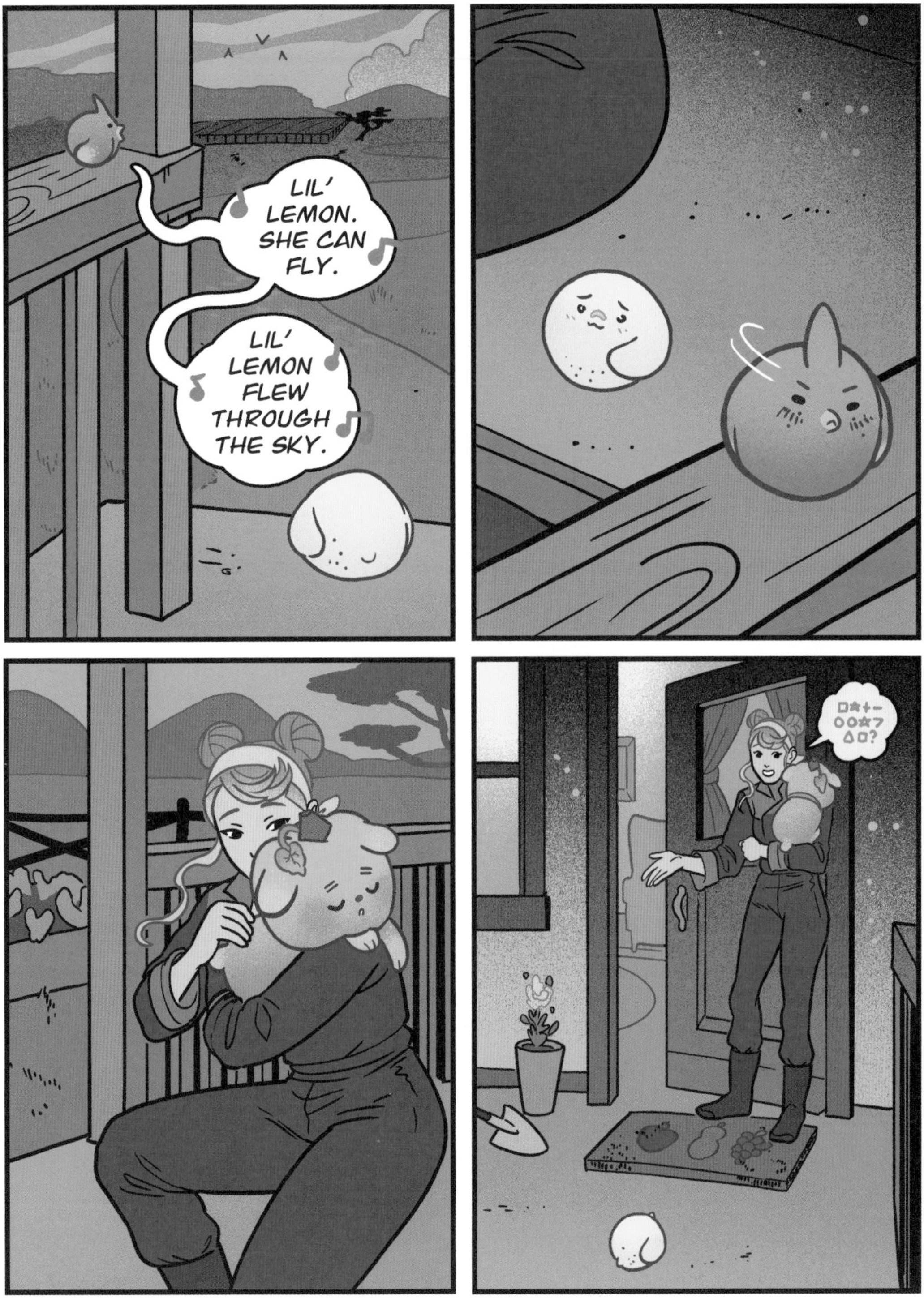
LIL' LEMON. SHE CAN FLY.
LIL' LEMON FLEW THROUGH THE SKY.

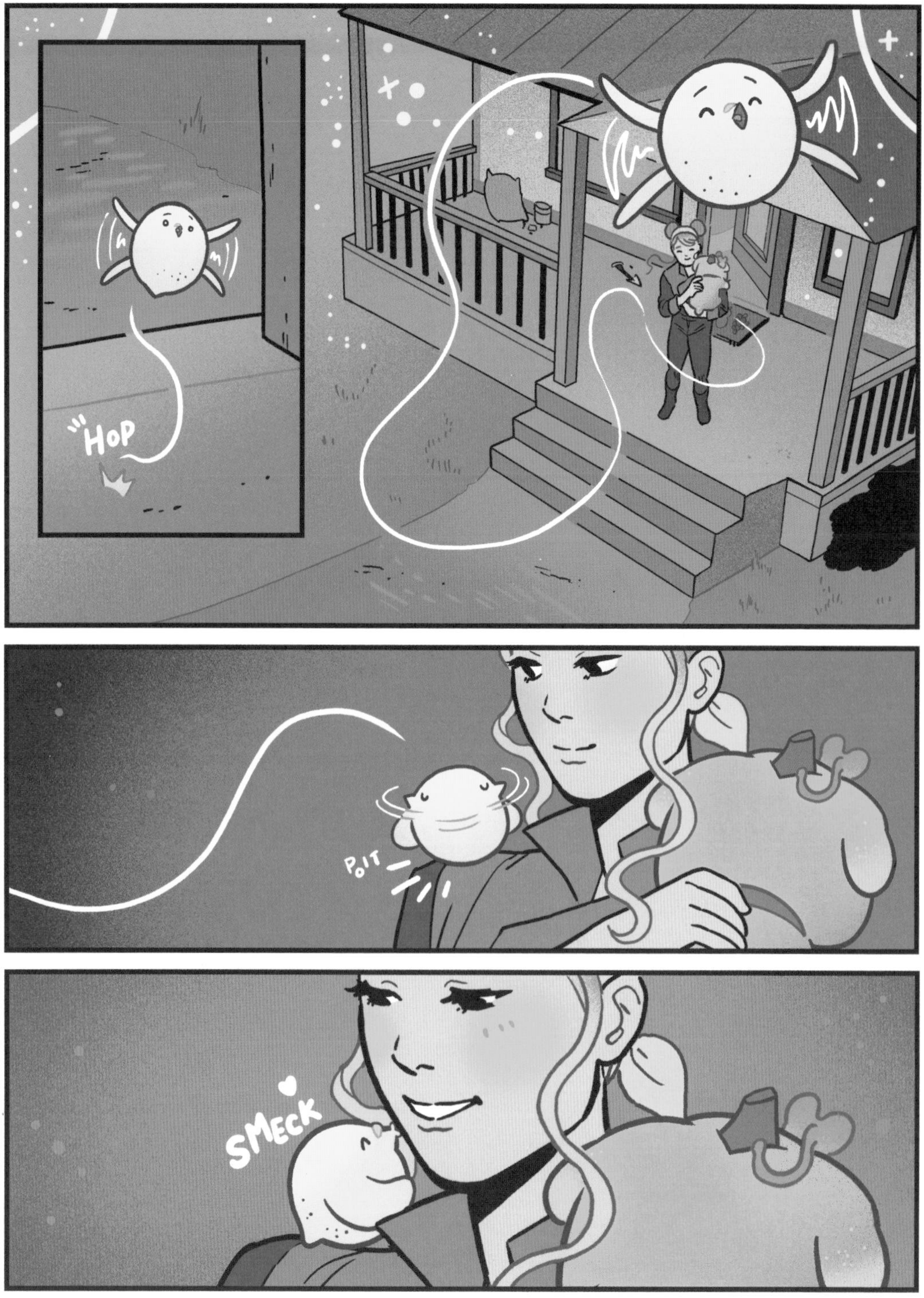
HOP
POIT
SMECK

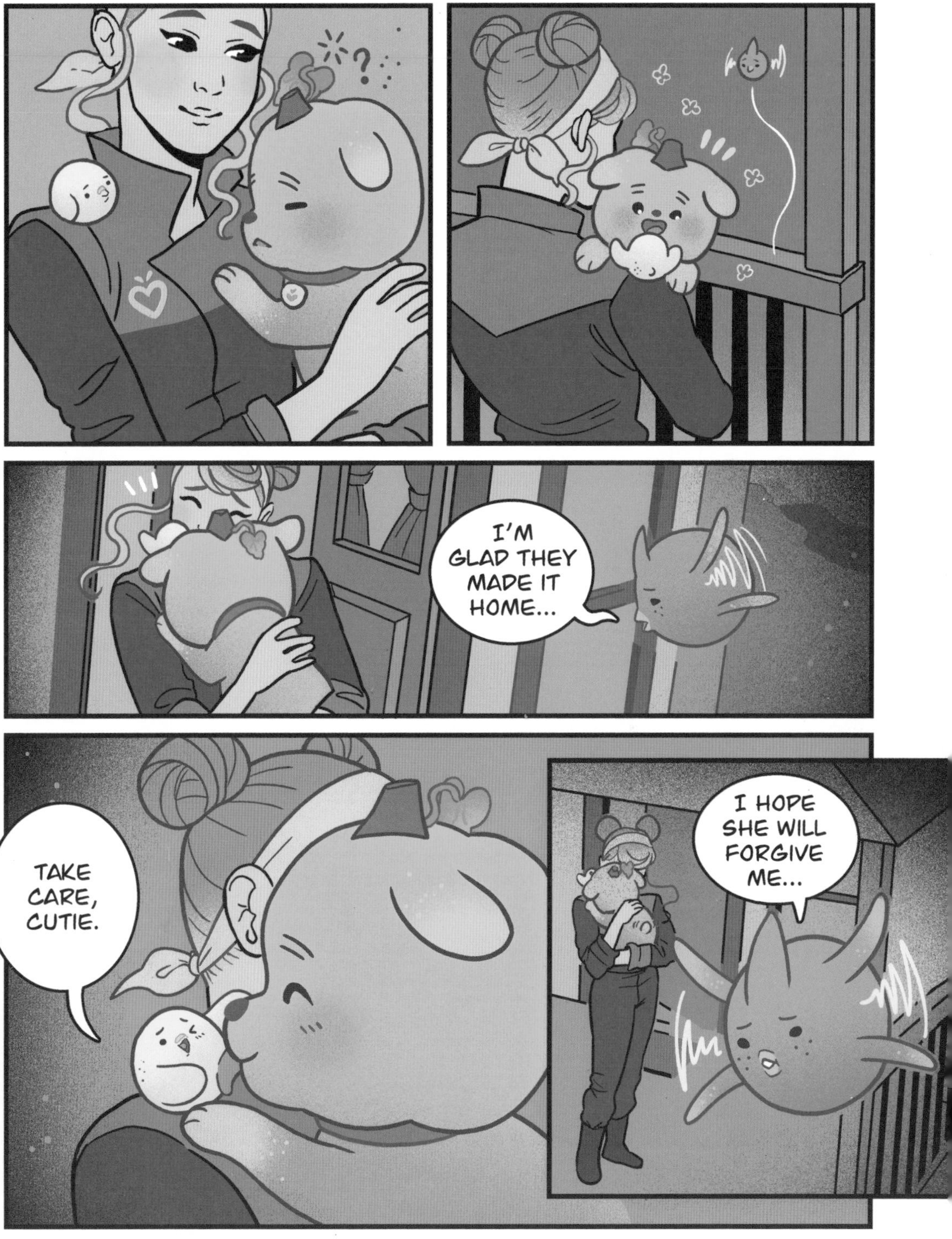
I'M GLAD THEY MADE IT HOME...
TAKE CARE, CUTIE.
I HOPE SHE WILL FORGIVE ME...

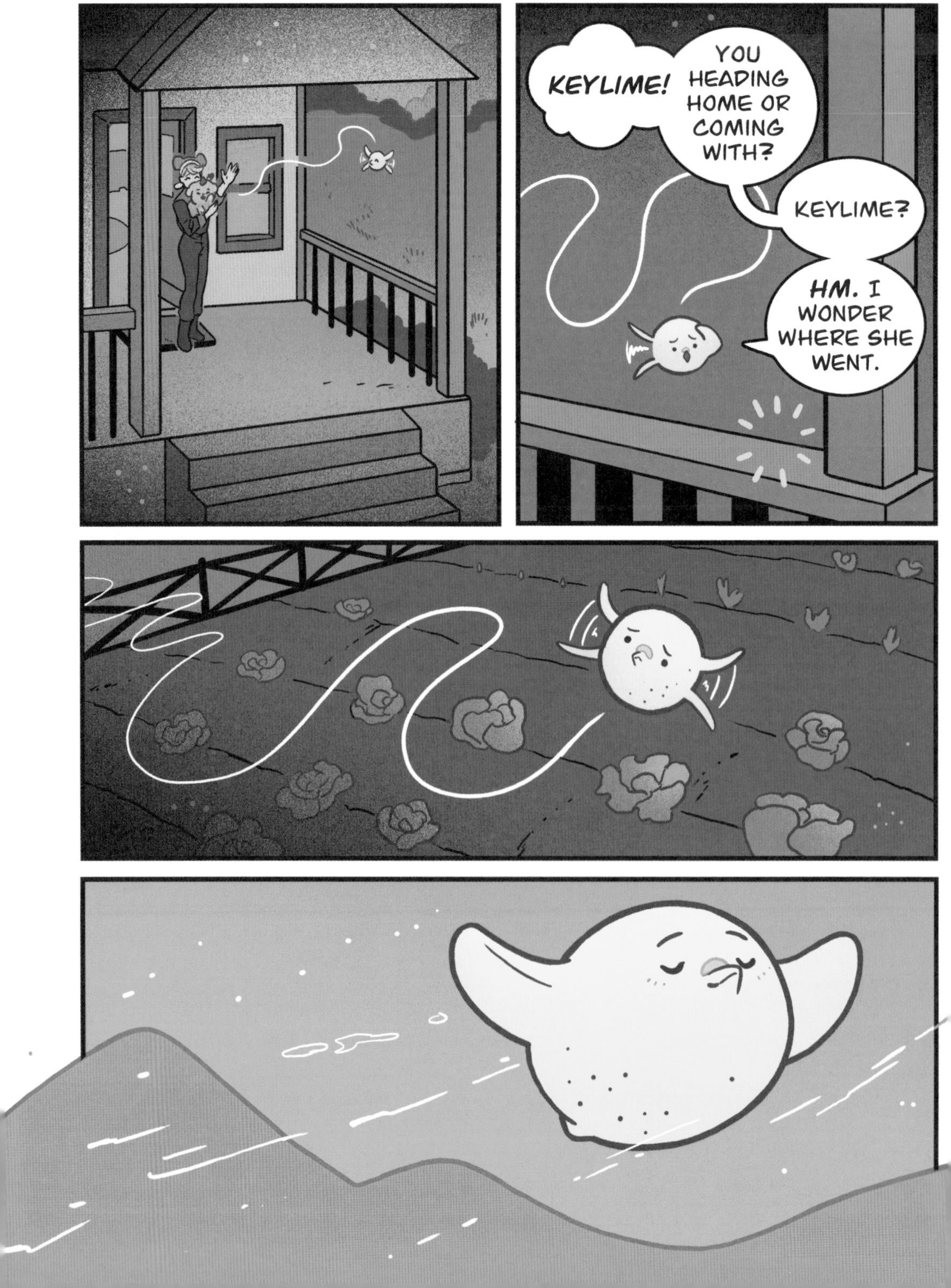
KEYLIME!
YOU HEADING HOME OR COMING WITH?
KEYLIME?
HM. I WONDER WHERE SHE WENT.

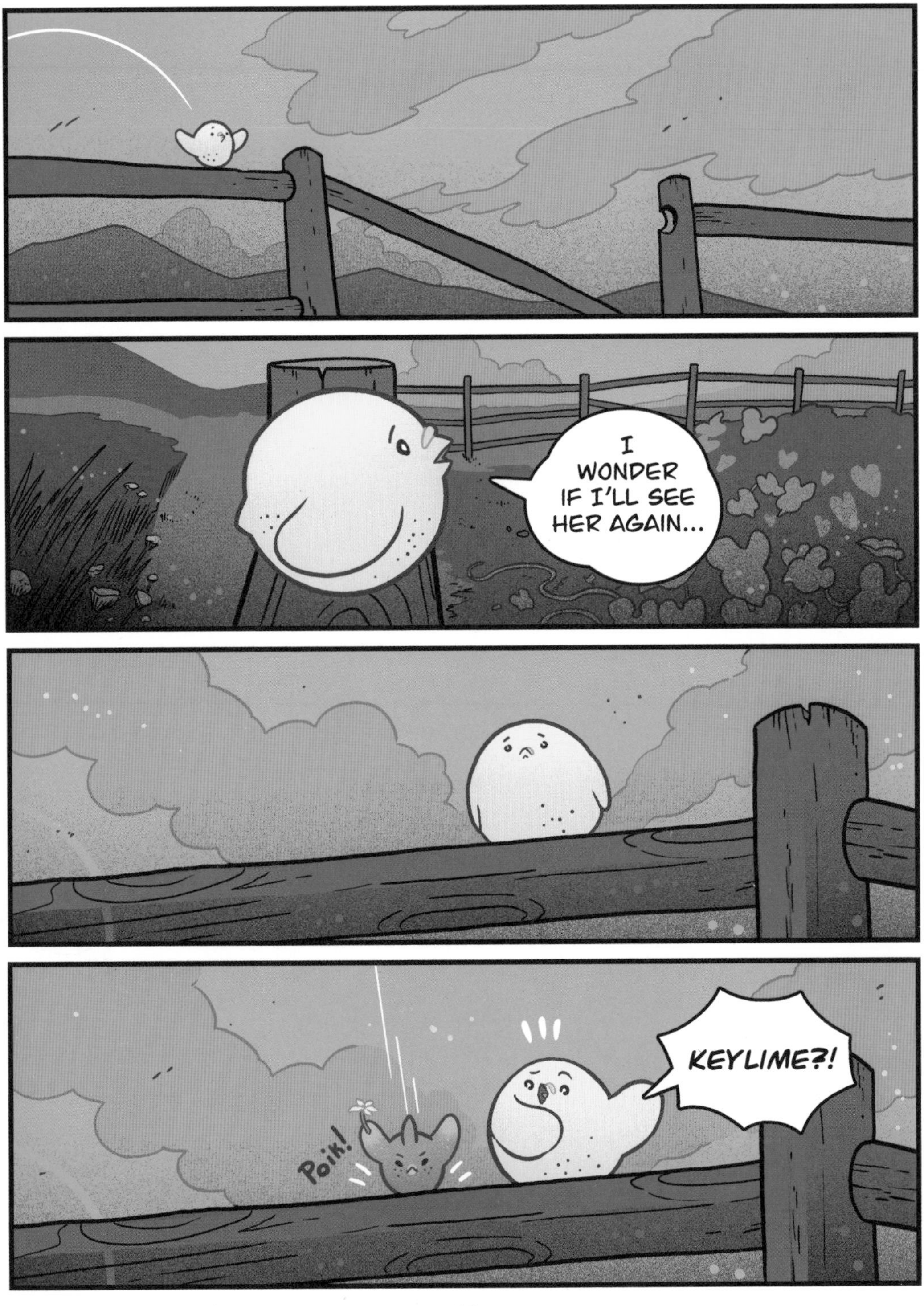
I WONDER IF I'LL SEE HER AGAIN...
Poik!
KEYLIME?!

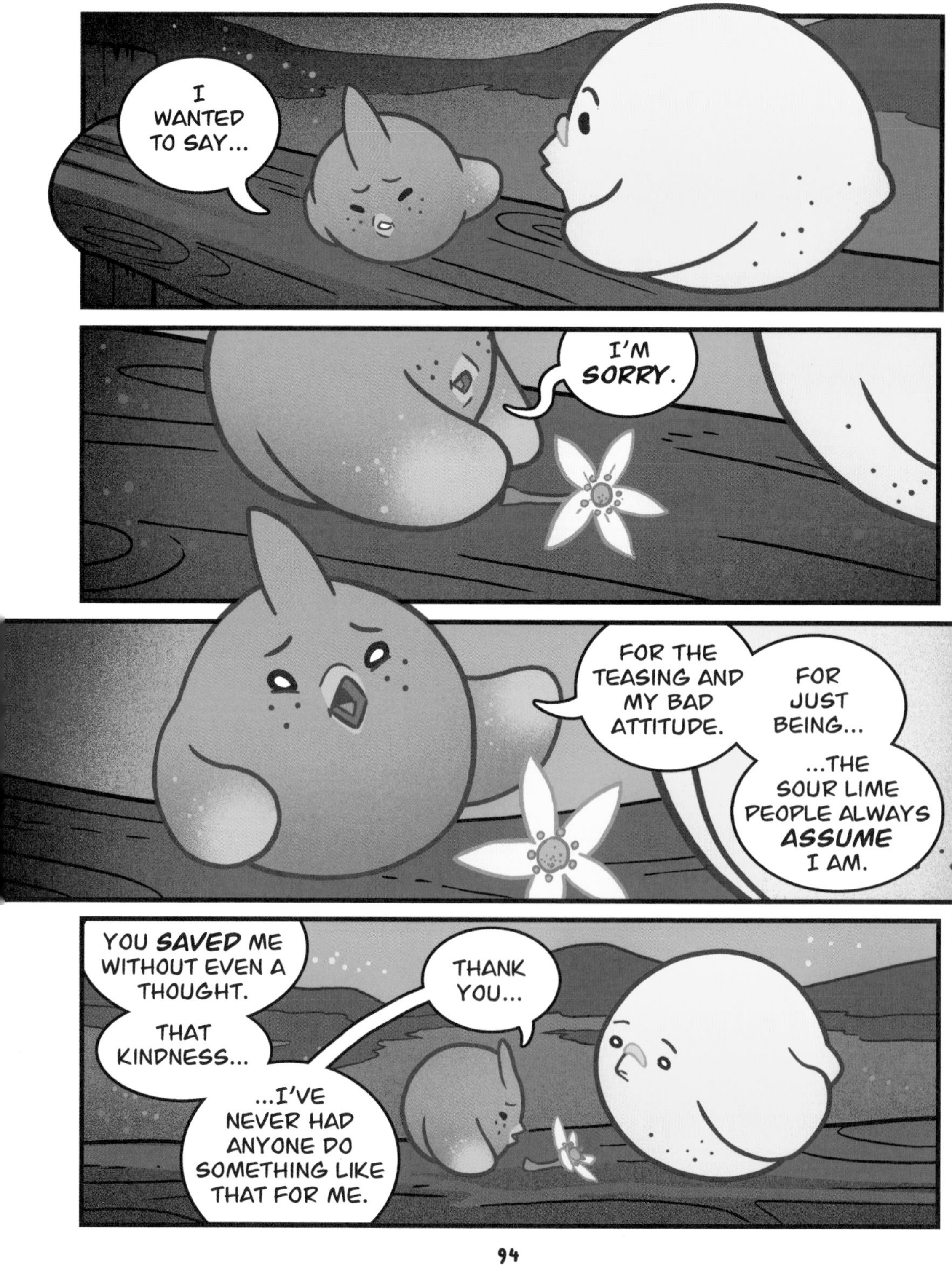
I WANTED TO SAY...
I'M SORRY.
FOR THE TEASING AND MY BAD ATTITUDE.
FOR JUST BEING...
...THE SOUR LIME PEOPLE ALWAYS ASSUME I AM.
YOU SAVED ME WITHOUT EVEN A THOUGHT.
THAT KINDNESS...
...I'VE NEVER HAD ANYONE DO SOMETHING LIKE THAT FOR ME.
THANK YOU...

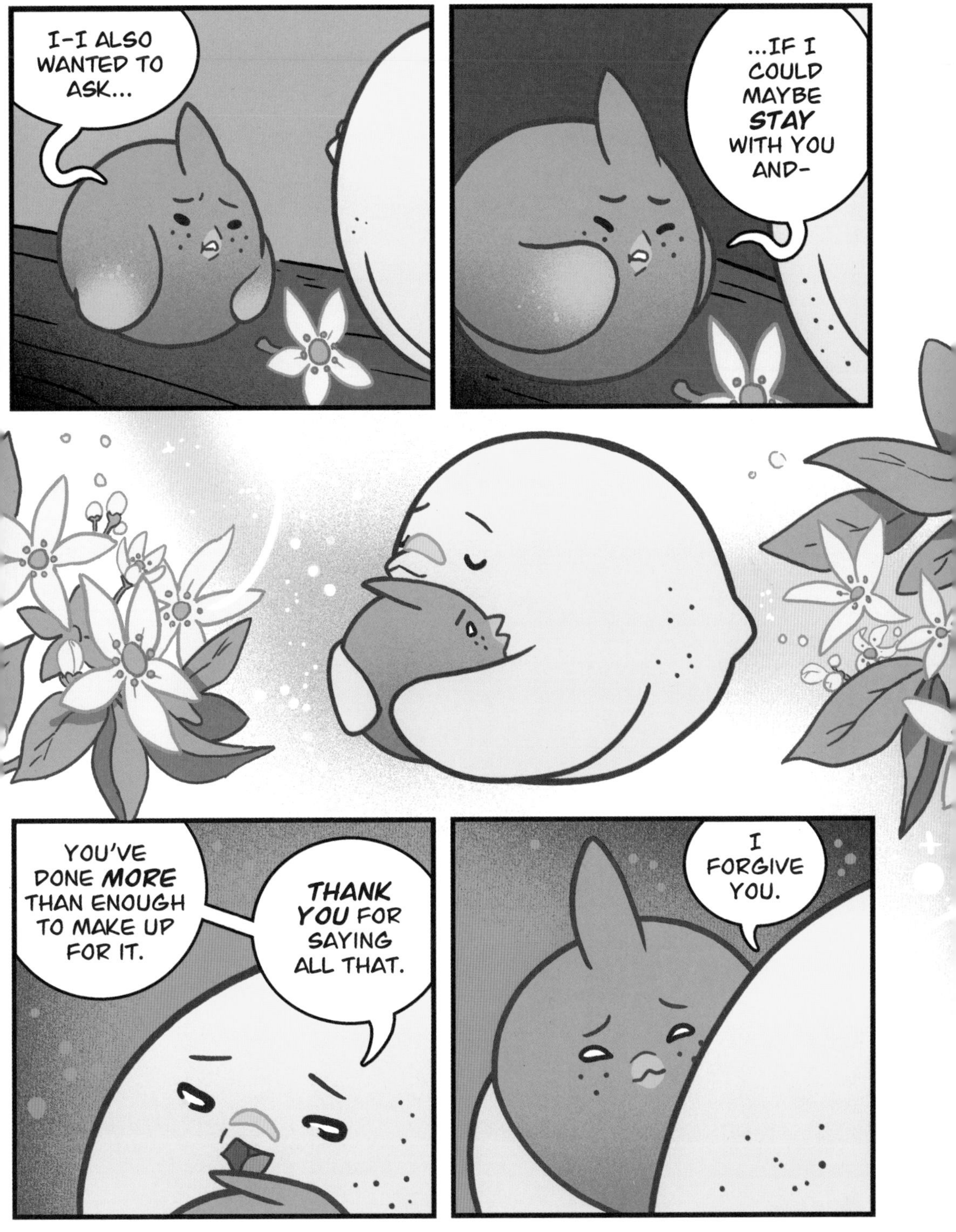
I-I ALSO WANTED TO ASK...
...IF I COULD MAYBE STAY WITH YOU AND-
YOU'VE DONE MORE THAN ENOUGH TO MAKE UP FOR IT.
THANK YOU FOR SAYING ALL THAT.
I FORGIVE YOU.

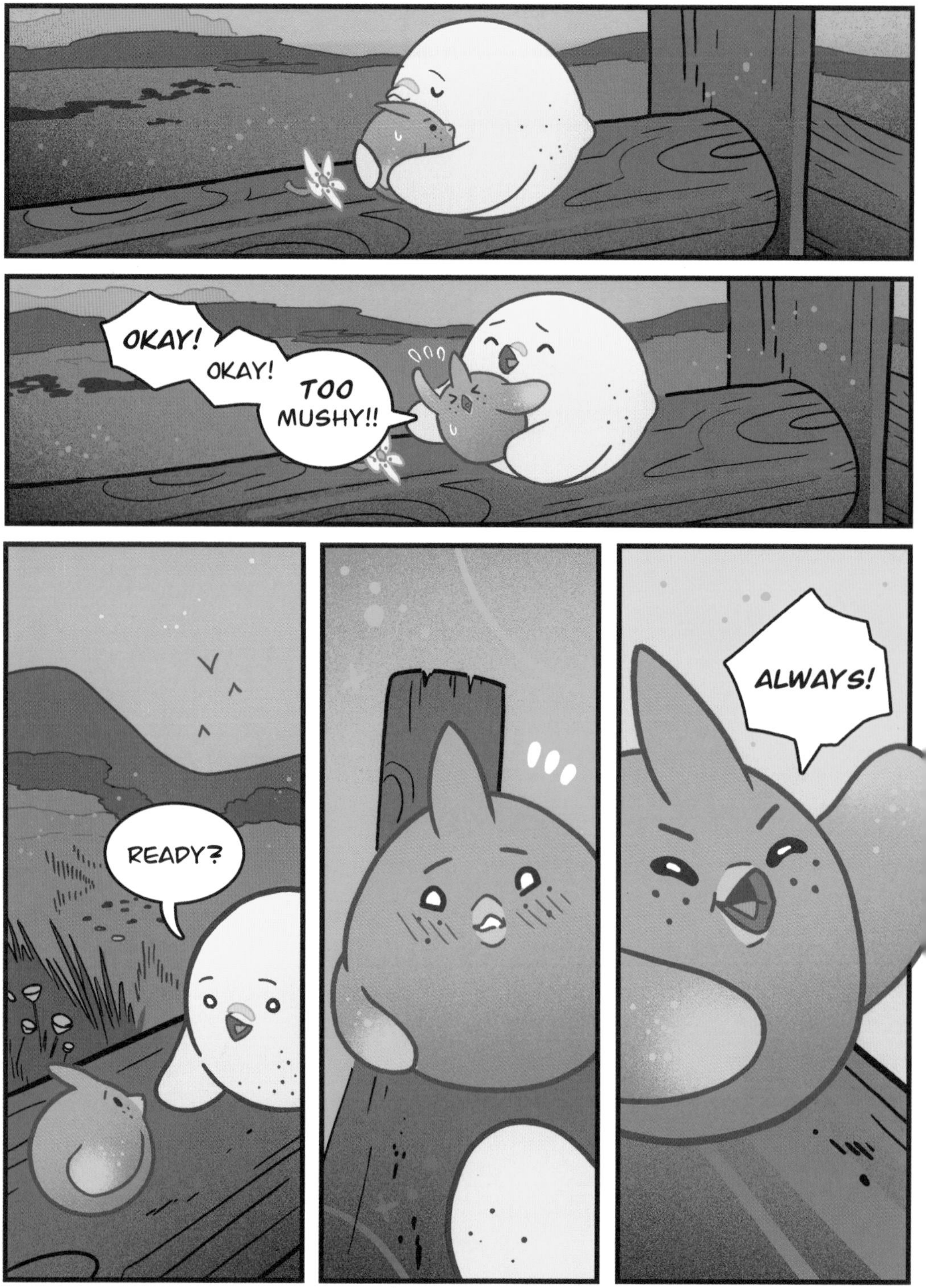
OKAY!
OKAY!
TOO MUSHY!!
READY?
ALWAYS!

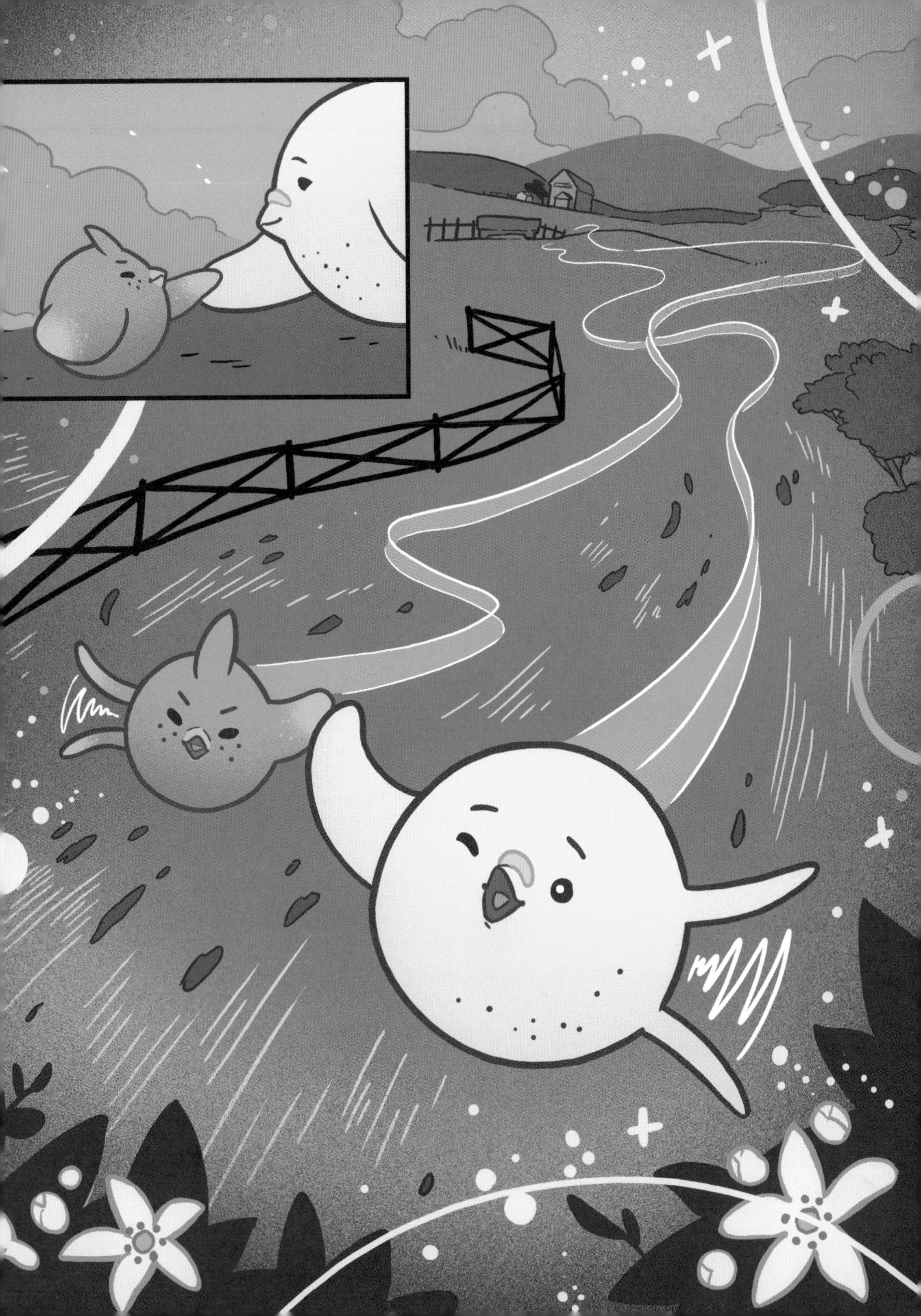

Acknowledgments

So many thanks to give! First, I want to thank Gina Gagliano, for this book would not exist without her query for more *Lemon Bird*. You saw the potential this little citrus bird had even before I did!

My agent, Charlie Olsen, for being the rock-star guiding-hand businessman who always gets my projects going on the right track. Same to my editor Whitney Leopard and my designer Patrick Crotty!

Mamaw and Papaw. You both gave me so many beautiful memories of creativity, fun, and laughter that I still carry with me to this day. It was so fitting that I was at your house when I found out *Lemon Bird* the graphic novel was being acquired. This book is for you both.

To my whole family. Mama and Daddo, I love you! Savi, my bestie comics sister. Kendall, my partner and my best pal. You keep me going. To all my friends, Kevin, Door, Julian, Coleman, Patrick, Robyn, Emily, Brad, Jess, Gabe, Tory. Thank you for cheering me on!

My supporters. My fans. To anyone who ever said my art brought them joy. I create for you. 🤍

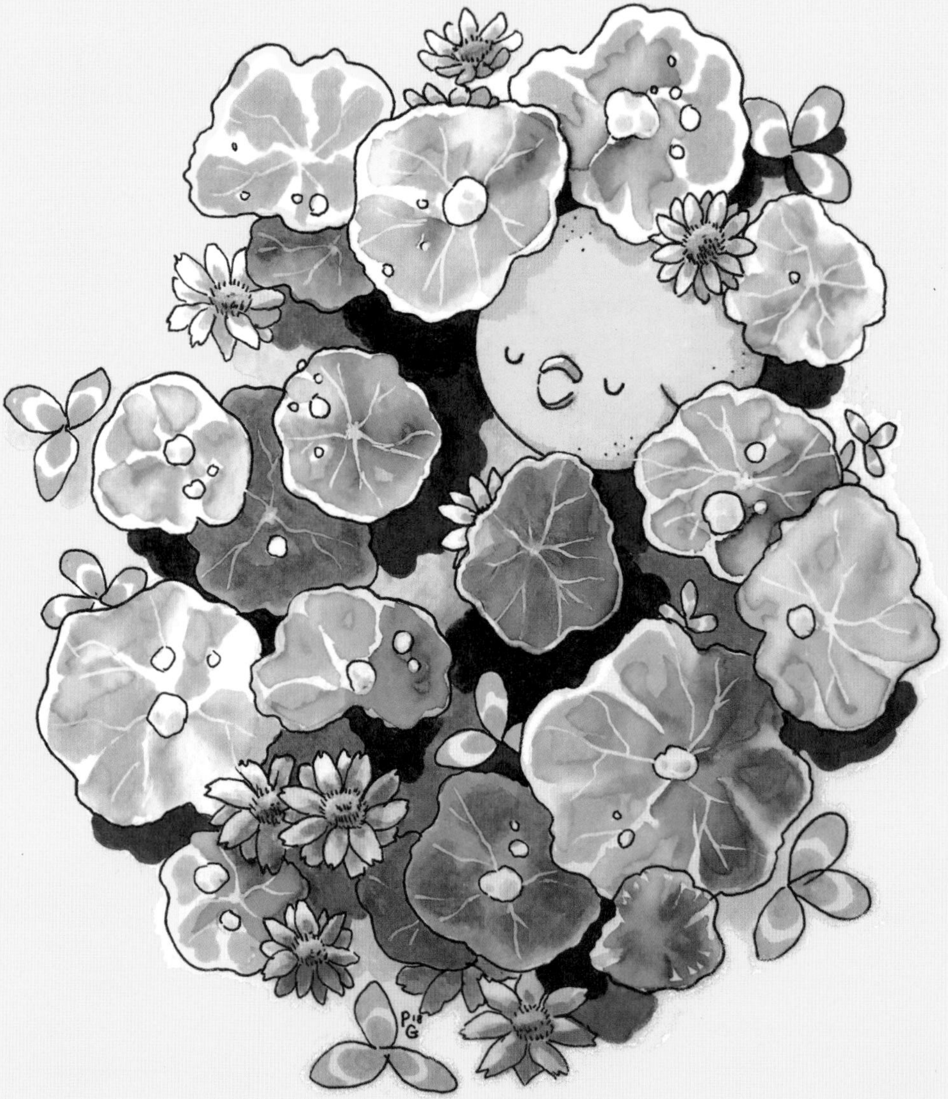

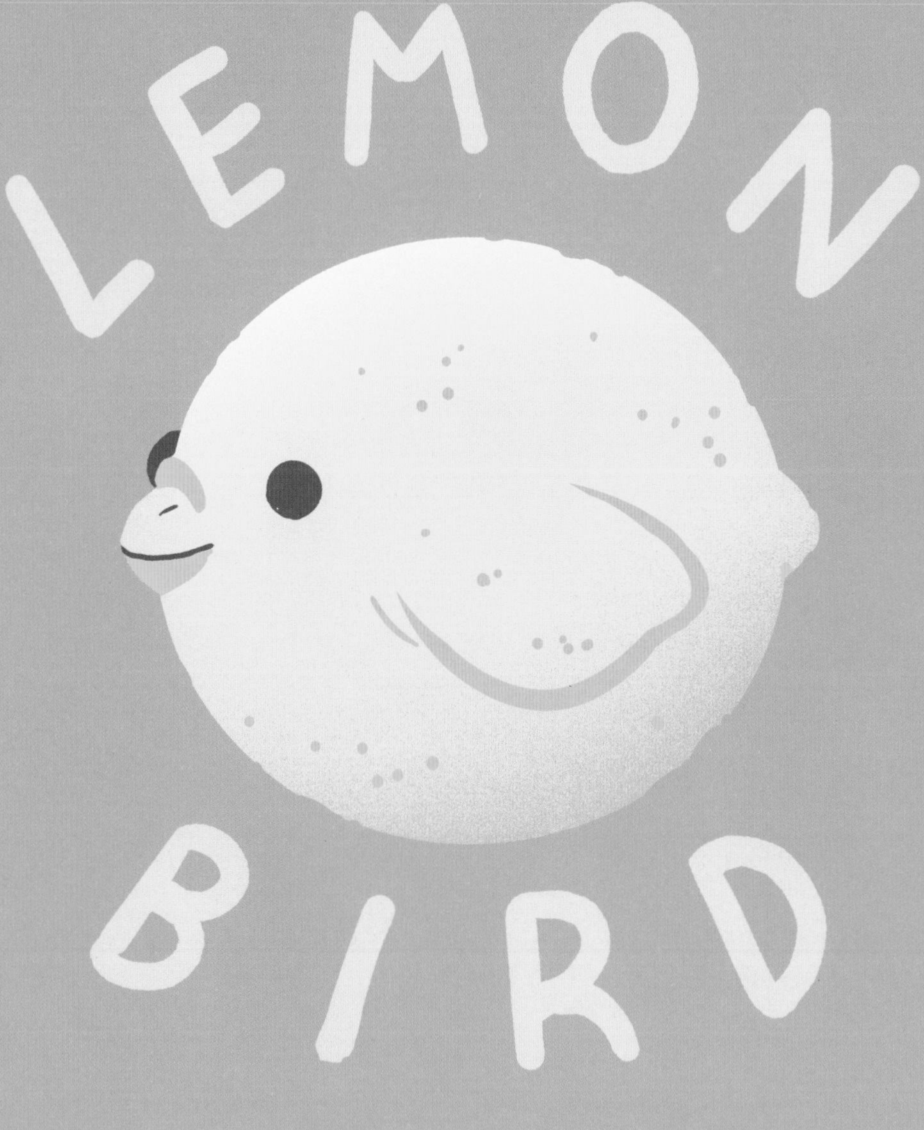
LEMON
BIRD

HOW TO DRAW LEMON BIRD!

**STEP 1: DRAW A CIRCLE.
(DOESN'T HAVE TO BE PERFECT!)**

**STEP 2: LET'S ADD SOME
LITTLE FLIPPERS FOR HER
WINGS!**

**STEP 3: STACK TWO LITTLE
TRIANGLES ON TOP OF EACH
OTHER FOR HER BEAK.**

**STEP 4: ADD THE SMALL
FACE DETAILS AND YOU'RE
DONE! SHE'S READY TO
FLY!**

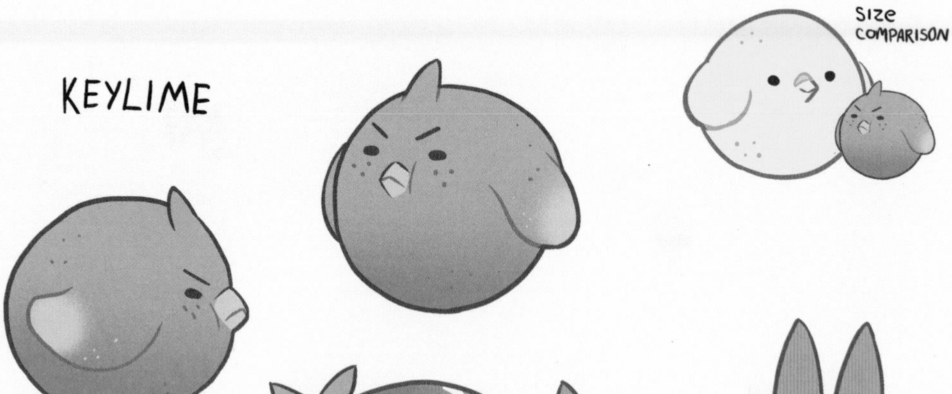
SIZE COMPARISON
KEYLIME

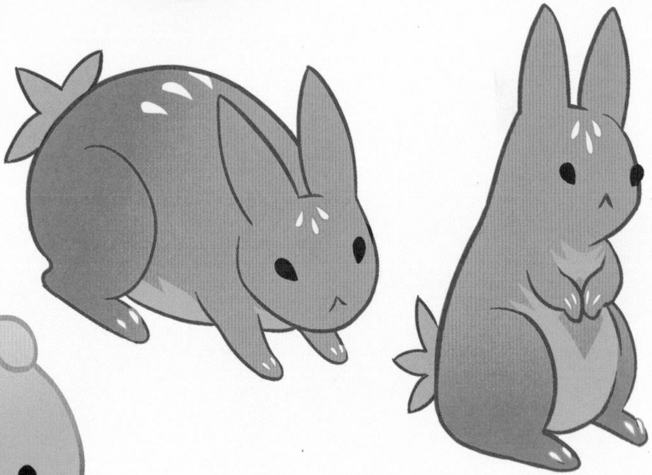

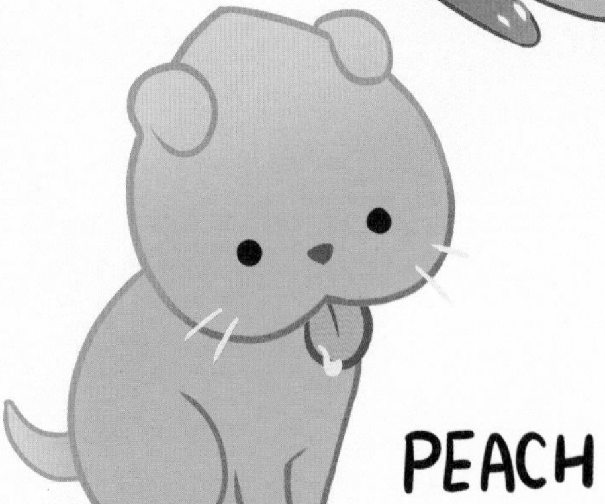
PEACH

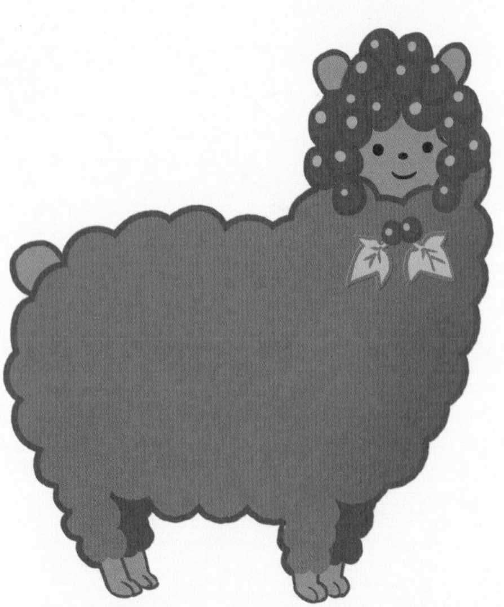

Here are some Fruit Animal mix-ups! What fruit and animal would you combine?

PEAR BEAR

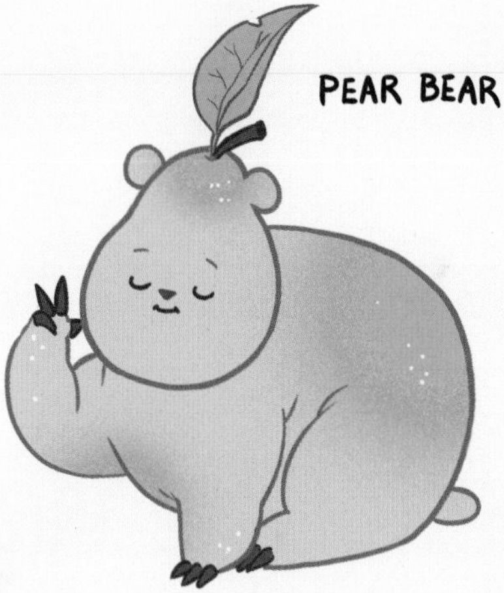

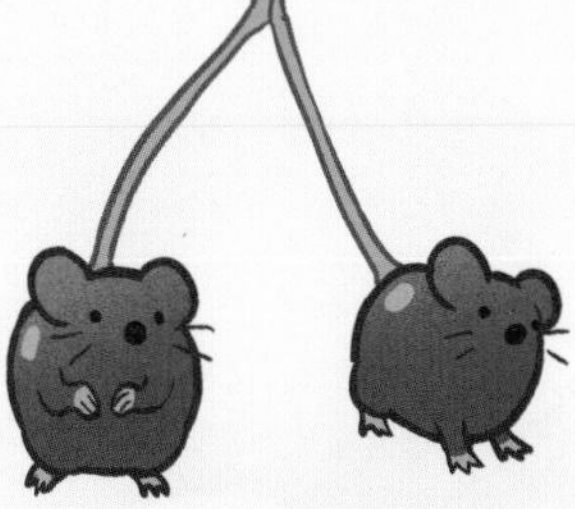

CHERRY MICE

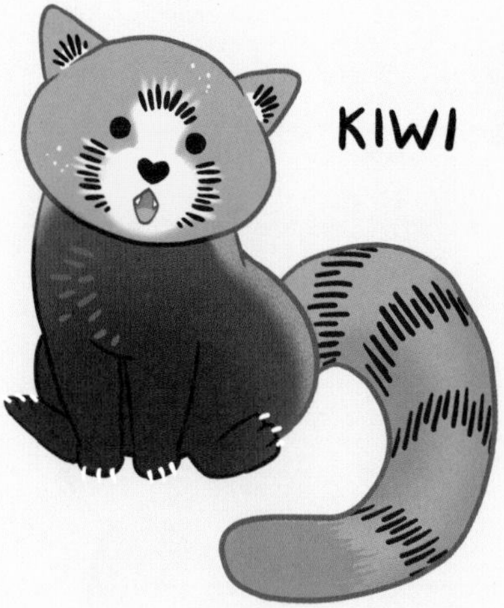

KIWI

BOARNANA

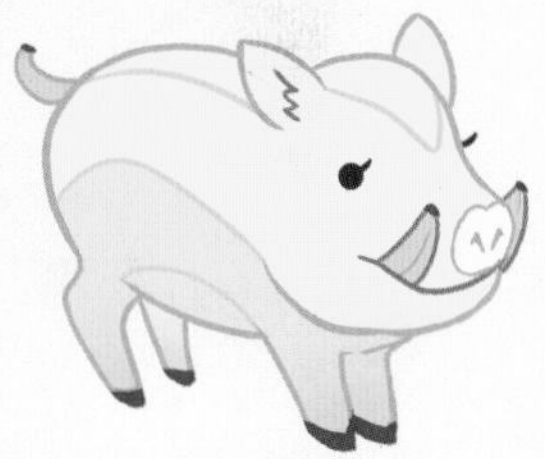

CATALOUPE

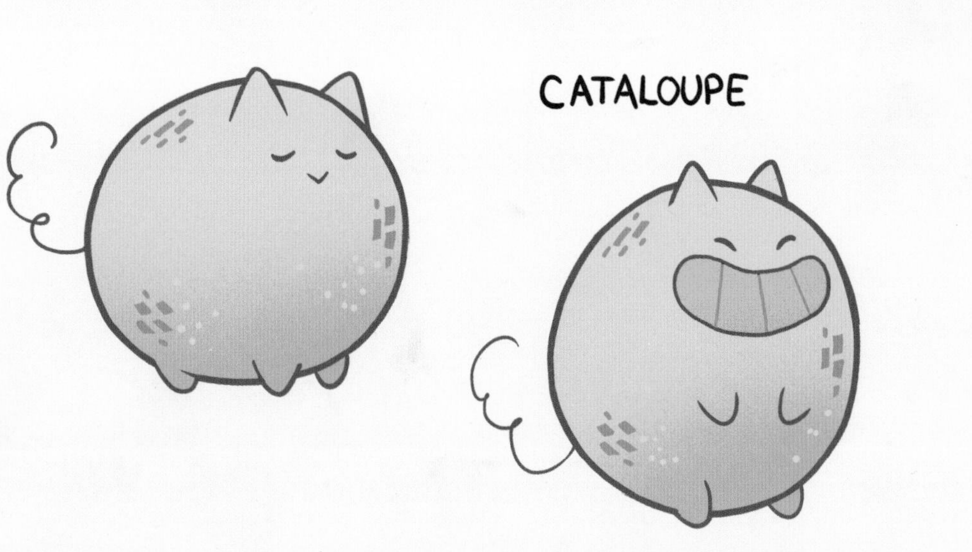

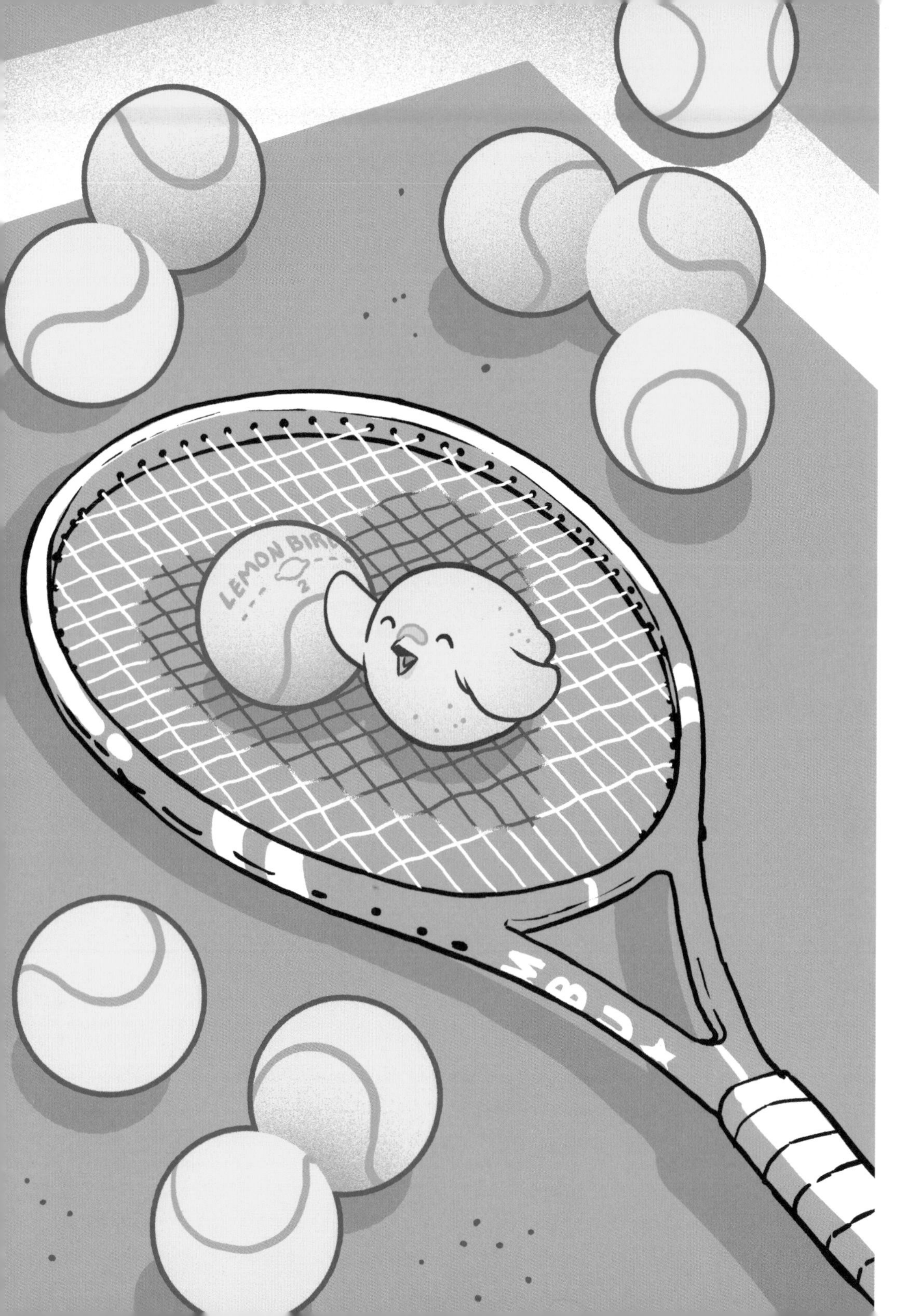
LEMON BIRD

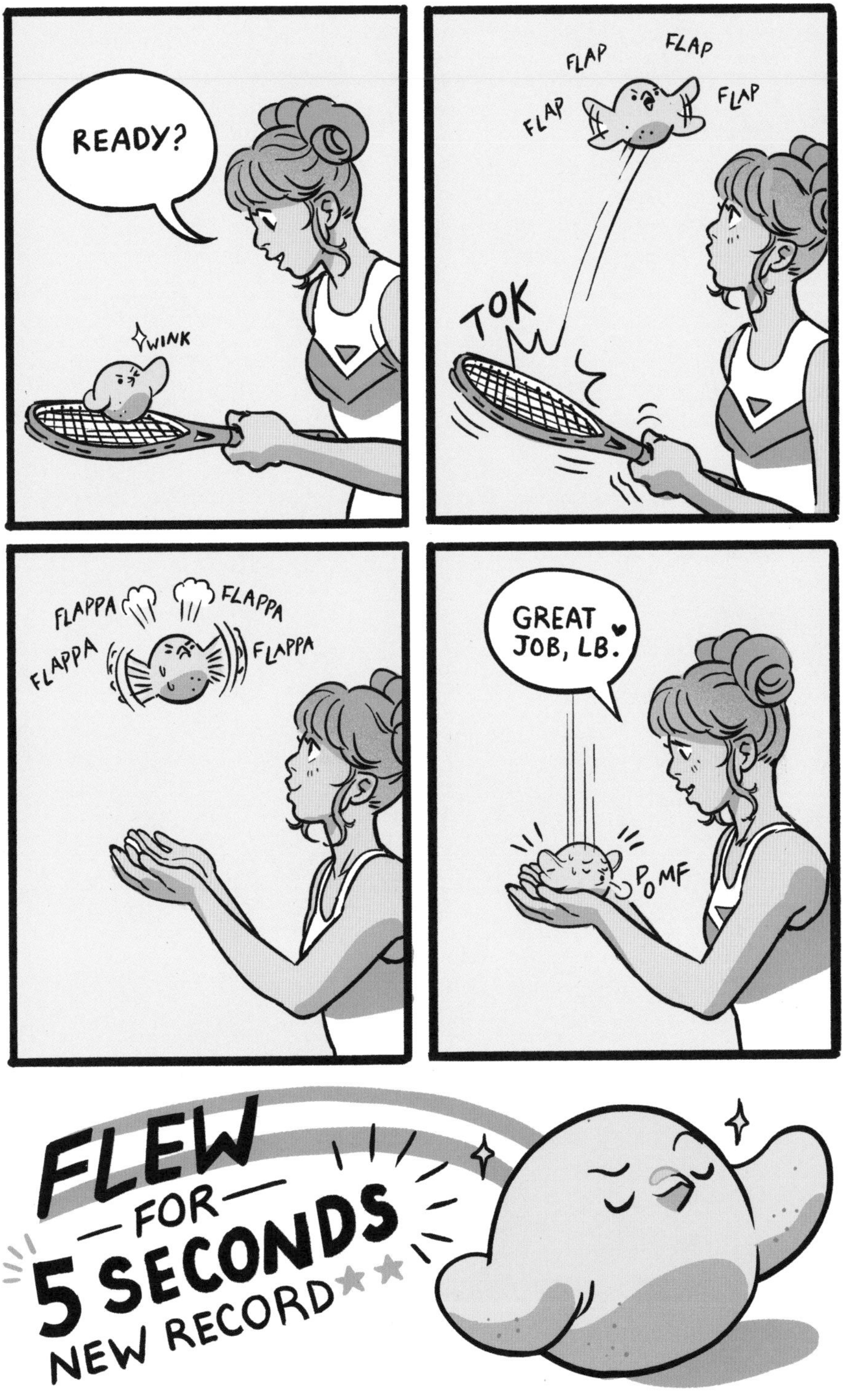
READY?
WINK
FLAP
FLAP
FLAP
FLAP
TOK
FLAPPA
FLAPPA
FLAPPA
FLAPPA
GREAT JOB, LB.
POMF
FLEW
FOR
5 SECONDS
NEW RECORD

Paulina Ganucheau is an artist who lives in Virginia with her dog and two cats. She grew up in New Orleans, where she and her sister would make comics together. She's been drawing ever since. Paulina attended art college in Georgia and has been published by many companies, including Marvel, DC, and Scholastic. A few of her other books are *Zodiac Starforce*, *She-ra: Legend of the Fire Princess*, and *Wonder Woman: The Adventures of Young Diana*. *Lemon Bird* started off as a fun little joke, but soon turned into a passion project. The idea came from a calendar Paulina had of vintage scientific illustrations. One particular month was of a parrot sitting next to a lemon, and thus *Lemon Bird* was born. Besides drawing, some of her hobbies include watching pro wrestling, cloud photography, and following dogs on Instagram.

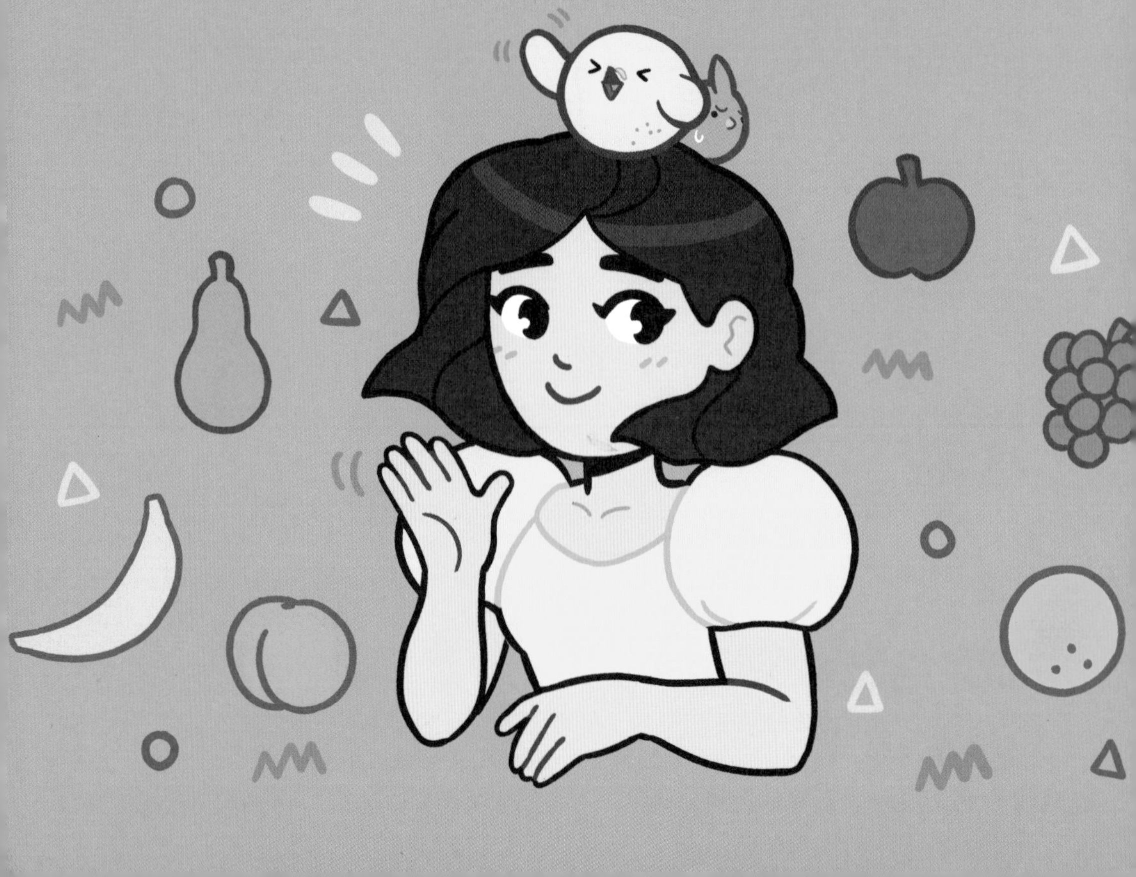

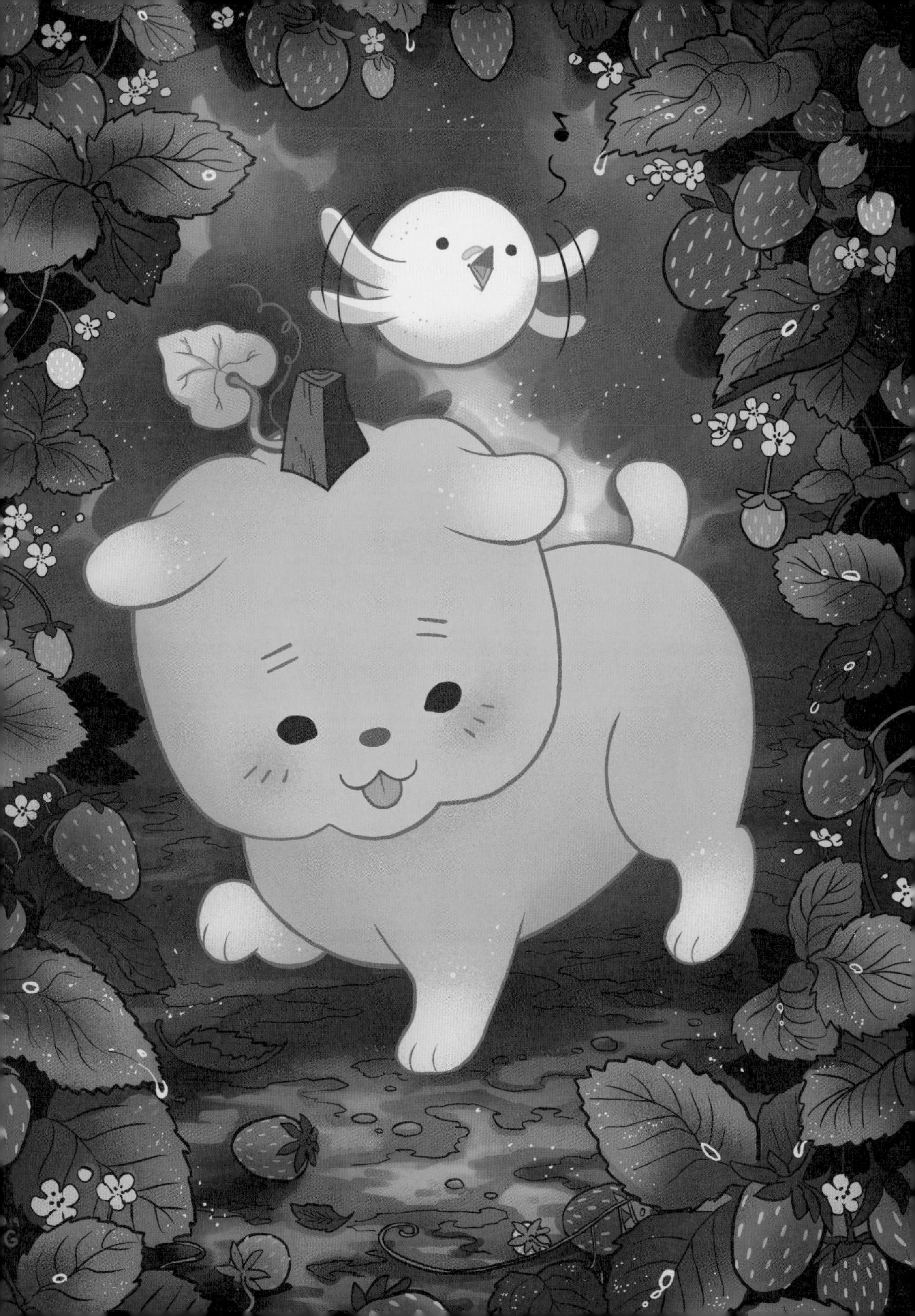

AWESOME COMICS!
AWESOME KIDS!